Veterinarian Mark Canis has a special gift that makes him one of the best at what he does...

But the gift has a price - and that price is about to go way up.

Can Mark make it all work out when his world is ripped apart? Ask the dogs. If you are like Mark, they will answer you.

Fast-paced and exciting, The Whining Mill offers a glimpse into the human condition from a new perspective.

The Whining Mill is a triumph of love, loss, courage, and lots and lots of dogs.

The Whining Mill

By

David I. Schoen

Consultant Editor: Sheryl Heitner

Illustrations: Lexis Mollica

Random Scholastic Press

Random Scholastic Press Randomscholasticpress.com

An independent publishing house.

New York, NY

For information address: *inquiries@randomscholasticpress.com*

This book is published under arrangement with Random Scholastic Press.

Cover by: David I Schoen

Consulting Editor: Sheryl Heitner

Drawings By: Lexis Mollica

First Random Scholastic Press Printing September 2012.

Printed in the United States of America

A 14 0 8 3 1 2 0 1 2 1 2 2 9 6 4 5 5 X 8 5

ISBN: 098823503X   ISBN-13   978-0-9882350-3-8

Books By David I Schoen

*Professor Dave's Owner's Manual for the SAT
(paperback and e-book editions)
Professor Dave's Owner's Manual for the SAT and
ACT Essays (paperback and e-book editions)
Professor Dave's Owner's Manual for the SAT
Teacher's Edition
Professor Dave's Owner's Manual for the SAT
Student Workbook
Professor Dave's Owner's Manual for SAT
Vocabulary (available October 2012)
Professor Dave's Owner's Manual for the ACT
(available December 2012)*

DEDICATIONS

To Pookie, for everything that has been and everything to come.

To Steven, a better version.

To my parents for being the rocks they are.

To my sister, Jennifer – I miss you, and if you read this whole book, I'll make you a super-duper drink!

To my students, who constantly remind me why I do what I do, and make it all worthwhile.

Thanks to Geo for his sage wisdom and for reminding me to always care about quality.

To Dean Koontz, who gave an interview that made this work possible.

And to all the dogs out there who unconditionally give their love because that is simply who and what they are – love givers.

Chapters

…So we beat on, boats against the current, borne back ceaselessly into the past.

-F. Scott Fitzgerald, *The Great Gatsby*.

Prologue - The Man in the Dark

The man leaned over the table, a cigarette dangling from his mouth, and he affected a vicious grin. "So, he's too slippery? He's too smart for you? What's the problem?"

The recipient of that evil grin looked extremely uncomfortable, and sipped from the can of soda he had been offered earlier. "No, it's not that. It's just, it's just hard when you don't want, you know, anyone badly hurt with this thing."

"Aw, what's the matter, you're in love or something?" With this, the cigarette man turned and walked the length of the room, which was shrouded in darkness. He turned, about seven feet away, and stopped. The room stank.

"This is serious money. Some wimpy, candy-assed vet is not going to stop this. Your job is to make sure he can't, and you're doing a lousy job. What would you do if you were me?" He raised his eyebrows anticipating an answer he seemed ready to bite off as soon as it came. He wiped his right hand over his thinning hair, and let out a sound that was something between a sigh and a grunt.

The soda-drinking man responded, "Just give me a little more time. I'm getting there. I'm almost inside. I will find a way to get him out of the picture until your 'big plan' is done." He said this last part in a sardonic tone, which was probably not a good idea.

Soda-man continued, "You said you didn't want anyone hurt, I'm trying to make that happen. But he's home a lot, his office is right there, and we both know his wife-"

"Girlfriend" the cigarette man interrupted.

"Fine, girlfriend," the soda-drinking man continued, "is untouchable, at least according to you."

At this, the cigarette man smacked the can of soda out from under the nose of the soda-drinking man, and leaned in so his face was inches apart from the soda man's.

"That's right, she's untouchable. Don't forget that. Anything happens to her, you won't see the next sunrise, I promise."

The soda-drinking man had several thoughts at this point. He had known the cigarette man a long time, but he had never truly seen the full darkness in his soul until now. He felt a mixture of fear, entrapment, and excitement at the prospect that this project, if successful, would make him very wealthy.

The cigarette man seemed to forcibly calm himself down, and spoke again.

"Let's just review it again. This is very simple. This vet is the only guy that I think could throw a wrench into what we're doing. From what I've been told, he'll know what's going on. I'm not going to explain that any further, just know it. You need to make sure he's not going to be a factor for at least a month. I don't care how, and I don't want to know about it. If possible, don't hurt him too badly, but I WANT HIM OUT OF THE PICTURE FOR A WHILE, GOT IT?"

"Yeah, yeah, I hear you, okay." The soda-drinking man rose tentatively, and started towards the door. "I'll keep you posted." With that, he exited into the bright sunlight, feeling hundreds of eyes on him as he walked.

The cigarette man lit another, and started to shake a bit. This was touchy, but the payoff was too much to ignore. If it was done correctly, no one would suffer permanent damage, and he could have everything he hoped for very soon. He wished he could do more himself, but that simply was not possible. It had to be this way. He hoped he was not making a mistake, but shrugged that thought off immediately. He had done worse. However, this time, it was a bit more personal than he liked.

***

1 - That Darn Gum

We are, simply, the sum of what we do in this life. Some may tell you the journey is half the fun. I disagree. I believe it is closer to seventy-five percent. We are not just the total, the end, the product; we are the nicks, cuts, bruises, and smiles we collect along the way. The way I see it, if the smiles and the laughter outweigh the injuries, you win.

My journey through life to this point can be measured in pants.

We will get to the pants later.

One afternoon, not too long ago, my only thought was, "I need a smoke." I hate these kind of gatherings -well - hate is too strong a word. Let us just say I was a bit uncomfortable at them, which is saying something since I am usually at home wherever I am or whomever I am with. Before you get to lecturing me, yes, I am in the medical profession, and yes, I know I should not smoke. It is my only vice, and I am working on getting over it – albeit – slowly.

The sun was hanging lazily in the sky, but summer had not yet tightened its grip on Nyagg, which the locals call "The Agg", and it was pleasantly cool. I excused myself from the conversation that had me tugging at my collar frequently and headed out onto the back porch. There were eleven other people at the table, so I would not be missed immediately. I soon discovered I was not the only lost soul seeking solace from the social conventions of in-law gatherings. Another man had sought the peace and separation of the back porch. I think his name is Jerry, or Jack, or something; I know he is one of the boyfriends of one of my girlfriend's siblings. He was standing where I had planned to go.

I was at the house of the parents of my girlfriend, Sarah, whom you will get to know well through these pages. Her father, Lou, is a bold, loud man who has been everywhere and done everything - at least twice. Her mother, Sophie, is more soft spoken, but carries herself with a manner that says, "I'm really in charge here." They are lovely people, and they adore me (as far as I know,) but I can only take so much sometimes.

The gentleman who had preceded me onto the porch nodded in recognition as I walked out, as men will do, and as I reached the railing, we both turned to face the expansive yard. A breeze kicked up and made the trees dance, as if for our benefit.

"Hey man, Mike, right?"

"Mark." I corrected.

"Yeah, yeah, Mark, right, sorry, how are ya, man?" He extended a beefy hand in my direction. 'Drake." pointing at himself, saving me the admittance I had remembered his name incorrectly. "You're a vet, right? That's friggin' cool." Yes, Drake, it is.

I smiled at him. I shook his hand back, careful to put a bit more strength in the grip than I normally would. Peacocking, my girlfriend Sarah would call it, but hey, I am a guy. It is what we do.

The porch we occupied, attached to the house of my girlfriend's parents who I can only take so much of, was suddenly an oasis of peace and serenity. We were just two men, strangers on a train, enjoying a smoke in the afternoon breeze. I like my girlfriend's parents, I really do, but sometimes her father's stories of the "good old days" can be a bit tiresome. I find myself wondering how many of them are actually true – or how many have an inkling of truth and then are embellished in the telling. I have heard the same story about the time forty men came to his rescue when he found himself in the wrong place at the wrong time, but I think the nationality of the rescuing men has changed a few times. It could just be me.

Drake and I stood smoking and leaning and glancing across the large backyard, sharing a common "glad to be here and not in there" moment that neither of us needed to voice. Cigarettes never last long enough in these circumstances.

A minute or so later, I felt a bump against my leg. It was not from the direction of Drake, but from behind me and to my left. As I looked down, Drake followed my gaze and jumped back involuntarily at the sight on the porch.

A small, grey squirrel was desperately trying to get my attention by repeatedly bumping his nose against my pant leg.

"Holy crap, what the heck?" inquired Drake with genuine surprise in his voice. He seemed suddenly embarrassed by his reaction to the tiny creature once he had regained his composure.

"I don't know, let's see..." I replied, and leaned down towards the small rodent, putting my arm down to the ground. As I expected, the squirrel scampered up my outstretched arm, and settled in my hands, now cupped in front of my chest, and looked up at me expectantly. Drake took another exaggerated step back and mumbled something about those things having rabies and carrying disease. I mumbled something in reply while searching the squirrel for the reason he sought me out. I spotted it almost immediately. He had a wad of gum stuck to his fur just to the left of his mouth. It looked like it had been there a while, and it was probably driving the poor thing nuts. I laughed at my own joke. Nuts, indeed. Ha ha.

"I see, little guy, I see, hold still." I transferred the calm and composed little squirrel into the crook of my left arm and took out the pocketknife from my pants pocket. I opened the scissors with one hand, and slowly put the two blades between the gum and the squirrel's face. One quick snip and it was done.

I lowered my arm, the squirrel jumped down, turned and looked at me, then scampered off the porch.

I put the knife away and looked up at Drake with an expectant look on my face. He was at the back of the porch looking at me with a mixture of disbelief and trepidation. He finally spoke.

"What just happened?" he managed.

"Looks like he got some gum stuck..." I began, but Drake interrupted me.

"NO. I mean, like," he stammered, "what the heck just happened?"

At that fortuitous moment, my lovely girlfriend, the light of my life and the best person on the planet, appeared from around the side of the house and made her way to the porch with that "I know what you're up to" look on her face.

Drake leaned in to see who approached, and settled back for a moment, still looking tense and a bit shaken.

Sarah noticed his countenance and asked, "You okay, Drake?"

Drake, in a misguided attempt to reclaim his manhood simply shook his head, pointed at me, bobbed his index finger up and down a few times, and went back into the house. Sarah looked at me expectantly.

I said, in muted, nonchalant tones, "Squirrel. Gum. Stuck. Scissors, well..."

She smiled knowingly, let out an audible sigh, and retreated in the house the way Drake had gone. Before going, she muttered, "Don't stay out here too long, mister" with mock consternation in her voice. I smiled. I turned again to the backyard, spied my now clean-faced little friend scamper up a tree trunk, and I lit another smoke.

This kind of thing happens to me all the time.

***

2 - A Furry Book Critic

Nyagg is a small town between two giants. I live here, I have my veterinary office here, and Sarah's parents live here. Sarah, as I mentioned before, is my girlfriend. I find myself saying that a lot, since she is such an awesome soul, and I suppose I still do not truly believe she chose me to love. I am just lucky I guess. Sarah did not grow up in Nyagg, but I did. Her parents moved here from somewhere farther east on Long Island a few years back, and Sarah attended the same high school as I had, but I am a few years older than she is so we did not cross paths in high school. We actually did not meet until a few years after she had graduated college. A fresh college graduate seeking a teaching position, Sarah moved in with her parents in Nyagg –and I became a lucky guy.

I often wonder about her parents' move from Eastern Long Island to Nyagg, but her father is not very forthcoming about the reasons, and Sarah does not know. I get the feeling something in her father's business or dealings precipitated the move, but I am not sure.

When I said Nyagg is situated between two giants, I mean giants financially. Originally settled in the 1700's by the Tabak clan, Nyagg rests on an exclusive chunk of real estate on Long Island, New York's north shore. Surrounded by affluence and influence, Nyagg keeps its middle class head down most of the time. The best cars in Nyagg are the ones that pass by on the single lane road that joins Glen Cove to our east and Great Neck to our west. It is a great place to live.

On that particular sunny afternoon, Sarah and had I left her parents' house after a few more hours of uncomfortable tolerance and drove home to our split-level ranch-style house a few blocks from her parents'. I had heard the story of the forty men in the bar again before we left, and this time they were Columbian. I think they were Italian last time, I do not remember. At least they both end in 'ian.' They certainly were not Amish.

The house we live in now, the split-level ranch-style, is the house I had grown up in, well, kind of. My parents relocated to Florida a few years back, and I bought the property and the house from them. Before they had even crossed the Queens line I had the house razed and built the ranch/office combination I had always dreamed of. My father says it is still weird to come back here to the oh-so-familiar with a strange house occupying the land. Back to Sarah's parents' house for a moment - Drake had stared at me the rest of the evening, which I found infinitely amusing. I made sure to offer no explanations just to further enjoy his discomfort. I do enjoy this most of the time.

The best thing about my relationship with Sarah is that we get one another. I know when to leave her alone, I know when to dig and find out what is on her mind. She can read me just as well, but since I am a man, that is easy. We are much simpler creatures. There is a tacit communication that exists between our souls (she accuses me of over-romanticizing sometimes) that makes it unnecessary for us to speak. What a great girl. On that ride home, we said nothing, I drove with a silly half-smile on my face and Sarah checked her mail and appointments on her smartphone while we made the quick journey to our place. Poor Drake.

Me? My name is Mark Canis. I am 37 years old, not tall, in pretty good shape, and I have a great sense of humor. At least I think so.

I am not sure why you should care who I am or even that I exist. I am not a celebrity; in fact, I am a pretty ordinary guy. I am a veterinarian, a good one, and I love my work. Those that know me would say it differently though, they would say my work loves me.

No one is beating down my door for my services, although I do have a healthy practice that makes a nice living. Sarah is a teacher, and between the two of us, we do all right. To my parents, I am still a child, and to my friends I am a bit of an oddity. To me? Well, I am just me.

My entire life I have found that I truly did not care what others thought of me; that is, until I met Sarah. She was the first one who made me worry about my appearance, my breath, and whether or not I had matching socks on. The funny thing is she really does not care about those things. There was another girl in high school, who you will hear about, but her ministrations to my appearance and wardrobe back in high school were simply products of the time and my complete lack of education in the subjects. It was Sarah, my girlfriend now, who truly changed me.

My life is no better than yours is, I am sure, but there are some things that happen to me that do not happen to the average person. Things involving animals happen with me in a way that do not happen with other people often, if ever. One of the things I hesitate to point out so early in this manuscript for the risk that I may lose you, dear reader, is that I was commanded to write this tome you are holding by an American Eskimo named Max. Not the human kind of American Eskimo, the canine kind. Pure white, with a sharp, engaging face and a curled-up tail, American Eskimos are simply beautiful to behold. I never knew dogs were aware of the human need to write things down; that is apparently ignorance. Dogs know much more about us than we think.

Before you toss this manuscript off as a whack-job fantasy or science fiction journey, I must implore you to read a bit further. This is a partial *memoir*. I say partial because I am still alive. I am sure more fun is in store. The story you are about to read is not only a wild and interesting yarn, but also it is true. I lived it. Vicariously, so will you.

I mention that Max ordered me to write this as a partial disclaimer. This book was not my idea. It was his. Now that you are wondering (since you are still here,) let me explain.

Max is an ordinary American Eskimo dog. Bright, energetic, an enigmatic grin plastered on his furry face all the time, much like any other American Eskimo dog.

What is different (or is it 'who is different?') is me. I can feel what Max is thinking. I can communicate with Max in unspoken terms that we both understand. I have always had this ability. I had always wanted to become a veterinarian — and this was a convenient fact since the state has these silly little laws about treating animals and operating on them without those letters DVM behind your name. In one manner or another I have been doing it since I was about eight years old, so I figured I would get the letters. My evaluations at veterinary college were laudatory. "Incredible instincts. Great command of myriad animal types. Superb manner with patients." Yeah, yeah. I knew all that already. I needed the letters behind my name to open up shop, so I got them. I enjoyed that journey too.

Max is the property of an old and dear friend of mine, Carlo Rockman. Carlo is a retired police detective who served this area for over thirty years. Carlo and I met while we were both on the job, as they say. I, a struggling undergraduate working a summer job while home from college, and Carlo, a newly shielded detective, found ourselves at the same Mobil gas station on the overnight shift. I was working the pumps; Carlo was on an extended stakeout to catch car thieves who had recently taken to grabbing cars at gas stations while their owners fueled them up. Our nightly vigils at the pumps became bull sessions, which grew into philosophical musings. Carlo was worldly and wise then; he is now a philosophical force to be reckoned with. When the world is running down, I run to Carlo to have it pumped back up again.

Max, the American Eskimo, came into Carlo's life just before he retired. A case brought Carlo to a housing tract on the south shore of Long Island where a double-murder suicide had just taken place. A scared, shivering Max, just out of puppyhood, stood vigil over the scene when Carlo and his partner arrived. The pup immediately gravitated to Carlo, and since his owners appeared no longer able to fill his food bowl, Carlo took Max home with him. They have been together ever since.

One day at a backyard barbecue that Sarah and I attended at Carlo's, Max brought me a piece of paper. The events in this memoir had recently unfolded, and I suppose Max felt some rather human need to see it on paper. At first, I could not understand the reason behind the dog's insistence on me taking piece after piece of paper from him, and I finally stopped accepting the bizarre offerings. It was not until someone handed me a pen and I began to scribble on the paper that Max settled down and stopped bringing me sheets. Where he was getting them from is still a mystery, but that panting grin when I began to write was unmistakable. A true canine literary agent, Max was.

Therefore, I continued to write. You are holding the result in your hands. They say the publishing world is "dog eat dog," but Max hates that expression.

Max is also a great editor. Carlo, one of the few people in the world who knows a little about my gift, has read every page of this memoir to Max throughout its creation. When Max put his head down or let out a whine, Carlo would make a note of it and pass it on to me. Max is a tough critic, but the final version you are reading is better for it.

When I looked deeper into the pages that Max had rejected with his body language, I detected a pattern. If I expressed self-doubt, Max would put his head down. If I digressed too much, a prone Max would let me know. Max is obviously an action junkie, anxious for the story to be told in a succinct, fast-moving way. I told you he was tough.

I am getting a bit ahead of myself here, so I need to back up a bit. The barbecue at Carlo's, which introduced me to the literary agent side of one of my favorite canines, happened much later. The barbecue was one of the first relaxing moments I had had after the events of the few weeks prior. I promise, dear reader, you will get the whole story. There are some important background things we need to cover first. So let's go.

***

3 - An Unusual Collapse

There may be some of you, at this point, that think you have picked up a children's tale, another *Dr. Doolittle* or its ilk, but I assure you that is not the case. In the telling of this trial there may be some juvenile references, but you will soon see how they fit in to what I can only assure you is a memoir best suited for adults.

Let me also assure you that I am a good guy. Why do I feel the need to tell you that? It is one of my character weaknesses. I constantly assess myself against my peers, my neighbors, and my friends. I am concerned with this not for vanity or outward appearance. It is for one reason and one reason only. Carlo, my good friend and mentor who you will meet in a moment, once told me: "Mark? The best thing a man can do on this Earth is be the best version of himself he can be." I try to live by that advice. I have always been an avid reader, but when I first read *The Road Less Traveled* in high school, I found it typically banal as most high school students do. After the conversation with Carlo about being the best version of oneself one can be, the poem by Robert Frost took on a whole new dimension. Those English teachers in high school occasionally did know what they were talking about.

One of my favorite books growing up was a mystery by Agatha Christie in which the narrator turns out to be the murderer. I promise you that is not the case here, and who said anything about murder? I am really just a typical, normal fellow who has something strange (or wonderful if you ask Sarah) about him.

When do we truly know someone? When do we truly know ourselves? Does it take our interaction with others to determine who we are – or – is who we are a product of our interaction with others? For answers to these questions, see my future volume on philosophy.

It all started, as I mentioned earlier, when I was about eight years old. My little sister, Emily, is two years younger than I am. Ever since she was old enough to talk, Emily wanted a dog. "Doggie!" was her first word, not "mama" or "papa" as is the typical case for English speaking toddlers. No, Emily clearly said, "doggie."

My parents were not keen on getting a dog, as neither of them had grown up in a household with pets. However, watch enough TV, see enough happy family scenes with canine friends bouncing happily along and you can get the idea. My parents were wonderfully flexible that way.

My father was afraid of what every father was afraid of in this scenario. For two weeks, everything would be great, and then he would be the one walking the dog in the rain, sleet, and snow. That turned out not to be the case.

My sister's birthday is in February, and on the sixth celebration of her emergence into the world, we piled into my father's Plymouth Duster and headed to North Shore Animal League, a pet adoption haven near our home.

Pets are something of a fascination in the United States, as you can find one in almost every home. Pets in every shape and size from cats to dogs to ferrets to hamsters to fish and everything in between fill our homes and our lives, and cost us billions of dollars every year. I often wonder if we are not the pets, and they the masters. It feels like that sometimes. In fact, if you count each fish individually (as opposed to counting a fish tank as a single pet), pets outnumber people in this great nation of ours by a healthy margin.

Once at North Shore Animal League, my father parked the car and my sister and I alighted and sprinted to the entrance. I jostled her a bit to go in first since I observed the rules of the annoying older brother like a master. Once we were inside, we walked over to the counter where a kind young woman smiled at us and asked us if we needed help.

My sister said, very sweetly, that mom and dad had given her permission to get a dog and could she see some that needed homes?

At that moment, my life changed.

I felt something as we approached the counter, but as I was just a boy of eight, I did not give it much attention. At that age, we are not always aware of our surroundings, or of our internal feelings, until they are pointed out to us. It is the reason young ones will venture out in pouring chilling rain with nothing on but a Harry Potter t-shirt and shorts. This something I felt tugged at me, like a sour stomach or a fever that is not invented to miss a day of school, but a real one.

I stopped and paid attention to the feeling in my body. It was more than a feeling, it was a sound with physical reality to it, and I *sensed* it as much as I heard it.

So much sorrow, then hope, then wonder, then confusion, then hope again, then several unrecognizable feelings. A jumble of emotions was pulsing through my body but the emotions felt unreal. In other words, they were outside of me, yet I could feel them as strongly as if they were mine. Were they? I was confused myself, and not aware at the time that I was empathetically feeling everything that was being thrown at me by the occupants of the shelter.

My mother and father had caught up with us and with that unerring sense that mothers have, my mother looked at me with alarm.

"Are you alright, Mark?"

"Yeah, mom," I replied unsteadily, and I proceeded to collapse in a faint to the floor.

***

4 - Discovery

We are creatures of water, tissue, and electricity. We are fragile beings. A swordsman once wrote, "The human body is a bag of water – poke holes in the bag, the water leaks out, and the body dies."

Dogs are also creatures of water, tissue and electricity. What most people think separates us from animals, is our capacity to think – to feel. This is not true. After all, are we not animals as well? I think so, although I have encountered some folks in my life that might be better classified as plants.

If I were to tell you that dogs feel envy, joy, sadness, loss, fear and excitement as much as we do, you may not believe me. I know for certain that it is true.

If I were to tell you that dogs are capable of advanced levels of thought – using tools, reasoning problems and figuring out situations, you may not believe me. I know for certain that it is true.

Cats are a different story; we will get to them later.

After my fainting spell in the animal shelter, my next memory was of an unfamiliar place, but a familiar face. I looked up and saw the fuzzy image of Dr. Klein, our family pediatrician. A smiling, white-haired Dr. Klein was shining a penlight at my face and I winced. We were not in his normal office in Nyagg; we were somewhere else I did not recognize. However, I knew Dr. Klein.

"There we are," he said, his smile widening.

I looked gently from side to side and saw my mother, looking ashen, heave a sigh of relief as my eyes met hers.

For the next fifteen minutes, I sat in the chair in this strange examination room while my mother and Dr. Klein discussed what had happened to me. I caught most of it, but was unsure of the meaning of some of the discourse. I caught the words "testing", "physiological", and "psychological" but I was still quite dazed, and had no idea what big words like that meant at the time. Slowly, bit by bit, the memory of the previous hour began to take shape.

While Dr. Klein and my mother bantered about in the upper echelons of the English language, I settled into the very comfortable examination chair a bit deeper and began to think. I replayed the scene leading up to my entrance into the shelter slowly and carefully.

Sometimes when we try to grasp onto a dream or a memory, it acts like a ball of mercury. It squishes, wiggles, and avoids our grasp as surely as if we tried to grab smoke. This was what I felt like, although in my heart was the certainty that the memory was there and was taking shape. I grasped slowly, cleared my mind of other concerns, and tried to "see" what had happened.

I remember teasing Emily as I got to the door, then I remember an aroma, strong and not unpleasant. It was a mixture of cleaning chemicals, fur, and some other things I did not recognize. It was the kind of smell that could take you back years to that very moment and very spot in time and place if you were to smell it again decades later. Distinct, if you will pardon the buried pun.

I remember a year or two ago following my grandfather around his small backyard, by the grape vines that he kept, while he mowed the lawn with an old-fashioned metal push mower. I asked to help; he chuckled and handed over the handle of the mower. I could not move the archaic beast one inch. It was simply too heavy. My grandfather let me walk alongside him while he pushed the beast through the grass, and we finished the job together. We gathered the clippings with rakes into large black garbage bags and carried them to the front of the house.

The smell of the freshly cut grass permeated my nose, my brain, and my memory. To this day, when I get a whiff of freshly mown lawn, I am taken back to that day as if it were yesterday. I also remember the incredibly sweet glass of grape juice he offered me in the kitchen afterward. It comes as in involuntary flood of aroma, feeling, and emotion.

More recollection began to take shape of the incident at the animal shelter. I remember my nose was assaulted by an "aromacophy," if you will, of scents. I remember then feeling strange, unfamiliar power in my body. More and more the feelings - and the memory - took shape.

Familiar emotions from unfamiliar sources washed over me like a wave at the beach. I was taken under, and fainted. It was simply too much for my system to handle. Nowadays, I am often inundated with similar "waves," but I have learned to deflect them, filter them, and handle them with great alacrity. Not that day, though, as the waves were brand new.

Still a bit shaky, but pronounced whole by Dr. Klein, my mother drove me home. That is when I realized I was in a hospital. I had a quick moment of panic, but quashed it as quickly as it had arisen. How did I get here? Why was my family doctor there?

We lived in a nice, four bedroom colonial style house in the middle of a quiet street in Nyagg. Neither of us spoke on the drive home, which was not long. As we pulled into the driveway, I turned to my mother.

"Mom, what happened to me?"

My mother looked at me with a face that I still remember clearly to this day. It was a maternal mixture of reassurance, uncertainty, worry, and love.

"I'm not sure, sweetie, but Dr. Klein says you're fine. Maybe you should lay off the Mallomars a little, huh?" Mallomars were (and still are) my favorite snack.

Deflated and a bit unsure of myself, I replied, "Ok, mom." There was something off here, something I did not truly understand. I think my mother's uncertainty had a large effect on me emotionally although I was not aware of it at the time. When I got into the house, much more became clear very quickly.

***

5 - Holy Cow, Can't You Knock?

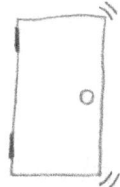

"OH MY GOD!"

The screen door of our ranch slammed in concert with the words as they were shouted across the deserted foyer, living room, kitchen, dining room, and den of our home. I am certain an unknown grandfather, enjoying his evening meal in peace in central Shanghai, dropped his chopsticks.

Since Sarah and I were upstairs, we were insulated a bit from the power of the yell, but both of us jumped involuntarily although we had heard it a thousand times before.

Sarah went downstairs after flashing me a "you know how it is" smile and started speaking halfway down.

"Hi Stef, what's up?"

Sarah's dear friend, Stefania, is a piece of work. First, let me tell you something that I have to get out early in this description, because it plays in a lot later as you will see. Stefania is drop-dead gorgeous. Now, I know what you may be thinking – I am madly in love with my Sarah, and I am, I assure you, but it is hard not to comment on the incredible beauty and energy that Stefania radiates. I know, I should not be concerned with the looks of another woman, and I am not, well, at least not to any point that it is an issue. But man, she is hot. I mean ohmygodyouknowhercanIbeintroduced hot.

Stefania and Sarah have been friends since they met in high school, though they are a few years apart. In fact, Stefania was an unknown bridge between Sarah and me; Stefania and I were in high school together, and later Stefania and Sarah were in the same high school together, but Sarah and I missed each other by a year.

I am frankly surprised that Stefania's vocal chords have held out this long. She does nothing halfway – whether it be saying hello, hugging, buying gifts, or driving – Stefania is pedal to the metal at all times. As beautiful as she is, if you are looking for a mate to spend quiet evenings at home with, Stefania is not your girl. Yes, she is single.

"YOU ARE NOT GOING TO BELIEVE WHO I SAW AT HEITNER'S" she gasped as she spotted Sarah coming down the stairs. Heitner's is a drugstore-coffee shop that has been a mainstay in Nyagg for over fifty years. Everyone in town knows Heitner's. They have awesome ice cream sundaes there, and they still make the ice cream in house. If you ever make it up to Nyagg, knock on my office door and ask for directions to Heitner's. I will probably offer to drive you there myself since one never leaves Heitner's empty handed – or empty stomached as the case may be.

Sarah walked past the yelling figure of her friend and waved her into the kitchen. She knew she did not have to say a word; the story would come out shortly and in machine-gun fashion.

"I was in Heitner's, and, you know how I love those milkshakes – they can make them with Splenda now so they're not so bad- and I was sitting there just minding my own business..."

Sarah interrupted by placing an arm on Stefania's, and asked, "Want coffee?"

"Oh yeah, sure, thanks." She then continued the narrative, and I admit I moved a bit closer to the door to make sure I heard the tale. Stefania is never boring. "So, I'm in Heitner's, and who comes in? I don't think he saw me, and thank goodness for that, because I was in my corner booth where I always sit, and..."

Sarah interrupted again, probably fearful there would be no oxygen in the room for anyone else if Stefania kept up this pace. "Take a breath. Relax. There you go, okay." Sarah rubbed Stefania's forearm in a gesture that never failed to bring Stefania back a few notches.

I also should mention, at this point, that there is a bit of history between Stefania and me. Long before I started dating Sarah, Stefania and I went out a few times. We actually did a bit more than just go out. This has not been a problem for Stefania or for Sarah as far I can tell, but knowing the little bit about women that

I do, I know I am fooling myself thinking that. The only saving grace I have is that it was Stefania who pursued me, which, at the time, made me the most popular person on the planet. Football players from high school who used to try to hang me in the locker-room from my underwear were inviting me to parties, games and all sorts of things I had never been invited to before. It was an interesting time. I was much younger then. I learned a lot. However, it is ancient history.

Stefania continued her narrative, albeit at a gentler pace but not at a lower volume.

"Craig." She let it sit there. It had no effect on me. Sarah reacted.

"Oh wow, really? Craig? THE Craig?"

I did not like the sound of "THE Craig" and strained a bit closer to ensure I did not miss anything.

"Yes, THE Craig!" answered Stefania, and I could sense her crossing her arms in her inimitable style. "I have no idea why he is here, or what, but it was him!"

Listening to the two girls go on for a bit, I figured a few things out about THE Craig. 1 – He used to date both girls, and neither relationship ended particularly well. 2- This is a man not to be trusted, which makes him no different from any other man. 3- Neither girl ever expected to hear about or see THE Craig again. 4- I had never been told about THE Craig, which for some reason pissed me off. My interest and my annoyance wrestled in my brain for dominance, but both agreed the best thing to do was listen further. I listened.

Stefania and Sarah went on for a bit longer, at which point I casually came down the stairs as if I was not privy to anything that had been said.

"Hey, Stef!" I called out as I spotted her in the kitchen, forgetting that Sarah did not care for it when I used that familiar nickname for Stefania. We men are stupid, are we not?

Stefania's answer was curt and perfunctory, as if she were trying hard to make me feel like a third wheel. She was successful. "Hey, Mark, what's up?" She immediately turned back to Sarah and opened her eyes wide as if to say "we shouldn't' talk about THE Craig with THE Mark in the room." At least, in my own mind anyway, I rated a capital THE in front of my name also.

Stefania and I, or I should say, Sarah and I (whoops) have an understanding when it comes to Stefania and me. We do not talk about it (it has been hashed and rehashed time and time again) nor do Stefania and I greet each other with anything more than a quick syllable or two. It can get a bit uncomfortable when we are out together, but again, men are stupid, and me being a man, I have no idea how else to handle it. I envy cats sometimes.

Speaking of cats, I mentioned earlier that they are quite different from dogs. I can explain this in a very simple way: Dogs have masters, owners, best friends, people whom they worship, obey, and trust implicitly. Cats have servants who bring them food, clean out their litter boxes, and are allowed to touch them when the mood strikes. In fact, now that I think about it, dogs have it over women, too, in myriad ways. When Sarah reads this chapter I may be on the couch for a few weeks, but I cannot resist this line that I overheard at a veterinary convention: "If you wonder whether your woman or your dog loves you more, simply lock both in the trunk of your car, leave them there for a while, and see who is happier to see you when you open the trunk." That makes perfect sense to me. Sorry, Sarah, I know where the extra pillows are.

I went out the front door, which caused a raised eyebrow from Sarah since I always explain where I am going and how long I am going for. I was dressed in a shirt and tie, so I knew she would assume I had some kind of meeting or the like. My veterinary office is attached to the house, and I rarely dress with a necktie for office hours. I think I did it on purpose, annoyed about the attention the aforementioned "THE Craig" was getting. I am a man, remember?

Every entrance Stefania makes is an event. The slamming of the front door (to which she has a key) is normal. We lock doors in Nyagg, but not with the surety or intensity that one would do so in other towns or in a city. We lock up at night, usually, and the front doors of most houses around here are open while the sun shines. It has never been a problem.

Stefania would make a lousy thief. I do not think she can be stealthy even if her life depended on it. Usually I am amused by her antics, but not today. My leaving without a word was a product of my annoyance, and I knew I would probably have to explain it later. I had some juvenile thoughts as I approached my Jeep – which was – of course – blocked in by Stefania's car. So much for dramatic exits. I sighed, slouched in defeat, and started walking down Florida Lane, the street on which my house sits. It was only about a half mile to the town center, and I guess that was my destination now, on foot. Men. Who the heck was THE Craig? There was only one Craig I had ever known in my life, and he was a piece of work. A few years younger than I was, he was bigger than I was, and we had an interesting interaction or two, which you will read about later. He had moved to a neighboring town relatively soon after we met, and he had never entered my field of vision since that move from Nyagg. Thank goodness for small favors.

I lit a smoke, and I began walking, with no specific destination in mind.

***

6 – Chelsea The Wonder Dog

I am eight years old again. Back in the house, fresh from my visit to the hospital, my mother and I walked in and saw Emily on the floor in the foyer. Emily was holding a small wolf with a big tongue and a curly tail. I froze on the threshold. The wolf had black eyes, a long, powerful-looking muzzle, and brownish-blackish fur. Emily was squeezing the wolf very hard and it did not seem to mind. Emily looked up at me, apparently forgetting I had just come from the hospital, and shouted, "Isn't she awesome?" My mother said nothing and went into the kitchen with a loud sigh.

Emily released the wolf and it ran over to me with its pink tongue flopping up and down. It propped itself up on its rear legs, and proceeded to bathe my face with spit.

Emily started speaking without breathing. "Her name is Chelsea, and isn't she the greatest dog?" I was still in a state of shock from the emotions I had felt at the shelter and the aftermath of same, and remained wordless, looking into the deep, dark, black pools above the nose of Chelsea. Chelsea promptly rolled onto her back, inviting me to pet her belly. A trusting soul very quickly, this Chelsea. I indulged the little wolf, and she whined with pleasure. "What is she?" I asked my sister.

"The doctor at the shelter said she's a vicious killer wolf-hound, so you better be nice to me!" she said in a strong tone.

My father, who had just walked into the foyer, smiled and said, "A Norwegian Elkhound, Emily, not a wolf-hound." He looked at me. Emily stuck her tongue out at me but I pretended not to see it. "All right there Champ?" My father has called me "Champ" ever since I was old enough to walk. I do not remember if I liked it then or not, but I know today I treasure it when he says it.

As children, many of the things we hear are taken at face value. It is not until we reach our older years that we understand the underlying psychological attachments we make to certain terms, ideas, and names. Parents, especially, have a huge and profound impact on their children with the names they give them. Nicknames, too. The modern practice of naming children with seemingly random names takes its toll as well. We have to be careful what we name our offspring. Sometimes, happy accidents happen. A misspelling of the birth certificate, perhaps, creates a neat new form of a name formerly used a different way. Alternatively, a new name can be created. However, please watch the initials. Oh, my, watch the initials. If you do not believe me, ask my friend from high school, Anthony, who now works at the Chase bank in town. His middle name is Scott, and his last name is Scatelli. Nice work, Mr. and Mrs. Scatelli.

Another example - in high school, there was a couple who had been boyfriend and girlfriend since they had met at the tender age of fourteen. His name was David Ira Schwartz. Her name was Debra Ann Thomas. It was not until the senior prom that someone noticed their initials and how they worked together. Interesting, huh? Was it destiny? Last I had heard he was working in Washington, D. C. and she had remained in Nyagg. So much for destiny.

My father and my mother resumed their discussion of Dr. Klein's comments. I continued to pet Chelsea, who now had half-closed eyes and was sinking into the floor in sheer delight from the attention.

Emily quickly moved towards the back of the house and called, "C'mon Chels!" The wolf-elk-hound thingy leapt up, and padded happily after Emily.

As Chelsea was leaving, I felt an absolutely clear, strong, and pure emotion. Joy. It overwhelmed me. It was sudden, strong, and came from nowhere and everywhere. It hit like the wave of heat hits when one opens an oven that has been cooking a turkey all day. There was no mistaking the feeling - it was joy. I felt like it was a holiday morning and I was opening up presents. It was crystal clear and strong. However, it was not my own. As children will do, I shrugged it off, and went into the kitchen to see if sympathy about my faint would warrant an extra Mallomar or two. Finding no Mallomars, I smiled at mom and dad and went to follow Emily and Chelsea into the backyard. I was still thinking and exploring the strange feeling that I could identify – joy – but I could not figure out where it was coming from. Then it hit me. The screen door, that is. Still woozy from my earlier stint, I wobbled a bit, but remained upright. I saw Emily and Chelsea bouncing around the backyard playing with a Frisbee and thought better of joining them. I headed upstairs into my room to lie down.

***

7 – My Self-Indulgence Is Interrupted

Now that I was feeling cranky and annoyed about "THE Craig" and had marched into town, I needed a destination. I had no office hours, so I was pretty much free to do whatever struck my fancy.

I am a loyal guy – I was not looking for trouble, but somehow I ended up at the local gin mill, a place called *Reflections* that had a surly reputation. It was on my way, and I think somewhere in the recesses of my mind I was thirsty and rationalized that they served water there.

I walked inside, my eyes adjusting to the dusty relative darkness of the bar after the sunlight of the spring afternoon. I noticed four or five people back by the pool table as I saddled up to the bar. A young woman, maybe twenty-two or twenty-three, smiled and approached me from the other side of the bar.

"Hey, Doc!" she began, and I raised my eyebrows.

"I'm sorry, do I know you?"

"No, but you know Effy, my bichon frisé. We were in last year when she broke her leg, remember?"

I did remember instantly. The adorable little puff ball had snapped her hock chasing a squirrel. An unusual injury, but not unheard of.

"Yes, yes, of course. How is Effy?" I grabbed a few nuts that were sitting in a brown bowl to my left.

"Oh, she's great, thanks, still chasing the little furry ones." Her eyes smiled, and I thought she was incredibly cute. I know I am not supposed to notice that, but I was still pissed off about THE Craig, so there. "What can I get ya?"

I asked for a Baileys on the rocks, which I guess is an unusual order in this establishment, for her smile waned a bit, her head tilted to the side, and she widened her eyes.

"I don't think we have any Baileys, Doc, but I have something close. That okay?"

I waved assent as I felt my cell phone vibrate in my pocket. I raised a finger toward the bartender to show "just a sec" and I walked back toward the front door of the bar and back out into the sunlight.

I did not recognize the number on the phone, but that was not unusual as I had calls from my office (when the caller pressed a number stating it was an emergency) forwarded directly to my cell.

"Dr. Canis." I stated in my most official doctor voice.

There was no sound on the other line except for that background noise that indicates someone is there.

"Do yourself a favor and take a vacation." said a voice that I did not recognize. It was a man, he sounded older, and he had a gruff quality that made the hair on the back of my neck rise. It struck me as strange, but the voice sounded affected.

"Who is this, please?"

"Take a vacation." – Click. The call ended.

I stared at the phone for about five or six seconds. I called back the number from which the call originated, and I was immediately greeted by a computer voice telling me the number I had reached was not in service. Strange.

I suppose my destiny that day was not to sample whatever Irish Crème substitute the pretty bartender had in store for me, for as I closed my phone and put it back in my pocket, I noticed a young woman I did not know walking something I did – a very large Great Dane. I did not know this specific dog, but I always loved the breed. Danes are big, mushy, friendly, unfortunately short-lived, and usually of great temperament. I noticed the dog limping a bit in its front right quarter, and watched as the pair ambled by.

As the two walked closer to where I stood, the dog began straining on its leash practically dragging its walker toward me. As the Dane made progress against its much lighter handler, I smiled and waited.

"Sorry…Sorry! A strong, clear voice said as the panicked south end of the northbound leash made its way toward me involuntarily. "She's friendly, I promise!" she added and the Dane increased its intensity to reach me.

Dogs do this kind of thing all the time. I can never walk down a street without every pooch in sight insisting on saying hello to me. I usually enjoy it and take a minute or two for a greeting, but occasionally it can be bothersome. For example, one day I was late for a meeting in Mineola, the county seat of Nassau County. I had parked a few blocks away, and was making my way rapidly towards the office where I was expected. A young lady of fourteen or fifteen was walking a gaggle of dogs, probably a neighborhood girl hired to do so by working neighbors. The group of pups literally pulled her across forty feet of pavement to come say hello to me. I was in a hurry, but there was really no avoiding a group hug, which I quickly gave, and continued on my way. An injured, hurt, or sick animal will find me with even more urgency. Trips to the dog park turn into mini-clinics for me, which is why I do not make it a regular habit to visit them. Besides, at present, I do not have a dog of my own.

Sarah and I had picnicked one afternoon in Cold Spring Harbor, a town a few miles to the east of us. We had a beautiful basket arranged (well, Sarah did) and we were looking forward to a romantic diversion near the water. The weather was perfect, and we were both in the mood for that sort of thing.

Shortly after we were set up for our feast, we heard a sharp series of barks coming from behind us. A German Shepard was leading his (or her, I did not know at the time) owner directly at us from across the grassy field. I sighed, looked at Sarah, who shrugged her shoulders, and put my sandwich away for the moment.

The owner was an older fellow who did not speak any English. He began to yammer at us in some foreign tongue, and his tone implied that this was all somehow our fault. He sounded annoyed. The dog came right up to me, and she (yep, she) circled me a few times, whining and pawing at the ground. I told her to sit (in English), which she did, and I looked at her face. I could see immediately something was wrong along her gum-line, and rose to my knees to get a better look.

The dog sat impassively as I opened the side of her mouth to see what the issue was. Her owner raised his voice, and in his foreign tongue starting practically screaming at me. I pulled my hands back in a position of resignation and said in clear English, "Okay, okay, take it easy. I didn't call her over, she came to me. She needs a vet, so find one, asshole." His tone and countenance had really annoyed me.

He tried to pull the dog away, but she would not go. Good girl. He then proceeded to pick up the dog, cursed at me again (at least it sounded like a curse) and quickly strode away. I sensed distress and sadness emanating from the pup, but sometimes there is nothing you can do. His attitude annoyed me to the point that I turned to Sarah, asked her to pack everything up, and took her to a nice restaurant for lunch. I was in no mood for a picnic any longer.

Back in real-time, I smiled reassuringly at the young woman struggling with the Great Dane and said, "It's okay, it's okay, let her come over." She visibly relaxed and the Dane covered the final few feet to me in pressed strides. As she reached me, the dog began to leave her front feet and rise up to her full height. Her owner frantically pulled on the leash, but to no avail.

I looked the dog in the eye, and with a firm "No!" held my hand out and toward the creature. She whined softly, then settled in front of me on her belly and waited.

"Hi, I'm sorry, hi, oh, wow, she never does this. I don't know…" she began and I gave her that reassuring smile again. I held my hand out toward her over the head of the Great Dane, who was now looking up at me from her prone position.

"It's really okay, hi, I'm Dr. Canis, and I'm a vet." I widened my smile a bit.

"Oh, wow!" she replied. "I was planning on making an appointment with one this week but I'm new here, and don't know anyone really yet." She was still a bit flustered from having herself dragged fifty unplanned feet to the front of a bar in broad daylight. She looked up at the bar at that point, and a confused look crossed her face.

"Not to worry, I'm not a drunkard," I chuckled. "Just found myself here after an unplanned walk." I was not sure why I felt an explanation was required, but offered one anyway for my auspicious appearance in front of a tavern in broad daylight.

I knelt down and stroked the head of the Great Dane, and the young woman said, "Her name is Spirit. She's 3." I barely heard her, as I sensed something coming from the dog that was not typical.

At this point, some clarification is needed. I cannot speak to dogs. Nor cats, nor squirrels with chewing gum stuck to their fur. No, it is more like a "feeling" that I get in the form of unspoken communication, and it is not always accurate. It is subject to my interpretation, and the difference in the brain of the human and the canine, so the land of misunderstanding is vast and fertile. I can also project feelings toward an animal, but that is not always received as I intend. It is not an exact science. I tried it with a spider once, but that did not work out too well. Either arachnids are on a different frequency or that particular spider did not care what I thought of his appearance in one of my extra pairs of shoes.

Animals, for the most part, have simple, uncomplicated feelings that I can usually glean when they are projected. Again, they are subject to my interpretation and classification. We humans accept the terms "happiness, "sadness," "jealousy," and the like because we are taught these terms and what they mean from an early age. Are they accurate labels of the full spectrum of the emotions? Are the feelings we experience limited by our lexiconic labeling of them? Food for thought. Come to think of it, I realized I was hungry at this point.

What was coming from the Great Dane, or "Spirit," as I should say, was something I could not get a clear handle on. Sadness mixed with frustration? Urgency? Wonder? Everything I was receiving was a jumbled mess of emotion that I had never experienced before. What I did recognize was a slight swelling in her right front leg that looked like an abscess of some kind.

"Have you noticed her limping a bit?" I asked, making an effort to keep my voice neutral.

"Yes, that's why I was looking for a vet. She's been chewing on the spot all week."

"I think she's got some kind of abscess, and I think it needs to be attended to immediately. What are you doing for the next hour or two?" I smiled at her, and patted Spirit again.

Again, that feeling. I was getting a lot of emotion from the dog, but not the normal one or two tracked raw feeling. There was more, much more than normal. What was it?

I took my cell out of my pocket and called Sarah.

"Hi." I began, tentatively.

As I have mentioned before, Sarah is a much better person than I am. After a few minutes, she pulled up in my Jeep and waved as she pulled into the parking lot. Most women would have grilled me on the spot if I had called them from a bar parking lot with another woman. I guess the dog helped, but still. Sarah said nothing, but I knew there would at least be a minor reckoning later.

I introduced Sarah to Spirit, and held out my hand towards her owner, whose name I did not know; she simply said "Cindy" and smiled. See? I did not know the girl's name! An intellectual victory for us stupid men! Now the score is something like twenty-seven trillion to six. At least I am doing my part.

Spirit happily worked her way into the truck and settled in the cargo compartment. Cindy got in the front seat next to Sarah who drove us back to our home where my office was. This was proving to be an interesting day.

***

8 – The Fence And The Mean Guy

Emily and Chelsea were getting along famously. Chelsea and I were getting along famously. She was the perfect home companion. Chelsea integrated into our family life as if she had been there from the beginning.

My parents were pleasantly surprised when Emily and I, usually at normal sibling odds, cooperated completely and placidly in the planning and execution of the care of Chelsea.

I would walk Chelsea in the morning while we were getting ready for school, Emily would walk her after school (she was home before I was) and we would alternate walking her after dinner. My parents were also enjoying Chelsea, and one of them would walk her before going to bed themselves. Chelsea had it good, we were all getting exercise, and there was peace in the Canis household.

Amazingly, Chelsea was "trained" in almost anything we asked her to do without much formal attention to the training. If we said something to her a few times, she picked up on it and would do it on command from anyone in the household almost immediately. Even more incredibly, if someone not in our family gave her a command, Chelsea would look to one of us for permission to execute the easily understood wishes of the visitor. Amazing.

One afternoon, my mother frantically bounced through the den of the house mumbling that she could not find her keys. Chelsea barked once, firmly, and led my mother to the basement door, which was closed. My mother opened the door and her keys were sitting on the top step. Apparently, mom had dropped them while carrying groceries to the extra pantry we kept in the basement. Mom lavished praise on the brilliant puppy and breathlessly told us all at dinner how Chelsea had done this incredible feat. Emily, looking nonplussed, simply said, "Mom, I taught her what keys are weeks ago!"

My walks with Chelsea were always interesting for me, as the raw emotions that I was receiving from the dog were hitting me unfiltered, unfettered, and still brand new. At this point, I did not attribute it to any special ability of mine. I simply thought that this dog and I had a special connection. I was also, despite my proclivity for torturing Emily, not using it against her. I was still unsure just what was happening, so I kept it to myself.

One particular day I remember, we were coming back down Bambi Lane, which is the street perpendicular to the one on which my house sat. I froze on the spot as the hair on the back of my neck began to rise up. Something from Chelsea had me pausing and nervous.

Chelsea stopped, lowered her head, and issued a low growl, which was something I had never heard her do before. Her eyes were fixed on the fence that separated the house we were in front of from the one next door.

Dogs have amazing senses. Amazing to the extent that we, as humans, cannot fully comprehend just how invaluable and incredible these creatures are when it comes to the sense of smell. An experiment was done in New York City in the 1980s (I wrote a paper on it in college) involving bloodhounds. Truly amazing stuff. The dogs were taken to Battery Park, which is at the southernmost tip of Manhattan Island. The three hounds were given a strong whiff of a mixture that contained talcum powder and a particularly strong perfume.

The powder/perfume combination was then taken by car, windows open, to the northern end of Manhattan Island, near Fort George. This is a distance of more than seven miles, across the acrid and incredibly heavily populated island of Manhattan. The mixture was released on the ground and shaken into the air when the cars with the research teams reached Fort George.

The bloodhounds, all three, were instantly in motion and, after four hours of trekking carefully through every type of possible aroma imaginable, stopping for lights, cabs, pedestrians, and two salted pretzels (for the humans), led their handlers directly to the spot where the bags had been released. Seven miles away.

Through the city. Does that give you an idea of how dull our senses are compared to theirs? I received an 'A' on my paper. That may have been because I cleverly included an interview with one of the bloodhounds that the professor really enjoyed. He thought I had been super creative and made that part up. You know better.

I asked Chelsea aloud what she saw, and what the problem was. She did not break her gaze at the fence. I never saw her so focused.

Fortunately, I do not startle or panic easily. The combination of sound, emotion, and movement that happened in the next millisecond would have caused most people to shriek. I started, but held my ground. Something large, ferocious, and angry was on the other side of the fence and took exception to Chelsea and me walking this particular route. What was strange to me is that I did not sense anything from this creature. Nothing. Usually I will pick up something from a dog, but I was coming up blank. I was only eight at the time, and not nearly as analytical as I am today, but I still remember feeling something was off. I was also a bit scared. I tried to turn Chelsea around and head back toward the house, but she would not budge. This was very unusual since Chelsea effortlessly and thoughtlessly obeyed every command anyone in the family gave her. This was long before cell phones were common, so I had no one to call. I was simply not sure what to do.

I heard a door slam, and someone said something in gruff tones, which caused the bane on the other side of the fence to trot back towards the house behind the fence. A man whose head barely cleared the fence came over, and looked down at Chelsea and me.

"Get out of here kid, and take that mangy mutt with ya!" His voice was thick with something I did not recognize, but it chilled me and I remember it sounding – unhealthy was the word that came to my young mind. Chelsea did not move.

"I'm just walking…" I began, but never got past that word.

He screamed. "I SAID BEAT IT!" At this yell, Chelsea, the most mild-mannered, sweetest pup in the world burst onto all fours and started barking fiercely at the man. This had the effect of startling me badly, and I started at a half-run back the way we had come. Chelsea moved with me, her face still turned back at the man, launching bark after bark at his red, pocked face as it stared at us over the fence. Half a block later, Chelsea faced forward, and walked back to the house with me without turning once. I sensed her normal carefree, easy manner was absent. She seemed tense, and unhappy. Angry, even. It was very strange.

I made a note to myself to walk Chelsea the other way from now on and debated telling my parents about the incident. I did not have to make the decision, as Emily made it for me.

"Oh my God, what did you do to her?" my sister screamed as we came back into the house. Emily dropped to her knees and wrapped her arms around Chelsea's neck. For one of the first times in my life, I was speechless. Something in Chelsea's manner tipped Emily off to the fact that we had just completed a non-standard walking experience.

I reported the event to my parents, while Emily looked on with daggers in her eyes. My father exchanged a glance with my mother as if to say "Who is that idiot?" as Emily and Chelsea went up the stairs.

My dad began, "You did the right thing by walking away, Mark. Stay away from that house in the future, okay, Champ?"

I nodded and headed towards my room. I did not think much about the incident thereafter, although someone in that house would play into my story in a big way much later, unbeknownst to me at the time.

***

9 – Nice Going, Mark

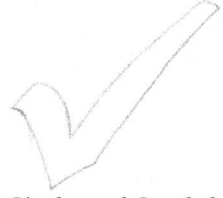

Back at my office, Cindy and Sarah helped me lift Spirit onto the examination table. Spirit was a big girl, at least one hundred twenty pounds, but she did not seem to mind the handling from her "mom" and two strangers. She settled nicely on the table and I scrubbed up preparing to take a good look at her. An uncomfortable silence permeated the room as Sarah and Cindy failed to communicate at all. I think it would have been easier if they started discussing handbags, makeup, or something like that. Anything, please.

I started with the standard heart, eyes, ears, and mouth examination of Spirit, and rotated her limbs thoroughly. I left the right front leg for last, which is where I observed what I thought to be an abscess. I was sure now. Not a big problem, but definitely something that required treatment before it festered or infected. Usually these can be surgically removed, and along with an anti-biotic regimen the dog would be fine in a few weeks. In this case, the abscess was open, which meant I could drain it right away, speeding up the healing process.

Cindy started to look a bit nervous at this point, and I smiled at her and asked if she needed anything or if she would prefer to wait outside in the waiting room.

She chewed her lower lip a second and said, "Well, no, it's not that, it's just, um, how much will all this be?" I had the instant sense that she was afraid this examination would be very expensive and beyond her means, whatever those were.

I smiled back and said, "Don't worry about it, it's on me. It was an unplanned visit as it were, right?"

Cindy gave me a brilliant smile and relaxed visibly. "Oh, wow, thank you!" She turned to Sarah and said, "Oh, and thank you too! Oh my God, people are so nice in this town!"

I took my time with Spirit, looking her over carefully while she sat there impassively tolerating my ministrations. I looked over at Sarah, and something resembling ice was in her eyes. Uh-oh. What did I do? Oh yeah, I gave this unknown woman, whom I had not yet had the chance to explain, a free pet examination on my day off. Well, not the woman, her dog. Good luck having sex in the next century Mark, way to go.

After about twenty minutes, which passed in complete silence, I was satisfied Spirit was all set and I wrapped some tape around the area. This special veterinary tape tastes horrible, and usually keeps all but the most determined pooches from chewing off the bandage. I explained everything to Cindy, looked nervously over at Sarah, and turned to put away my supplies.

Sarah broke the silence. Remember I had said she was a better person that I am? Apparently, she decided I would be the brunt of her anger later, so she graciously engaged Cindy in conversation.

"How long have you been living in Nyagg, Cindy?"

"Oh, not long," Cindy started, looking relieved to be conversing again. "My boyfriend and I broke up just after we moved here, and he was the reason I moved here, so it's been a nightmare, really."

Sarah replied, "Wow, men suck, don't they?" She looked at me when she said that.

Cindy giggled and spat out, "Yes, they really do. But you seem to have a good one here." She gave me a big smile. Thanks, Cindy, dig my love life grave a bit deeper.

I jumped in. "Do I know your boyfriend, I mean, is he from here?"

"EX-boyfriend." Cindy replied pointedly, and as my eyes caught Sarah's, the unmistakable pink of her tongue sticking out at me caught my attention. "We broke up after we moved here from Pennsylvania. I honestly think he just used me to get here – I signed the lease and everything, and then he basically threw me out of my own place. His name is Craig, although I call him 'asshole' now."

Sarah smiled halfway, and seemed to be thinking about something.

"Is he from around here?" Sarah asked.

"I think he lived near here when he was younger, but I'm not really sure. He picked the place. I had never been to New York before. Then, he kicked me out."

"Nice," said Sarah. "Then where are you living now?"

"Oh, I rent the apartment on top of the garage at Mrs. Sullivan's house. It's over on Tulipwood, do you know it?"

Dr. Mark, me, who never knows when to shut up, said, "Oh yeah, we know the Sullivans, they had two Chihuahuas for years who were patients of mine." I finished the sentence with an inane smile, which I bounced back and forth between Sarah and Cindy. "Where were you living before?" I asked.

"We had a nice two-bedroom apartment by the water, on Grove. He's still there for all I know. I have no contact with him anymore, and that's fine with me. He's an idiot." She said this last part with exasperation, and Sarah smiled in empathy.

"Yeah, they all can be, sometimes." Sarah replied, and again looked pointedly at me.

I briefed Cindy on care for Spirit over the next two weeks, and gave her sample packs of the anti-biotic she would need to feed her daily. I suggested putting it inside some cheese and feeding it to Spirit before she ate anything else. Cindy took the bag, and then made my life infinitely worse by grabbing me in a fast, hard hug and kissing my cheek. I cannot describe the face Sarah made at this, let it suffice to say I could probably donate my sexual organs to science at this point; I would never need them again.

Sarah offered to drive Cindy and Spirit somewhere in town, and Cindy gratefully accepted, asking to be taken home. Just as they reached the front door, Cindy turned and said to me, "You will probably meet the jerk at some point; after all, he sells puppies and stuff." As the words registered, the feeling that I had when I first sensed something from Spirit came back with a vengeance. Something in the words Cindy spoke chilled me. Although the room was warm, I was suddenly cold. What did she mean? He sells puppies? That was a strange thing to say, and certainly were there a breeder or a pet shop in town I would know about it. If I had had more guts, I would have followed Sarah and Cindy outside and inquired further. However, I am not that brave. Not yet, anyway.

***

10 - I Don't Like This Kid

I had heeded my father's admonition not to walk Chelsea past "the mean-guy" house, as my sister Emily had labeled it. I began to walk Chelsea the other way as a habit, and she quickly caught on and led me in the new direction every time we left the house.

When no one was watching, which was the usual scenario when I walked Chelsea in the morning; I would walk her "off-leash." Chelsea never gave me a reason to worry about this. I know my parents would not have been happy about it, and I was certain Emily would have found a way to bring me up on charges if she knew, but it made me feel cool, I trusted Chelsea, and it was easier than holding that dumb leash. Chelsea never ventured more than two feet away from my left leg. I would bring the leash with us in case we saw a police car, as there was a leash law in Nyagg, but it was never an issue.

One morning, Chelsea and I began our daily sojourn in the usual fashion. As we reached the cross street that runs parallel to mine, I noticed a construction crew doing something major in the street. Curious, as all young boys are when encountering a plethora of construction equipment, Chelsea and I wandered a bit closer to take a look. Chelsea dutifully scampered along at my side, nonplussed by the noise and the strange men in the yellow vests.

One of the men approached me, and with a smile, said, "Hey there guy," he leaned down towards Chelsea "and hi there pretty pup!"

Chelsea sat immediately and I sensed no danger from her. I smiled back at the man. I then realized I depended on Chelsea to warn me of 'stranger-danger,' a term that would not be coined for another twenty years. If Chelsea trusted the person we met, so did I.

He continued, "You guys should head back down this street," pointing at a cross street, "we're digging up some pipes here and it's a bit dangerous. You and your dog shouldn't walk past this way. She's beautiful, by the way." Chelsea stood up at the compliment. I swear this dog speaks English.

"Ok, mister, thanks." I replied as politely as I could, and without giving it too much thought, headed down the side street he had indicated back toward my street. What I did not realize immediately is the side street he sent us down met my street at the corner by the mean guy's house. I was told not to come this way, but I saw no choice except to re-trace my steps all the way back past the construction crew. For some reason I did not want to do that.

I looked at Chelsea, she looked at me, and we both started walking purposefully toward home via the new route. I attached her leash, which Chelsea tolerated with her typical equanimity. Along the way, Chelsea stopped and did her business, which I was always equipped to pick up, and I had the strong impression she knew where we would pass and wanted to be ready for anything. That may have been a silly notion, but I had it anyway.

When we reached the corner – the corner of doom – in front of the house of doom - I heard that low growl from Chelsea's throat that I had heard the day we had first encountered the mean guy. Eyes locked on the house and walking purposefully, Chelsea and I strode intently on the other side of the street towards our home. The side we walked on was on a higher plane because of a long berm, and we were able to see over the fence a bit into the yard of the mysterious house with the mean owner. We saw no dog, no mean guy, nor anything unusual. I spotted a dilapidated swing on the porch, noticed that the house needed painting, and began to relax.

As we reached the far end of the fence, we heard a shout. "Hey! I thought I told you not to walk that mutt around here!" came a scream from somewhere in the direction of mean guy's house. Looking up and back, I noticed the mean guy shouting at me from an upstairs window. Next to him was a boy about my age with a huge grin on his face. The boy saluted me, that is to say, he raised the middle finger of his left hand in a deliberate gesture, which I assumed was a salute since I did not know any different at the time. I remember thinking to myself, "What's up with these people?" and I hurried Chelsea along. She stuck with me, increased her speed to match my pace, and soon we were a few houses away. I was shaking, not sure why. Something about that house spooked me, not just the mean occupants. It was something else. Chelsea and I continued home and went inside as if nothing out of the ordinary had happened. Chelsea headed for the kitchen where I heard mom greet her, and I headed upstairs to get ready for school.

My daily routine as a youngster was pretty standard. After walking Chelsea, I would gather my things, throw them in my super-cool Star Trek knapsack, grab my lunch from the kitchen, kiss mom, and head out to wait for the bus that stopped at the corner away from mean guy's house. I followed all these procedures that morning, but there was a surprise waiting for me at the bus stop. It was the middle finger kid, with a smile plastered on his freckle-pocked face.

"Hey, dumbshit!" he started as I reached the bus stop. I had that heated feeling on the back of my neck that I would get whenever I felt like I was in trouble.

I remembered my father's advice for handling situations like this, and I ignored the boy. Did not work, dad. He came right over to me, towering over me by at least six inches, and said, "I said, HEY DUMBSHIT! What, are you friggin' deaf as well as ugly?" Two other kids, ones that I knew distantly from riding the bus with them for a few years, looked nervously in my direction but said nothing.

"What do you want?" I asked, and my voice came out a bit weaker than I had intended.

"I want to kick your ass, that's what I want. Where's your little ugly mutt to protect you, huh, dumbshit?"

I did not know what to do. I had never encountered such a foul, awful human being before. I was simply dumbfounded.

It occurred to me, in that moment, rather, in the few moments I had before I found myself on the ground, the brunt of an unexpected punch to my stomach by freckle-boy, that no one had ever been mean to me before. This was a profound moment in my life. In those few seconds, my stream of consciousness awakened and I *thought*. I felt like I had aged ten years in a few moments. I had lost my innocence. I saw this evil on the six o'clock news every night. This was the 'real world' that, up until this point, I had been insulated from. This kid was going to kill me and there was nothing I could do about it. He also had no reason to do so, and I remember being struck by the irony of that. I remember thinking what a nice kid I was – and I wondered for a minute who would walk Chelsea in the morning after freckle-boy put me in my grave.

I sat, stunned, not remembering how I had become earthbound. I heard the nervous laughter of the other kids, but I suppose that was not their fault, taking freckle-boy's side was probably the prudent move at this point.

"Not so tough without that little mangy mutt, are you?" freckle-boy said, spitting each word down at me. He then leveled a kick at me, which narrowly missed my face and brushed off the side of my head. I got up quickly, and sprinted back to my house.

"That's right, run away you little girl. Run home to mommy! Waa, waaa…" his taunting voice could be heard in my head as I headed home. I realized I did not have my knapsack, and Captain Kirk was left there, unprotected, with freckle-boy.

I noticed the bus coming up the block, but I did not stop and head towards it. I was going home, and nothing could stop me. As I broached the front steps of my house, Chelsea barked a few times sharply probably because a visitor at this hour was so out of routine for the Canis household.

I burst into the house and ran upstairs. I heard my mother call, "Hello? Mark, is that you?" Chelsea ran up the stairs too, and looked at me. She tilted her head and I cursed at her. "Go away, you stinking beast, this is your fault!" I screamed, and immediately felt awful for doing so. I felt the sadness in Chelsea immediately, and that just made it worse. Chelsea lay down at the doorway to my room and I could swear I saw a tear in her eye. Could this day get any worse?

My mother came in and said, "Mark, oh my, what's the matter?" At that point, I realized I was in a full-blown cry, and ran into her arms. I sniffled and cried more, but could not answer her.

I was overwhelmed by several things: my stomach hurt, and my pride hurt worse, I had snapped at Chelsea which made me feel terrible, I had lost my Star Trek knapsack, and I was late for school. Wow, that was an eventful few minutes, I thought. I turned from my mother and sat on my bed.

I tried to explain to my mother why I was there, but I could not form words. She sat next to me on the bed, put her arm on my shoulder, wiped my face with her apron, and waited.

"I got beat up, mom."

"What? By who?"

"That kid from down the block. From the mean guy's house."

"What were you doing down there?" she asked, "Didn't your father and I say not to walk Chelsea that way?"

"I didn't!" I shouted, louder than I had meant to, and continued, "The jerkoff is on my bus!" The last part came out half-scream half-cry and my mother looked annoyed and concerned at the same time.

"We do not use language like that in this house, mister, calm down, clean yourself up, and I will drive you to school." She calmly arose and walked purposefully out of my room.

I screamed after her, "I'm NEVER GOING TO SCHOOL AGAIN!" and slammed my bedroom door. Chelsea had followed my mother out of the room, and I suddenly longed for her to bury my face into. Nothing was working out this morning.

***

11 – I Almost Face the Music, But I Don't Know This Tune

Next day, Sarah and I were to have dinner with her parents. You know how much I was looking forward to that, but after the events in my office with the Great Dane (which had still not been discussed) I knew I had better keep my mouth shut and be a good boy.

We were to meet them at a Japanese restaurant not too far from here, since for some reason they never liked us to pick them up. When we pulled into the parking lot, the reason for us not picking them up this time became clear.

Sitting in the parking lot was a shiny, brand new Cadillac two seat convertible sports car, with Sarah's smiling dad standing leaning upon it. We pulled up slowly in our Jeep, and I moved to the left so Sarah's side of the car would be by her dad as we pulled into the adjacent parking spot.

"Sweet, huh?" her father said as we alighted from our Jeep. I nodded my head up and down as if to say "wow, nice" but I really did not care for the car. I would never say that though. Sarah took everything in stride, especially when it came to her father, and spoke the appropriate accolades.

"It's beautiful dad, when did you get it?" She went over to her father and planted a kiss on his cheek and stood admiring the car.

"Just today. It's custom. Had them install the big speakers and it's got all the bells and whistles. I love it." He glowed at the car, and nodded in my direction as a greeting.

"It's great, enjoy it." I said, mustering as much enthusiasm as I could, although I did not feel it. We had very different tastes in vehicles.

Sarah asked, "Where's mom?"

· "Ah, forget her, she's cranky. C'mon, let me take you for a spin."

As there were only two seats, I stood unsure as of what to do, and said to Sarah, "Yeah, go! I'll go inside and wait with your mother." I had assumed Sarah's mother was inside the restaurant already, and since no one corrected me, I waved and headed up the steps.

Sarah and her father have an interesting relationship. Sarah is a strong-willed, dynamic girl, but her father seems to reduce her to childhood instantly. She simply cannot seem to say no to the man. I wonder often if I am jealous of her relationship with her father, but I do not think that is it. I suppose they are just so different that I do not see the connection. I know that is ridiculous, he is her father, but it still never added up for me. Sarah is grounded, sensible, loyal, and even-tempered. Her father is an overgrown teenager with a wild streak or two or twenty. Go figure.

The growl of the shiny car's engine caught my attention as I turned back, and Sarah waved to me from the topless automobile as it zoomed into traffic on the heavily travelled road on which the restaurant was located. I sighed to myself and completed the trek up the stairs.

I was greeted by a uniformed maître'd who asked, "How many, sir?"

I explained that my girlfriend's mother was probably already seated, and as I did I saw her wave from near the window.

I leaned over and kissed Sarah's mother Sophie and sat down across from her while taking in the opulent room. "Nice place," I said casually, and smiled.

Sophie let out an exasperated sigh. "Mark, I swear, that man," obviously referring to her husband. "He drives me nuts. He comes home today with that car, meanwhile, they're about to turn off the electricity since we haven't paid the bill in three months!" I stared at her. This was the first time I was let in on family stuff like this, and it made me a bit uncomfortable.

"Wow, I didn't know you guys were having problems like that." I said weakly.

"No, no, no," she waved me off. "It's not like that – we're fine. He just forgets things – and when he gets something like that car into his brain, nothing else matters. Recently he's been buying all sorts of things, and I just keep forgetting to tell him to pay the damn electric bill. It's my fault, really."

That bothered me. Why was she self-effacing? This did not make sense, and it was very contrary to what I was used to. In my household growing up, mom was in charge of the finances as far as I knew, so this was a new arrangement to me. I felt that little tweak of 'I shouldn't be hearing this,' but at the same time, I felt like I was being brought into the 'inner circle.' It was a strange mix of feelings.

Sophie went on to brag about all of the new things that had been appearing in the house recently. The old tube TV was gone one evening suddenly replaced by a 42" plasma. There was a decorative vase on the table that had never been there before, and it looked expensive. In addition, a new painting was hung above the mantle that Sophie knew nothing about until she saw it.

"He just buys things and doesn't say anything?" I asked.

"Yes." She sighed. "That's his way. I'm not complaining, really, I love the TV. You have to see it next time you come over. "

As we finished this little treatise, Sarah and her father walked in, his face still beaming. He reached for my hand and gave it a hearty shake. "That thing moves, let me tell you." He said as he sat down. Sarah's eyes met mine and they went wide as if to say, "Oh yeah."

Once we were all in place, a waiter quickly came over and took our drink orders. Usually in a restaurant I will enjoy a cocktail or a beer, but tonight I just ordered lemonade or iced tea, whichever they had. Sarah's parents were not big drinkers either, so none of us ordered anything with kick.

We chatted amicably about this and that, killing the time before our appetizer arrived, and I ventured out into uncharted territory.

"So, Lou, what made you decide to get the car?" I asked as casually as I could. It was obvious some major money had made its way into Lou's pocket recently, and it made me curious.

"Ah, you know, you only live once." was his static reply. "I always wanted one of those, just never got around to getting one. It's nothing compared to the convertible I had in the 60's, man, now THAT was a car."

No explanation further was forthcoming, and Sarah looked at me and raised her shoulders in an "I don't know" motion. I pushed.

"That thing must be what, sixty, seventy grand?"

"Ah, don't worry about it." He quickly replied. "A good friend of mine knows the dealer; I got a great deal on it." End of subject, I suspected. My kick from Sarah under the table confirmed that.

The meal continued in normal fashion, with Lou ordering for everyone, which I disliked but tolerated, and with more casual small talk about nothing. I was now more curious about the sudden influx of funds. I never truly had a handle on Lou's business dealings. I knew he was an importer of some kind, but no one seemed to know precisely of what, where, or how. He was flush one week, broke the next it seemed, but never failed to pick up the check at dinner. This time was no different.

We left the restaurant and Lou told Sarah he would drive her home – and told me to take Sophie with me. Okay. Sarah shrugged her shoulders and got in the sports car.

I took Sophie by the hand and led her to the Jeep. "Don't try anything funny, lady, I have a girlfriend." I joked as I helped her into the truck. She laughed and winked, but I could see she was a bit hurt by being told to ride with me.

I dropped Sophie off at Sarah's parents' house, and waited outside for Sarah. I expected her to drive up with her father momentarily, and I figured if I waited outside we could do the quick 'gimme back my girlfriend' transfer and not have to go inside where I would have to endure stories. I mean, I would if that is what Sarah wanted to do, but I was hoping to avoid it. Sophie did not say anything, but silently went into the house.

My cell phone vibrated, and I answered. "Hi babe."

"Dad and I are going for ice cream, lover," came Sarah's voice from the speaker, "head home after you drop mom and I'll meet you there later."

"Okay." I hung up. We usually end our conversations with a pleasantry, but not this time. Sarah was usually uncomfortable saying anything sweet over the phone while she was with her dad, but she had called me lover. That struck me as funny. I interpreted it as, "I'm sorry I'm not coming home right away but you know how it is so I'll see you at home and don't worry about it – but don't say anything about it either."

I was pissed off now. Only Lou could make Sarah like this, and I resented it. First of all, we had yet to discuss the Great Dane incident or THE Craig situation, and I was a bit anxious to avoid the first and dive into the second. Now I was stuck not exactly sure what to do or where to go. I laughed to myself as I considered going to *Reflections,* but wow, twice in one day? Not a good idea.

I headed home, parked, and went inside.

Headlights and an engine growl woke me a few hours later. I had fallen asleep on the couch, which was unusual for me, but it was also unusual for me to be home late at night alone.

The flash of headlights illuminated the den, which is at the front of our house, and I heard a car door slam. A bit disoriented, I suddenly had a rush of all the emotions from the night. What a mixture my mind concocted. Let's catalog: I was annoyed at Sarah for going with her dad instead of coming home with me – but at the same time, I knew not to go down that road. I was anxious about discussing Cindy and Spirit, since I knew that was coming. I was also feeling amorous, as late night is my witching hour for that kind of thing, and I argued to myself that I would have a hard time satisfying that thirst. Then I thought through the whole new car, new TV, new painting, new vase thing over at Sarah's parents' house, and wondered about that. This gave me a quick, sharp headache, which circled me back to the amorous feeling that quickly went away, I got annoyed about that – WOW – I was working myself into a frenzy as Sarah made her way from the driveway to the front door. So what did I do? Right. Pretended I was asleep when she came in the front door. I have no idea why. I just shut my eyes and listened. I heard the screen door swing (I have to remember to WD-40 that tomorrow) and then I heard the key in the lock. The inner door swung open slowly, and in walked Sarah.

She spotted me on the couch, and said, "Hi, hon, I know you're up, you never sleep on the couch."

Pretending to be in a stupor, I replied, "Oh, hi, babe, how was it?"

"How was what?"

"I dunno, um, whatever you did after we left dinner."

"Fine. We just talked. He's very excited about that car."

"Yeah, I got that feeling. You like it?"

"It's beautiful. Really rides nice. He loves it."

With that, she headed up the stairs without another word. I am so bad at this kind of thing. I had no idea what to do next. Should I just follow her up the stairs and jump her? Should I run the shower and ask if she wanted to join me? Should I wander into the bedroom and smile and wait for what came next? Should I go mow the lawn in the middle of the night?

I was a brilliant student in high school. I was a great student in college, and I was top of my class in veterinary college. Yet, a situation like this makes me feel like a moron. I just had no idea what to do.

Annoyed with myself now, I stood, went to the sideboard, and I poured myself some brandy. I sipped it, and coughed. Wow, that was harsh. I do not even like brandy. See what I mean?

I did not have to make the next decision for Sarah came down the stairs still dressed in her clothes from dinner.

"I think we should talk." Oh, man. Words that set the thunder off in any man's brain. Oh boy, I was in for it now.

I followed her into the kitchen, and sat at the center island on a stool.

I asked, "Want anything?"

No reply.

Out of the blue, here is what came next: "So, do you want to explain why you walked out of the house today, dressed in a shirt and tie, and went to a bar and met a blonde woman?"

A great football coach once said, "The best form of defense is a great offense." Apparently, Sarah had played on one of his teams at some point.

"Yeah," I began, but I chickened out. "Um, hon, can we do this tomorrow? I have office hours in the morning."

"Fine."

Those words are doom. Never let the last thing your woman says be, "Fine." Trust me on this one.

"Wait," I said, "Ok, let's chat a bit." I tried to keep my tone light, but I do not think I pulled it off.

Let me give my fellow males out there a little advice. Ladies, you can stay tuned in, but it will not make a difference, the men out there reading this will not take this advice any more than they will stop for directions next time the GPS takes them down the same dirt road seven times consecutively.

Ok, men, pay attention: Just come clean right away. Tell her everything, do not embellish, and deal with it. Women have this innate sense when they are being bullshitted, and that will always come back to haunt you. Go honest from the get-go.

This puts me in mind of my old friend Tom, with whom I worked in a small veterinary practice before I opened my own shop. Tom was an assistant, but he was much older than I was, and always had sparkling advice for anyone that would listen. That was usually me. One day, Tom noticed me noticing a pretty young thing that had brought her Siamese cat in for a checkup.

"Watch out for cat-ladies," warned Tom, "they'll get ya every time."

Not sure what he meant, I asked, "What do you mean?"

"Well, son, it's like this." That is how Tom talked. "A woman like that is too good looking to be trusted. See, the better looking they are, the more dudes out there that are going to try to bang her." Tom had such a gentle, kind way with words.

He continued, "That leads to jealousy, problems, fights, all kinds of horseshit you don't need. It's like the song says, 'If you wanna be happy for the rest of your life, never ever make a pretty woman your wife.'"

He smiled at his lyrical recitation, and gave me a look that said, 'see how damn smart I am?' I was still confused.

"You mean, only pursue ugly women?" I inquired.

"No, no, no" he admonished. "But when you're looking to settle down, a hot one like that is nothing but trouble." He continued, taking a pose of the great wise man lecturing the innocent, brain-dead disciple of life. In other words, me.

"Let me tell you about women, son. You see, the woman is a different kind of animal. She has needs we can't possibly satisfy, thinks about things we have no idea about, and needs to be constantly bullshitted to be happy."

I stared at him probably the same way a new puppy stares at

his owner the first time he is told to "Sit, now lie down, and now roll over." In other words…what???

"You see," the great wise Tom continued, "Women don't want the truth if the truth is going to hurt. Let's say your wife comes home and finds you banging the maid on the dining room table right next to the Thanksgiving turkey. Whatrya gonna do? That's right, deny it. Deny, deny, deny. That way there will always that one percent of doubt, even though she caught you red-handed. Got me?"

I stared at Tom for a long time. His enigmatic smile sat there staring back at me. I remember thinking, "What an idiot." I can safely say, at this point in my life, that the best thing I learned from Tom was to never take advice from an idiot. See, not all of us men are complete fools!

Digression complete, time to face the music. Sarah stared at me, and I was at a loss for words.

What happened next almost broke my heart. She stood, and said, "You know what? I don't want to know. I'm going to bed."

I felt like someone had shot an arrow through me. Sarah had never spoken to me like that before, and I was stunned. I even forgot about wanting to get laid. I had no idea what to do.

I sat at the kitchen island for what must have been forty-five minutes. I then did something I had never done before. What a night for firsts this was turning out to be. I went into my office, which is accessible through a door off the kitchen. I took off my shoes, pants, and watch, laid them down on the end table in the waiting room, and went prone on the waiting room couch. The scent of dog and cat hair immediately permeated my nose, but I did not care. What the heck happened? I stared at the ceiling until I finally fell asleep.

***

12 – Ah, So That's Who it Is

My father today is an even-tempered guy, as I remember him being when I was young. I ended up staying home from school the day of 'the bus stop massacre', as my mother never came back up to my room after I had reported the incident, to take me to school. Mom had seemed somewhat confused, as if this sort of thing was out of her area of expertise to deal with. I know better now – she was just trying very hard not to let me see her anger and rage.

My father, even tempered as he was, went nuts when he came home and heard the story. "What happened?" he shouted at me after stomping up the stairs after the brief conference with my mother.

"This kid, dad, he punched me, then he …" I started, but he interrupted.

"Did you say anything to him?"

"No, dad, I promise. I just walked up…"

"Why do you think he punched you?"

I yelled, louder than I had meant to, "Because he's an ANIMAL dad!" I burst into tears again, and saw my father's face show a mixture of disappointment and anger as he turned away.

Chelsea came into my room, and lay down next to me looking at me with those big, black eyes. I felt her sadness – and realized it was because I was sad. For some reason, this picked me up. I sniffled a few times, wiped my damp face, and put on a smile. "It's okay, girl, it's not your fault. He's just an idiot," meaning the kid at the bus stop. Chelsea's tail started doing the Texas–two-step and I immediately started to feel better. I actually laughed at loud at her change in countenance and bounced off my bed. "C'mon, girl," I said to Chelsea, "let's go outside." This is what dogs can do for us, and it is priceless.

Something strange was occurring downstairs, as I heard the raised voices of my parents, something I do not think I had ever heard before. I froze on the stairs, and Chelsea stopped short with me. I tried to listen, but only caught snippets as my parents were in the kitchen on the other side of the house. I heard "going over there" and "what will that accomplish?" and "He's my son!" and "How will challenging him help?" and lots of other statements and questions like that. I suddenly felt guilty, as if their raised voices were my fault.

I continued down the stairs, and made some noise as I crossed through the dining room with Chelsea. My parents stopped speaking and I walked into the kitchen with Chelsea in tow.

My father spoke to me. "Mark, I don't want you walking Chelsea anymore in the mornings. Your mother or I will do it."

"But, dad," I started, but he cut me off.

"No. This kid is obviously some kind of bully and I don't want any more trouble. I will speak to people about it and see what can be done, but until then, you can walk Chelsea with one of us in the afternoon or in the evening."

I felt deflated. I also suddenly felt a burning in my chest and a desire to go the house of the mean guy and his equally mean freckle-faced devil offspring and beat the living crap out of both of them. Chelsea's ears perked up at the sound of her name mentioned so many times, and I sensed uncertainty from her. I patted her on the head and led her into the backyard. I did not understand this whole situation, but I suppose I learned one of the most important lessons of life that day: People affect people. Neighbors affect neighbors. Living in close proximity, as many of us do, we have a profound effect on those around us, both good and bad. I vowed to never be taken by surprise as I had at the bus stop that morning, and I vowed to never treat anyone else that way. It was too painful, too humiliating.

I heard my father walk out the front door, and heard my mother call after him, "Arty, don't!"

He did not return immediately, which meant he was going to do whatever my mother had implored him not to.

My father is not a big man, nor is he supremely muscular or

tough. One thing about him I admire to this day I first saw that afternoon. In later years, we would discuss it, explore it, qualify it, and laugh about it, but that day my father taught me an incredibly valuable lesson: "Be nice. Be kind. Be polite. But, never, ever, ever, ever take shit from anyone." Amen, pop.

Twenty minutes later my father marched back into the house and called, "Mark?"

I appeared through the kitchen door and walked to the front of the house, Chelsea at my side, my mother joining me as I reached the foyer.

On the front porch, in all his freckle-faced glory, was the kid from the bus stop with an incredibly ugly Walrus standing next to him. Okay, it was not a Walrus, it was a man, but I clearly remember the term "Walrus" popping into my head when I saw him. It was mean-guy, in the flesh.

My father stepped to the side and I looked into the face of the Walrus, who was trying to look stern but had a smirk on his face.

My father spoke. "Mark, this is Mr. Zornig and his son, Craig. He says you called him crater-face at the bus stop this morning, is that true?"

"NO!" I shouted, louder than I had intended. Chelsea was next to me, and she lay down and growled softly. Good girl.

My father looked at the boy now, backing me up.

"You did too!" he shouted, and turned to his father.

The Walrus spoke. "Alright, whatever happened, it's done now. Say you're sorry, Craig."

Freckle-face replied, "But, dad!"

"Just say it!" groaned the Walrus.

"Fine. I'm sorry."

The Walrus looked at my dad. "Okay?"

"Yeah, I guess so." Replied my father, with a danger in his voice I had never heard before.

As they walked away, I clearly heard a word spoken softly, followed by a chuckle. I clearly heard the word "pussy." My father started to move – he had heard it to – but he stopped. Without a word to me, he spun and went into the house.

I stood there for a long time and wondered if it would ever be safe to go out again. As it turns out, the behavior of the Walrus and his offspring prompted my parents to drive me to school from that point forward. My father was afraid of what he would do if there was another confrontation, and my mother simply agreed to keep the peace. It meant an extra fifteen minutes of sleep in the morning, so I was happy. Not nearly as happy as when we found out the Walrus and his offspring had sold the house and moved not two months later. Peace was restored to Nyagg, at least for the time being.

***

13- The Longest Day of My Career, So Far

Bright and early, I went into the bathroom in my office and surveyed my choices. My couch sucked as a bed, by the way- my back may never be the same. My office lavatory is primarily for my patient's owners, and comes in handy. It has a stall shower, and I could not remember if it had ever been used. I needed it now – since nothing short of a nuclear bomb was getting me up the stairs. Like most men, I will let my pride get in the way of better, more rational choices.

I tentatively turned the faucet in the stall shower to the on position, and I was rewarded with spurting brown fluid that flowed for a few seconds, sputtered, and then turned almost water-color. I waited, tested the temperature, and decided it was fine.

I had no shampoo or soap with me, so I improvised, planning to squirt a few blasts from the hand sanitizer near the sink as soap and shampoo, so I moved the container into the shower and began to undress.

Remember when I said Sarah was a better person than I was? A moment later, I heard the office door open. A voice said, "Moron, come upstairs and take a shower." There was a laugh in her voice that made the word 'moron' okay. "You don't have clean clothes down here." I turned at looked, and she was smiling. I walked over to her, and kissed her. At that moment, I realized how much I had missed her last night. She turned and headed back into the house.

In my more functional, familiar, and stocked shower, I let the water cascade over me and thought about the past few days. There was a lot happening, and I needed to sort it out. First, THE Craig. I wondered for a minute if it was the same Craig that I had had the incident at the bus stop with all those years ago. THAT Craig and his Walrus father had moved away not two months after our bus stop incident. Whatever, wherever, or whomever precipitated that move would get a large donation from me were it or they to open a church.

The only connection there, that I had just recently made, was the name. I would never forget hearing the name of my tormentor, Craig, when he and his father appeared on my front porch after my father's visit to their home. I played the whole THE Craig thing through my mind, then thought about the Great Dane and Cindy at *Reflections*. Why did I give the woman free services? Was it some unrecognized attempt to hurt Sarah because I was angry about THE Craig and her conversation with Stefania? That did not sound like me, I told myself, and dismissed the idea. I do pro bono work all the time – I open a free health inspection booth every year at the town fair – so helping a poor dog owner was not that much of a stretch for me.

I thought about the mysterious phone call. I decided, then and there, soap in my hair, that I would consult Carlo on that. I started to hum as I felt better, putting things into perspective and into focus. The thought of Sarah reentered my mind, and I was suddenly unhinged again. It dawned on me how fragile my world seemed if there was something amiss with Sarah. I suppose that, more than anything else defined love for me. I needed Sarah to be happy for me to be happy. That is when I made a rash decision, but not so rash after all. I would make a shopping trip after my office hours today. Finally.

I turned off the water, and reached for the towel that I had forgotten to place on the heated rail next to the shower. Great. I opened the shower door and saw Sarah standing there holding open a big, white, fluffy bath sheet. She glanced down my body, suggestively, and said, "Nice, sailor. New in town?" I felt myself begin to stir.

I moved towards her and I guess my eyes gave away my thinking.

"Hold it, macho-man, I am leaving in a few minutes, and your first patient is due in twenty minutes. I'll see you later."

She kissed me, wrapped me in the towel, and was gone from the bathroom.

I felt better, and felt sure the shopping decision I had made was the right one. Life was good.

One of the great things about my situation was the fact that I most definitely had the best commute of anyone I know. It was literally (I measured it, yes) a twenty-seven foot commute. Traffic was never an issue. Well, truthfully, there was this one time the cleaning lady was on her way up the stairs and I was on my way down and I had to pause a few seconds to let her pass, but that did not make the traffic report on the morning radio stations.

My office, which you know by now, is attached to the house, and it is a simple but functional affair. I have a waiting room with a receptionist's desk behind a glass partition, two small examination rooms, and a surgical room that I do not use very often. I have a small personal office that I use to discuss things with patient's owners when warranted which is where I keep my laptop, a television, a small refrigerator and shelves of books. It is a little man-haven of sorts, but I am usually more comfortable in the main house, especially since Sarah moved in.

Off one of the examination rooms is another room I call "the hotel" lined with a few cages that I use when a patient has to stay overnight or longer. The cages are large, spacious, meticulously clean spaces that I insist remain that way. I also have a small play area off the "hotel" with a small fenced in area with a drain in the middle of the cement floor where patients can run around a bit. If the situation warrants it, there is access to the backyard as well which is completely fenced in for just that reason – sometimes I let patients play outside.

My practice is mostly word-of-mouth, and I do no advertising. I have an excellent reputation, which is enough in this neighborhood, and I draw extensively from the affluent neighboring communities. I know all of my patients very well, and take all cases except the most dire. I am more of an office practitioner, and although I am well versed in surgery, I tend to send the more complicated surgical cases to two veterinarians in neighboring towns that I know well and am comfortable with. I like to keep it light as possible.

My receptionist is a terrific woman who has worked with me for years. Her name is Gina, and she tends to the mundane aspects of the practice. She schedules everything, monitors supplies and reorders when needed, and basically runs the place. I also have interns who come and go, but my favorite assistants are the high school kids, mostly girls, that come and help on a volunteer basis mostly because they love pets. I have had male assistants as well, but when it comes to loving pets at that age, the majority of applicants I get (I run an ad every year in the school newspaper for assistants) are female. They are a big help, entertaining waiting patients and gleaning the reasons for visits saving me the need to do so. Overall, the office runs very smoothly.

Gina was not due in for another twenty minutes, so I sauntered to the coffee maker, which is kept clean and well stocked by the aforementioned Gina. I chose a Columbian this morning, popped the pre-measured cup in the machine, closed it, and hit brew.

I heard a car pull into the driveway and I looked at my watch. It was too early for it to be Gina, and too early for my patient. I walked to the waiting room, which is at the front of the house, and looked out. A large pickup truck with darkened windows was idling a few feet from my office door. Due to the angle of the sun and the darkened windows of the truck, I could not see who was driving or if there was anyone else in the car. I waited. After a few minutes, the truck backed up, and shot out of the driveway, screeching a bit as the driver hit the pedal hard. Strange. I did not get the license plate number as it pulled out too quickly. I do not know why I felt I should get the license plate number, but something about the truck felt wrong. Add it to the list of things I could not explain at that point. I also made a mental note to add it to the things I planned to talk to Carlo about. I took my coffee over to the mini-fridge in my office and added a dab of cream.

Gina arrived on time, as usual, greeting me with a smile and made her way behind her desk carrying a brown bag with her morning treat. I smiled back at her and picked up the appointment clipboard she always prepared the day before.

"Looks pretty basic, huh? Good morning."

"Good morning, Doctor, nice to see you." Gina always called me 'Doctor', and no insistence of anything else would change that.

My first patient of the day arrived, a beautiful Himalayan cat, all white, whose 'mother' has been bringing her to me for years. The cat, "Charlie", had just had the incredibly cute 'lion cut' grooming done, and looked simply adorable. Her mom, a woman whose name I did not remember, smiled at me and greeted me as she put the carrier in which the cat resided down on the table and walked to Gina's window. I turned and walked into my small office. I heard the door open and close, which meant one of my myriad assistants had probably just arrived. Singsong greetings and mushy musings to the Himalayan cat confirmed this.

My day went along as usual, except that it seemed time was moving more slowly than usual. This was probably because of the shopping trip I had in mind after office hours.

One quick story from the day before we go shopping- at about 11:30, a young man and his mother came in unscheduled. I listened from my office and my heart sank a bit. Here is what I heard:

"Good morning, hello, can I help you?"

A small voice, thick with emotion, spoke. "It's Milo. He's my goldfish. He's sick."

Gina is just wonderful with these things. I heard her say, "Oh my, young man, I'll see if the doctor is free to take a look at him right away."

I walked into the office pretending to not have heard a thing, and said, "Hello there young man, what's up? I'm Dr. Canis."

He turned to me, with sad eyes, holding up a glass bowl that contained an obviously very dead, floating goldfish.

He broke into tears and flustered, "It's Milo, Doctor, something's wrong with him!"

My heart broke. I had hardly noticed the woman with him, probably his mother, until our eyes met. She tilted her head to the side, and in that instant I knew this was a wonderful mother who had brought her son and his floating goldfish to the vet's office because he had asked her to.

Very often parents do not take the time to indulge the inanes of youth, and that is a mistake. Moments like this resonate in a child's memory forever. I know one wonderful mother, a dear friend of mine, who took the time to go through a major rigmarole every time her young daughter lost a tooth. She would instruct her daughter to leave the tooth under the pillow, and encouraged her to write a polite note to the tooth fairy explaining how the tooth had come out and asking, again politely, for a reward in exchange for the tooth. She told her to seal the note and the tooth in an envelope so no one else could see it. After a few hours, she would retrieve the sealed envelope from under the pillow, steam it open, remove the tooth and the letter, and replace it with a letter from the tooth fairy and a monetary reward. She would then reseal the envelope and replace it under the pillow. This went on for years. Imagine, for a moment, the appreciation and love her daughter felt for the time and effort her mother took to make that happen when she was old enough to understand. I know when she has children of her own she will probably do the same thing. By the way, if you are under twelve years old and reading this, forget what I just said, the tooth fairy is REAL and I just made all that stuff up about the steaming of the envelopes. Take the time to indulge your children when you can, it is worth it.

I said to the youngster, "What's your name?"

"Paul."

"Ok, Paul, let's bring Milo into the lab and see if there's anything we can do for him, okay?"

Paul nodded, tearfully, and followed me into the surgical room at the back of my offices. I turned and said, "You may come along too, if you like" to the mother that had brought him in.

She smiled at me and said, "No, thank you, if it's okay with you, I'll wait out here."

"Fine, we won't be long." I turned and continued into the back room, gently holding the glass bowl that Paul had entrusted to me at this point.

Back in the surgical room, I put my stethoscope in my ears, and held it up to the bowl. "Hmmm..." I muttered. I then took a tongue depressor and dipped it in the water, held it up to the light, and studied it intently for several minutes.

I put down the tongue depressor, looked sternly at Paul who anxiously met my eyes, and sighed. "I'm sorry, Paul, but Milo is beyond my skills to help. I'm sorry."

Paul took it well – better than I expected, and said, "What happened to him sir?"

"Well, Paul, it's hard to tell. Perhaps he was just old, perhaps he ate a bit too much, but I can tell you this – he looks like he was a very happy *Carassius Auratus*."

Paul looked confused. "A what?"

"Oh, I'm sorry, you know we doctors tend to talk in technical speak. That's the Latin scientific name for 'goldfish.'"

"Oh, yeah, okay." Paul replied, a serious look on his face.

He sniffled, looked up at me, and said, "Thank you, doctor."

I carried the bowl with its non-moving occupant back out into the waiting room where Paul's mother waited. Paul ran to his mother and hugged her about the waist.

I spoke directly to mom. "I'm sorry, ma'am, but there was nothing we could do for Milo. Might I suggest a visit to Aquarium World on the way home? I'm sure this young man will be an excellent fish-caretaker in the future, and some lucky fish would be proud to occupy this bowl."

She smiled at me and said, "Thank you doctor, that's an excellent idea. Um," she paused, "Can you see to the disposition of Milo?"

"Certainly. Kathy?" I called for the assistant of the day. "Could you bring this into my surgical room and put it on the table? I'll be back there in a minute." I turned back to Paul and his mother. "Just give us a minute; we'll take care of it."

Paul looked up at his mother, and said something that made it all worthwhile. "He's a really good doctor, mom." She smiled at me, and I turned around before she could spot the gleam that had formed in my right eye. Gina saw it, though. Busted.

I went into the back room, gave Milo an honorable burial at sea, at that great cemetery we call Flushing, and asked Kathy to rinse, disinfect, dry the bowl and return it to Paul. I snuck to the side alcove near Gina's desk and whispered, "No charge." She smiled again at me.

The rest of my office day was uneventful, a Chihuahua for a standard checkup, a golden retriever with a bad tooth, and a few non-distinct cats that had one thing or another to be looked at and tended to. Nothing unusual or especially exciting.

One comment I get from the owners of many of my patients is how well behaved and calm their pets are when they are in my office. They do not know that I try very hard to radiate such calmness to great effect with most animals. I have never had a bad experience with a pet in my office. Most patients trust me almost immediately, even the most boisterous ones, and I am quite adept at communicating my caring, trustworthiness and calm demeanor to them. I have an unfair advantage over most veterinarians, but as you know, I do not play it up. Dogs, especially, seem taken with me almost immediately, and I can even get Their Royal Highnesses, The Cats of The World, to behave and trust me. Ferrets do not care who is around them, they just want to have fun.

In the course of my career, I have treated dogs, cats, ferrets, turtles, chinchillas (wow, great fur), snakes, hamsters, gerbils, mice, rats, one pony, fish, sugar-gliders, an ocelot, hens, roosters, and even an African grey parrot. My specialty is dogs and cats, but with that wonderful network known as the World Wide Web, most anatomical information is readily available when I have a new species to examine and I can do my homework relatively easily. Anything I do not feel comfortable handling I refer to a list of trusted colleagues that Gina keeps up to date near her desk. Like I said earlier, smooth sailing.

The end of the patient list was finally reached, and I told Gina of my intention to hit some stores after office hours. She raised an eyebrow at that, and I was tempted to tell her why, but I resisted. She informed me she had a few things to order, then would lock up, and I could head out at my leisure. I thanked her and went into the house to prepare for my shopping excursion.

As I got to the top of the stairs, I wobbled. I froze in place. Whoa. What was that? I stood motionless for a long moment. There was a strange feeling ebbing at the ends of my perception. I took another step and nearly lost my balance. Floods of memory came rushing back – the day we found Chelsea at North Shore Animal League – it was reminiscent of the feelings I had then.

I am much better equipped to deal with "animal emotion waves" as I sometimes call them than I have ever been. Momentarily forgetting why I had ventured up the stairs, I sat on the top step by the landing to steady myself and concentrate.

Almost as quickly as the feeling came, it was gone. The memory lingered. I reached for it, but it was gone. It was not distinct, clear, or absolute. It was a "wrongness" that I was certain emanated from an animal or animals nearby, but that was all I could glean from it. I thought about it again, and the term "whining" came to mind. Complaining, unhappiness, worry, and then squalor. These terms all came to mind as I sat. Strange.

I waited another four or five minutes, then rose, found myself steady, and went into the bedroom to grab what I had come upstairs for.

***

14- Dolphins, Here I Come!

My father, at dinner one night, seemed especially cheerful. Emily was about seven at the time, which made me about nine, and we were sitting down to the family meal we ate promptly at six o'clock every evening for as long as I can remember.

It was late spring, and summer was just around the corner. My father was a teacher, a math teacher, and his mood tended to improve exponentially (ha ha, dad) as the end of June approached.

He turned to Emily, and said with a hint of banter that was rare for him, "Who wants to see dolphins?"

Chelsea peeked up, Emily's mouth went wide open, and she said, "Wow! Really? Can we?"

My mother placed the bowl of steaming pasta down on the table and said with a smile, "We are going to take a trip down to Florida to visit grandma and grandpa as soon as school is finished, and we will make a stop at SeaWorld on the way, okay?"

Emily and I both said, in concert, "Yaaaay!" I loved the idea. I liked going to my grandparents' in Florida, I had the place all mapped out. I was like a local gang leader down there. I knew the maintenance guys, I knew when they cut the grass, and I knew which kids were cool and which kids would tell on you if you jumped into the pool, which I believe was a felony in most retirement complexes in Florida in the 70's. There were tennis courts, swimming pools, a lake that was always stocked with fish, and cool things to do everywhere. The idea of going to SeaWorld appealed to me also.

My parents both smiled and we began to eat.

After a few munching minutes, my mother said, "Now, both of you, remember, we will be driving, and I expect you to behave in the car." All of a sudden, Emily's face sank.

"But mom and dad," she began, "what about Chelsea?"

Chelsea looked at my father as if to say, "Yeah, pop, what about me?"

My father said, "Chelsea will go stay with Mr. and Mrs. Katz while we are gone; I have already spoken to them."

"What?!?" Emily screamed, and crossed her arms. "They're weird!"

"Emily," my father said firmly, "that's not nice." They are very nice people and it was very kind of them to agree to watch Chelsea for a week."

"A WHOLE WEEK?" Emily shrieked. "NO WAY, I'M NOT GOING!" With that, she rose, waved at Chelsea, and the two of them stomped into the backyard. More accurately, Emily stomped, Chelsea padded. Chelsea looked back at me on the way out and I shrugged my shoulders.

My mother and father looked amused, not angry, which surprised me. I learned, at that point in my young existence, that parental rule could be absolute. Emily was going, Chelsea was staying, and that was that.

The fateful day arrived, and my father and I walked Chelsea to the Katz'. Lexis and Steven Katz were a few years older than my parents were, and dad was right, they were very nice people. Mrs. Katz leaned over and greeted Chelsea with a two handed face rub and crooned to her for a while. She spoke to Chelsea as a grandmother speaks to a visiting grandchild, about how much fun they were going to have and about walks they were going to take, and I found myself smiling. I sensed from Chelsea happiness at the attention, but also a little confusion. My father and Mr. Katz spoke briefly, shook hands, and my dad handed Chelsea's leash to him.

Chelsea obediently followed the Katzes in their front door, but was looking back at my father and me. I stopped, looked at Chelsea, and tried to send her a message – namely - "Don't worry Chelsea, we'll be back." I think something got through to her, but not my exact intention. It was the first time I had ever tried to send a specific, direct message to her, or to any creature for that matter, but I do not think she understood me. I have not become much better or more accurate in the following years.

My father and I walked back to our house, and went directly

out front where my mother had just finished packing our car for the trip. My parents went through a checklist about the house – doors – windows – stove – check, and we were off. Emily was blissfully silent all the way to the Verrazano Bridge, which was a new record for her. As the reality of her situation set in, I suppose she decided there was nothing she could do about it and she might as well enjoy the trip. That was a much more mature stance than I would have taken, but then again, I was always a better complainer and whiner than she was.

The drive was mostly uneventful, except for me teasing Emily a few times earning a stern warning from my father. As I sat back and watched the traffic go by on I-95, I thought about many things. I thought about what I would do when I arrived in Florida, and about things that had happened this past year. I had done well in school, as I always did, and earned a great report card, which I noticed with pride my parents had packed to show my grandparents. Emily was never quite the student I was, but she did very well also. The ride was relatively peaceful, and we spent the first night somewhere in South Carolina at a nameless motel after eating a good meal at a nameless restaurant.

The first part of the drive to Florida is always fun – watching the signs for that very famous tourist attraction and shopping plaza in South Carolina with its entertaining signs stretching all the way back to the Delaware border. I remember falling asleep for a good portion of the next day's drive, and I awoke at another motel – this one surrounded by palm trees.

My parents announced that we had arrived at SeaWorld, and would spend the night before exploring the park the entire next day. The plan was to "do" SeaWorld in the morning and afternoon, then complete another two-hundred miles to my grandparent's house in Southern Florida that evening. Sounded like a good plan to me. Of course, at that point I did not know I would be spending the night at Winter Park Memorial Hospital just outside Orlando. Neither did my parents.

Next morning bloomed bright, sunny, and warm, and Emily and I were excited to get to SeaWorld. We checked out of the motel, left our car in the lot, and hopped on a shuttle to the famed theme park. I was genuinely excited, as was Emily.

We spend the next few hours exploring the exhibits, eating a light breakfast, and watching some of the live shows. The real treat came when my father walked over to us and announced he had bought tickets for Emily and me to go swimming with the dolphins.

"Coooool! Emily squealed, and headed off with my mother to a restroom to change into her bathing suit.

My dad asked if I needed to change, but I had my suit on already and did not care if it would be wet later on. Nine-year-old boys truly do not care about that sort of thing, ever. He smiled and put his hand on my shoulder. He then said something that I will remember forever. He looked across the park but spoke to me. He said, "You're a good boy, Mark. I love you. You're a good boy."

I looked up at him, but the sun was behind him and I could barely make out his face while I squinted to see. He had a gentle smile on his face, and he looked peaceful and content. I also remember thinking how handsome he was. I will remember that moment forever.

Emily came bouncing back with my mother in tow and we four headed to the newly constructed Olympic size pool which was now a "swim with the dolphins" attraction at SeaWorld. Dolphins are beautiful, intelligent creatures, and I felt building excitement as we approached the queue. The line was not long, blissfully, and in minutes, we were greeted by a smiling young blonde woman in a blue one-piece bathing suit.

"Hi, y'all!" she said to Emily and me. "Welcome to Dolphin City. Now remember, don't be scared, do not poke the dolphins in the eyes or anything like that, and have a good time! Yell 'OUT' if you get nervous and one of us will come and get you, okay?"

We both nodded, nervous with excitement, and waded into the slowly descending pool towards the few other people that were in the water and the myriad grey shapes that were moving effortlessly through the pool.

Everything was fine for a bit, but then it was not.

To the best of my recollection, and after hearing the stories from my parents, Emily, and the young woman in the blue bathing suit, here is what happened:

There were six adult dolphins and two juvenile dolphins in the pool that day. All had been around people their entire lives, and loved the attention and the playtime. When I reached the center of the pool, something changed. At once, all eight dolphins converged on me. They surrounded me, bumped me, and leapt over one another to get closer to me. I do not remember thinking or feeling anything, it all happened too fast. The sun was blocked out by something large and airborne, and I remember nothing else. According to my father, and the story that has been embellished over the years, he yelled at the operator of the dolphin attraction that one of his dolphins had tried to mate with his son. We laugh about it now, but at the time, it was not funny.

Apparently I lost consciousness at some point, for I do not remember anything else. My father, another man in a blue bathing suit, and the woman in the blue bathing suit swam rapidly towards my collapsing form at the center of the pool. The dolphins held me above water, so I was never in danger of drowning. The man carried some sort of buzzer implement which he activated causing the dolphins to scurry to the far side of the pool immediately. My father picked me up, slapped my face a few times, and called my name. Of course, if you listen to Emily's version of the story, I fainted from fear of the gentle, intelligent creatures. That was not it.

I was taken to the hospital for observation even though I was clearly breathing and appeared healthy. Well, there was the fact that I was not awake, which I should have been. My father rode with me in the ambulance (which again, I do not remember) and my mother and Emily followed in the family car.

I awakened to a hospital room full of people. There were a few doctors in the room, my entire family, and my grandparents. What were they doing here? It seems my mother had called them from the hospital and they insisted on driving up immediately.

The doctor asked everyone to kindly step out of the room except for one of my parents, and it was my mother who shooed everyone out including my father. She sat on one side of me, the doctor stood on the other.

"Mark, can you hear me?" he began in a singsong tone that reminded me of Dr. Klein but was not as kind.

"Yes, sir, I can hear you fine."

"Good, good. Do you know what day it is?" he asked.

"Tuesday." I replied, confident of my answer.

"That's right, good. Do you know where you are?"

"In a hospital, I think. In Florida. Right?"

The doctor smiled for the first time. "Yes, that's right. Do you remember what happened?"

I did not. I felt cold although it was warm in the room and I was covered by a blanket. I tried to recall where I was before I woke up in this bed, but I could not. My mind was blank. I remembered the shuttle, I remembered going into SeaWorld, then I remembered going into the attractions with everyone. Slowly, the memories were coming back. I must have looked like I was supposed to look at this point, because my mother told the doctor she was calling my father back in and went out into the hall. She reappeared with my worried looking dad a few moments later.

The doctor indicated my parents should follow him to the other side of the not large room, and they did. He spoke to them in low tones, too low for me to hear, and I focused on the ceiling of the room which featured a rotating fan that I remember was spotlessly clean. Strange the things we remember at certain times. I remember thinking, "How do they clean that thing?"

The next morning I was pronounced whole and well and my parents checked me out of the hospital. I did not know if we were continuing to my grandparents, or any other details. We were not, at least, not all of us.

My father and Emily were to drive to my grandparent's house (they were his parents) but my mother and I were flying home to New York that afternoon. The doctors had found absolutely nothing physiologically, neurologically, or psychologically wrong with me, but implored my parents to take me for further testing back in New York. I was disappointed but also uncharacteristically reticent. I said nothing, and I remember not feeling much of anything either. I just followed.

On the airplane, my first memory of what had occurred at the pool finally snuck through my subconscious and announced its presence to my conscious brain. It was coming back slowly, and I was careful not to physically react to the return of the memories so as not to spook my mother any more than she was already spooked. I noticed her checking me and making that half-mommy smile frequently throughout the flight, which made me feel guilty. I felt like I had ruined the family vacation.

Back in thought, the images were taking shape and becoming more solid in the haze that was my memory. I felt the dolphins' complicated, overlapping, intelligent thoughts and feelings. They were playing, teasing, and – laughing? Yes, laughing. I had the distinct feeling they were actually making fun of a woman that was in the pool with us who must have weighed more than three hundred pounds. Yes, they were! I had the strongest feeling they were comparing her to a beach ball – the big round toys they were tossed often by the Dolphin City staff. Wow, that was pretty cool.

I remember then feeling the young ones reacting as if one of their own had entered the pool. They were coming to inspect me, to see which pod I belonged to, and whether I was friendly or not. They thought I was a dolphin? That did not make sense. I was at the point now where it all became clear, right up until the moment I passed out. It was a replay of the animal shelter where we adopted Chelsea, but with more intensity and more complexity to the wave of emotion and thought that washed over me. I do not know any other way to explain this – but at that moment, I knew that if it were to ever happen again, I would be able to deflect it, consume it, filter it, and deal with it. Nothing that powerful was likely to ever wash over me again, but if it did, I would be ready. I did not fear this empathy. I embraced it. It made me special, and it made me different.

I turned to my mother. "Mom?" She looked at me with that half-smile. "Do you think the dolphins are going to get into trouble for what happened to me?"

She laughed a bit. "No, honey, I'm sure they won't be in any trouble. I'm just not sure how long it will be before they re-open Dolphin City. No one is exactly sure why they reacted to you that way. Until they find out, they may not open the pool back up to people."

This made me feel bad. I knew the dolphins meant no harm, in fact, I was absolutely certain they enjoyed swimming with people as much as we enjoyed swimming with them. I wondered if there was a way I could communicate this to the people at Dolphin City. I laughed at that notion. 'Dear Dolphin City,' my letter would begin. Yeah, right.

The flight was uneventful except for the revelation that I had had somewhere over the Atlantic Ocean. I could handle this thing, even control it. This was cool. I could not wait to reunite with Chelsea and try out my newfound control.

***

15- I Go Shopping, Yay.

I like to think I am a pretty reasonable guy. I will go along with much of what any crowd wants to do. I am wrong. In retrospective internal examination, I have discovered something about myself that I am not very proud of yet extremely proud of at the same time. I do not do things that I do not want to do.

The modern world does not allow this attitude to guide one's life for very long. Certainly not many people want to get up at five in the morning to go to jobs they do not enjoy, but they do it. The responsible ones do, anyway. There was a movie I enjoyed in which one of the characters lectured his son about this very topic. He admonished him for worshipping some of the criminal element in the neighborhood, raising them up in status, and thinking down on the common man. The father told his son, "You know what's hard? Getting up every morning and going to work every day. That's hard. That's what makes a man." In some ways, I agree with this. However, to be honest, I find that I have a wonderful life for the simple fact that I seldom do things I do not want to do.

You may be thinking about the comments I make when I have to go to Sarah's parents for dinner. That is not what I mean. After all, Sarah is with me, there is adequate booze and a place to smoke, and the food is always good. I mean more painful, full time drudgery. I have been lucky to avoid it for the most part. Very lucky.

After my brief incident at the top of the stairs, I grabbed the one secret I keep from Sarah. Sarah and I have slowly integrated our finances over the years we have lived together, and we are both superb money managers with similar philosophies. We have never had an argument about money, which is a good thing, since money is the culprit in most relationship problems. It helps that I make a good living and so does she, but also we have similar tastes, levels of tastes, and moderate attitudes. I told you she was the perfect woman.

The secret I am referring to is an American Express card in my name that has remained dormant for years except for the annual fee, which I pay in person at the American Express office. I do not know why I have a compulsion to keep this card a secret from Sarah, but I have had this account since I was eighteen years old and it is very special to me. It was my first credit card, and I have maintained it in perfect standing for almost twenty years. I was upgraded to gold, then to platinum, and I know for certain the card is good for about eight or nine thousand dollars before AMEX would even call to make sure the charge is being initiated by me. I am sure I could push it to fifteen or twenty thousand if I ever needed to. I have not.

I had taken it out of my jewelry case, and had put it in my pocket. I planned to give it a workout today – and planned to tell Sarah about it afterwards which would be inevitable as you will soon see.

I hopped in my Jeep, moving a bit quickly now, since Sarah would be home any minute and I did not want to cross her path on my way out. To ensure that did not happen, I took a longer, less direct route out of town than I normally would have.

In my neighborhood and surrounding communities, things are expensive. If you want to blow ten or twenty grand in an afternoon of shopping, it is very easy to do nearby. I was smarter than that, and headed for the parkway that would bear me out farther into Nassau County where the prices were better and the clientele not as stuffy.

Driving amidst rush hour traffic, I again took a moment to appreciate my situation. I felt bad for the people that endured this drive every day. I was here by choice on this particular afternoon/evening, but many did not have that option, this was their daily grind. That must suck.

I exited the Northern State Parkway onto the Wantagh Parkway, and looked for the exit for Hempstead Turnpike. I was on my way to a small mall that I had read advertisements for in the newspaper the past few months. One aspect of the mall caught my eye, and I paid attention. I was in a good mood. I turned on the radio in the Jeep, which had been silent up until now, and clicked the FM button. I rarely listen to music in the car; I prefer AM radio stations, mostly talk and sports. This drives Sarah nuts, and we play this little game in which I ensure I leave the car radio on the most objectionable station imaginable when I know she will drive my car next, and she does the same, ensuring rap music at maximum volume greets me whenever I drive her car or reclaim my Jeep from her. I clicked on the first button, which I think is the classic rock station, and the ultimate driving tune was just beginning, China Grove, by the Doobie Brothers. I will never forget that scene in *Field of Dreams* when Kevin Costner and James Earl Jones set off in the Volkswagen Bus on their way to Chisholm, Minnesota and destiny, and that song sets the pace.

The only issue with my movie moment was the fact that I was moving at a neck-breaking ten miles per hour. Other than that, the scene was perfect.

I opened the sunroof, cranked down the windows, and cranked up the tunes. Life was good.

Arriving a brisk thirty minutes later at my destination, I parked, feeling a bit nervous, and started towards the door. Suddenly, waves hit me. Nothing directed at me, and nothing specific, but waves of different emotions were coming at me loud and clear. A grizzled veteran by now, I tried to filter the waves and make sense of them, but I could not. I spotted the source of the waves immediately. There was a Petland Discounts store immediately adjacent to my destination, and I was receiving the standard static from the myriad creatures inside. If I had time, I would pay a visit.

Pet store visits are a different experience for me than they are for most people. I can tell if animals are content and are being cared for properly, and I can tell when animals are subject to neglect and abuse. I do something about it, too. One time I happened into a pet store (which shall remain nameless) not too far from our house, but a few towns away. There was misery everywhere. The cats were miserable, the dogs were miserable, even the hamsters were listless and grumpy. I reported the store to the ASPCA multiple times, and within weeks, the store was closed. So there.

I would visit Petland Discounts later if I had time. I had not explained to Sarah where I was going, so I expected she expected me to be home when she was. I would deal with that later as well. I do not lie to Sarah, but I would have a hard time selling this one, and I was certainly not telling her where I was. I would most likely go with the "my phone died" scenario if need be.

I went to the second floor of the mini-mall, signs directing me towards my intended destination. When I arrived, I saw many island booths set up throughout the floor space. Not knowing where to begin, I walked to the first counter nearest where I had come in. A dark-skinned, well-dressed man greeted me in an obsequious manner, and he smiled, showing a gold tooth which glistened in the fluorescent light.

"My friend, my friend yes, tell me, what do you wish to see?" he asked, his smile broadening as he spotted my watch, a stainless steel Rolex that was a present from Sarah on our first anniversary. We had flown for a week to Anguilla, and Sarah had purchased the watch for me and given it to me one magical night while we sat on the terrace of our hotel suite. I love this watch. In fact, this watch would probably cost me my life were I ever to be mugged, for I would not give it up no matter the weapon I faced. To the store, or more accurately, booth-owner, it meant I had money.

I spoke to the gold tooth directly. "I want to see engagement rings. Nice ones."

I never made it to Petland Discounts, I was too anxious to get home. Heavier by 1.67 carats and lighter by about $7,000, I returned to my Jeep and started back the way I had come. This was going to be some night. I reminded myself to pick up wine before I got home, even though we had a healthy stock in the house. I also wanted to get flowers, and although Sarah was not a huge fan of flowers, I wanted the night to be perfect. We still had a serious conversation ahead of us, but I would try my best to make sure this took precedent. I drove.

***

16- My First Foray Into The Sciences

Summer had come and gone, my dolphin induced fainting spell a distant memory, except for the tests that I had endured at Long Island Jewish Hospital for about a month after my return from Florida.

Doctors found nothing wrong with me. Keep in mind, I had never, at this point, discussed my "animal feeling" experiences with anyone, including my parents. I was simply afraid to bring it up when speaking to the "word-doctors," as I thought of the battery of psychologists I had endured, and never did.

Back home in Nyagg, I made it a point to spend some alone time every day with Chelsea. It was usually in the evening, after dinner, and Chelsea became used to the routine. Oftentimes she would be waiting for me near my room at about seven or seven-thirty in the evening. Both of us had had dinner, she had been walked (and still had one more late night walk with mom and dad ahead) and seemed content to spend this time with me as she knew I wanted her to.

I would sit Chelsea down across from me, and try to "move" feelings to her. Most times, I was rewarded with a confused head-tilt from Chelsea. I then had the brilliant idea to show her pictures. That was an enormous breakthrough. In fact, later, in college, I used my Chelsea experiments with photos as the basis for a term paper. The professor thought the entire thing invented, but loved the concept and the depth of study. Little did he know how easy it was to write, since it was all true.

I cut out pictures from magazines (this was decades before the Internet) and showed them to Chelsea along with a word that I associated with the picture. By doing so, Chelsea would react to the content of the photo, and I could quantify any feeling I had. Oftentimes nothing would happen, but occasionally I did get lucky.

I showed Chelsea a picture of a dog food ad, and she immediately reacted with happiness. At least I thought it was happiness, it felt warm and good. I showed her pictures of cats, and she reacted in a wary way, not hostile or benevolent, but as if on guard. That gave me another idea.

There have been myriad studies of the eyes of canines, cats, and many other species. There have been untold thousands of reports written on what dogs can actually see, what color tones they actually see in, and so forth. One very obvious point has been missed in all of these experiments.

Experts disagree as to whether or not a photo or a television show will create an accurate reproduction of the image or event for a dog, since a dog's vision is different from ours. The obvious point that I think is missed, however, is that no matter what a dog, cat or ferret actually sees, will they not see the same thing in the photo or on the television? Of course, they will. Whatever visual interpretation their eyes and brain make will be exactly the same when a static photo or a television show is put in front of them. Think of it this way: If a red fire truck is described to you as "yellow" ever since you were a baby, does that make it any less red to the rest of the world? Alternatively, more scientifically, do the light waveforms that make up the color red to the scientific community change because we place a different name on the spectrum? No. That is my point with dogs. If they only see shades of green, which some scientists believe, then the photos I was showing Chelsea would show up in the same shades of green, allowing her to see exactly what I wanted her to. Based on Chelsea's reactions, I believe this to be true and correct.

Chelsea and I repeated this nightly experimentation for months, until one evening Emily came into my room and caught me in the middle of showing Chelsea a picture of a large hotel fire. She instantly grabbed Chelsea and took her out of the room, telling my parents that I was trying to cast spells on Chelsea and that I should not be allowed to play with her ever again. I suppose being the annoying older brother has its drawbacks as well.

Outside, on my way to school, on my way home from school and everywhere in between, I started to tune into the waves of feeling from the animals I encountered. Squirrels were easy. Very simple creatures, their startles at being approached by humans or dogs were easy to detect, as were their almost mindless blankness upon alighting at a safe height.

Birds were, in the best way I can describe them, capricious. If a bird allowed me close enough, I would sense it (very, very tiny sensations) looking around, expressing danger, expressing hunger, minding the wind, and flying off without a thought. Simple, rapidly changing, and consistent. I could even close my eyes and tell what kinds of creatures were near me by the feelings I was receiving.

None of this seemed unusual to me, and I was enjoying my newfound skill. I had still never told anyone about it, and to be honest, with the exception of Sarah in my adult years, I have never told anyone the full extent of it. I suppose I am afraid they will think me weird, or possibly kidnap me and sell me to the government for experimentation. I am exaggerating now, but I think you can see the concern. People fear what they do not understand. Heck, I have been this way for years now, and I still do not fully understand it. For that matter, I avoid asking myself this obvious question: Why me?

The other idea that the cat photo had given me was this: Take a picture of mean-guy's house, and show it to Chelsea to see how she reacted. This was easier said than done in 1974, as the digital camera was still twenty years away. I did not own a Polaroid camera, which was the 1974 approximation, but my grandfather did, and I tucked away the thought to ask him to borrow it next time we visited.

***

17 – An Unplanned Stop

Before heading home with the fruit of my successful yet expensive shopping excursion, I stopped, as I had planned to, in Nyagg's main shopping area to visit the liquor store and the florist.

Between the two stores I had planned to visit is Heitner's, the family run drugstore/coffee shop that I had mentioned earlier.

I had the sudden urge for a milkshake, and pulled open the glass door. Behind the counter of the shop, which was a cross between a modern pharmacy and a fifties style diner - complete with counter- was Larry Heitner, owner, proprietor, and maker of incredibly rich, fabulous milkshakes and sundaes.

"Hello there Mr. Fancy-Pants-Animal-Doctor who has been too busy to come by here in a month of Sundays! How the heck are ya?" said Larry as soon as I opened the door.

His smile was white, warm, and wide, and it made me feel like a kid again, which is what I was the first time I had met Mr. Heitner.

"Hey there, Larry (I was still uncomfortable calling him Larry) I'm good, I'm fine, thanks." I smiled in return.

He was busy for the moment finishing an anecdote with one of the regulars of the counter at the other end, and I knew from experience he would be with me shortly. I had an idea. Ooh, sneaky, but an idea. I walked directly to the spotless counter and sat myself on a stool.

Larry came over with that wide smile on his face, and planted a firm handshake in mine. "How'r things in the animal kingdom, sir?"

I smiled to match him, and replied, "Fine, Larry, things are fine, thank you."

Larry has run Heitner's since the sixties, before I was born, and

I have been told that before him his parents had run the shop. Sylvia, his mother, was responsible for the expansion of the shop from a simple lunch counter to a "convenience store" long before convenience stores would dot every corner in America. This place has been in the Heitner family for three generations, which I always thought was really cool.

My father first brought me here when I was a child. We came one Sunday afternoon, without my mother or Emily, after a foray to the nursery where we purchased some shrubs for our yard. That men-only visit made me feel very special for some reason. Just the men, hanging out. I distinctly remember my father was greeted by a younger version of Larry much as I was greeted today. Memories and feelings like this are priceless.

Larry and his anecdotal recipient laughed heartily, and Larry came back before me with a smile still widening his face. "What can I get you, Fancy-Pants-Doctor-Sir?" He said it in such a disarming way I knew it was meant as a proud compliment. I suppose everyone in Nyagg is an adopted child of Larry's, which is how he made you feel.

"My good man," I started, affecting a truly terrible upper-crust British accent, "I shall endeavor to try one of your fabulous bovine-based libations in the chocolate variety." I cleared my throat loudly.

Larry laughed, sighed, and turned around to start making what I hoped would be the chocolate milkshake I had ordered in bombastic bad English Gentry.

Heitner's was quiet, which was good, because I had a question for Larry that I did not want anyone else privy to. The regular at the counter was a good five feet away, and only one other person, a lady shopper in the sundries aisle, made up the entire crowd.

Larry turned around while the blender behind him whined, and smiled at me again.

"How's that lovely young thing who for some reason likes you?"

I laughed. "She's great Larry. In fact, can you keep a secret?" I whispered, sotto voce.

"Absolutely not. So tell me."

I leaned in to the counter, conspiratorially, and showed him the ring, which I had in my shirt pocket.

He whistled and shook his right hand in a manner that said 'fancy!' "Wow, that's some rock! Another one bites the dust, ey?" He turned, poured my milkshake, and said, "This one's on me Fancy-Pants, congratulations."

I felt like a kid again, and smiled wide. "Thanks, Larry, thanks a lot. She's the best thing that ever happened to me, and I figured I should make it official. But, she hasn't said yes yet. "

"Ahhh." He waved that off as if it was a given. I love this guy. "Damn right you should make it official. That's a great girl. Wow. I'm very happy for both of you. Good for you." He turned, greeted someone that had just walked in, and I secreted the ring in my pocket once more.

In the "small world" category, guess who it was who walked into Heitner's at that very moment. Yep, Cindy. Remember her?

"Oh my gosh, Doc, hi!" she came over to me and embraced me from the back which was awkward and brought a raised eyebrow from Larry.

My man-brain kicked in, and I said, "Um, hi! Yes, um…" and I pretended to have forgotten her name. See how smart we men are? Clever, huh? Take that, eyebrow-raising Larry.

"Cindy! You remember! Spirit!" she said, exasperated. She rolled her eyes as if to say, 'how can you not remember?'

"Ohhh, yes, of course. How is Spirit's leg? Is she taking her pills?" I said, much too quickly.

"Yes, she's so easy, that one. She globs them down like nothing." Cindy tilted her head to the side and affected a soft, feminine tone. "Thank you so much for what you did, I really appreciate it. That was so nice of you."

Larry looked at me as if to say, "What the heck did you do?"

I scowled at him and he smiled and turned away.

I took a tentative sip of my milkshake, which was heavenly, and endured a few seconds of uncomfortable silence. I looked around Heitner's, waiting for something to happen, namely the movement to another part of the establishment by Cindy, but no. No, she planted herself on the stool next to mine, put down a small shopping bag, and sighed. Larry, of course, had diplomatically found something to do at the opposite end of the counter. His radar was on, though, count on it.

Heitner's is an interesting mix of old and new. There is the aforementioned counter, aisles towards the side with myriad products and sundries, and a modern set of tall drink refrigerators offering everything from sodas to the latest fad water drinks against the wall that abuts the front door. However, the gold at Heitner's was behind the counter. Those homemade milkshakes and ice cream, wow.

Cindy did not seem intent on going anywhere, and this put a crimp in my plan to ask Larry about THE Craig, which I had planned to do. I did not need to. Fate is a funny and fickle friend, is she not?

The door of Heitner's opened again, and I will give you three guesses who walked in next.

I did not have to say a word; Cindy took care of it for me.

"Hi, ASSHOLE!" she screamed as such volume I think my milkshake vibrated in front of me. Larry looked startled, but said nothing. The woman in the sundry aisle froze and looked at Cindy.

A middle-aged man, slightly younger than I, stood frozen on the threshold of the shop. I locked eyes with him a moment, and instant recognition, surprise, and shock went 'dingdingding' inside my head. With ultimate class, astounding panache, and true gentlemanly manner, the man gave Cindy the finger, turned around, and exited. Nice.

Cindy spun and spoke to Larry. "You shouldn't let scum like that into your nice place!" She seemed to be struggling with something. She gulped a breath, and then let it out. "I'm sorry, sir, I didn't mean to curse in your shop."

"Ah, that's okay young lady, I've heard worse. I take it you know that guy?" Larry smiled reassuringly.

"Yes, he's my ex. An asshole." As she said this, she put her hand up to her face. She hesitated a moment – as if she wanted to bolt out of the place but thought better of it since he might still be in the vicinity. The man had looked so familiar to me but I could not place him. I butted in.

"Cindy, why don't you stay a bit, and Larry here will fix you up – or at least start you on the road to obesity."

Larry looked at me with mock severity and said, "Hey! All natural ingredients, wise guy!"

I wanted very badly to ask the "asshole's" name, but did not.

I rose quickly, as the time was ripe to do so, and nothing else productive could happen here tonight. My place was at home. I suddenly needed to get there as quickly as possible.

Cindy said to me, "Do you know Craig? He's the one I told you about that sells puppies."

I froze. I turned, looked at Cindy, smiled, and nodded no. I do not think I could have spoken had I wanted to. I decided if I were ever elected President, I would outlaw the naming of babies "Craig" for at least two decades. That name was never a good thing in my life.

I thanked Larry, left a large tip, (without him noticing or he would have thrown it back at me) smiled again at Cindy and moved quickly to the door.

Safely outside, I forgot all about the flowers and the liquor store and headed to my Jeep. Could anything else happen? Sure, it could. All four tires on my shiny Jeep Grand Cherokee were slashed, hacked, and flat. Great. I wonder how that happened.

I walked to the train station to find a taxi and get myself home. I would deal with the Jeep in the morning.

***

18 – More Information Than You Need, But You Have To Read It To Find Out What Happens Next

It was a difficult time. Things in the world were rough. This memoir will not dive into them in any detail, but here are some highlights: International relations were not going well; we were not speaking to Russia. The US hockey team made us all feel better about that in the Olympics, but on the grand scale, that was not so important.

The American President was "kicking ass and taking names," at least according to my Political Science professor, but as a freshman in college, I did not really care about such things.

I had recently broken up with a girl named Stefania, who had introduced me to a side of the world I had previously not been privy too. I had read many books, watched a lot of television and movies, but until Stefania, I did not understand the emotional power inter-personal relationships could wield. Nor how much fun they could be.

Stefania and I had dated only a few short months, but the relationship changed my life. I grew up very quickly.

The day before I met Stefania, I was a semi-geeky high school student with a bad wardrobe and a propensity to hang around the science labs too much. I enjoyed chorus, drama, math, science, and especially caring for the animals that many teachers kept in their classrooms – both as pets and as the basis for humane science experiments.

I took every opportunity with these animals to "test" my powers, as I thought of them then, to see just what I could accomplish, and how far it could go. I determined that my ability was not anything magical, nor arcane, nor supernatural for that matter. In fact, I reasoned it was closely related to the talents of a fine psychologist who can empathize with his or her patients so well that his or her advice was succinct, pithy, and effective.

The difference with me was that my empathy came in the form of feelings, not words. Other than that, after much research in the field of psychology (I had ensured I took AP PYSCH in my senior year of high school) was simply well-trained empathy. I concluded that I was simply especially empathetic with animals, and nothing more. That was enough.

I was certainly empathetic to Stefania, but it was not the same. There was most definitely an element of animalism, but that was normal for any eighteen-year-old male.

For some reason, this beautiful, sexy, popular and gregarious person decided she liked me. I like to think it was my eminent charm, dashing good looks, and fabulous sense of humor – but that would be kidding myself. I have charm, but it is not eminent. I am average looking, although I do take good care of myself and always try to look my best. My sense of humor? That I will accept. I am the funniest guy I know. Watch – 'What happens when a frog parks his car illegally? He gets TOAD away?' Get it? See what I mean? The reason I never pursued comedy as a career is - for some reason people tended to groan after my jokes while comedians garnered laughter. I never understood that.

Stefania actively pursued me and my geeky self, which had ancillary effects. My group of friends changed slightly, although the new ones were mostly of the fair weather variety. My wardrobe changed once Stefania got a hold of me, for our weekly excursions to the shopping mall were mostly about making me presentable to accompany her. I held on to myself a bit though, there were certain outfits I simply would not wear, but for the most part, I followed her lead and liked the results.

Stefania also taught me about other things that to this day I like to think I still have a talent for. Those were eye-opening nights under the stars in my beat-up old convertible. Even today, I intentionally stay away from a certain pier on the north shore of Long Island for the memories they awaken in me much like my grandfather's lawnmower did.

The day after I met Stefania I was a changed man, and many of those changes took permanent hold in both my manner and my personality. No reflection on Sarah, but I think I am a better person for the relationship Stefania and I shared. I certainly learned a lot. Did you know boys and girls have different parts? Imagine! I like to think that Sarah is getting a better 'me' because of the time I spent with Stefania. What makes it a bit difficult is the fact that Stefania is still in my life. I have no romantic feelings for her any longer, my love for Sarah has firmly pushed them out of my heart, but it makes for uncomfortable times with Stefania around so much, now that she is the best friend of my beloved.

This changed man went off to college after high school, and I must say that most of my junior high school years and high school years were uneventful except for the aforementioned Stefania.

The Walrus and his son Craig had moved to Douglaston, I found out, which is technically in New York City, but not as far as I would have liked. Douglaston is in Queens, and as the crow flies (I know a few who have made the trip) it is only about three or four miles away. There were a few times that I believed I saw one of them or the other during my sojourns, but I was never sure, nor did we have any contact. That in and of itself made life easier.

For years, Chelsea made the Canis household a better place. After the Walrus family moved, our walking resumed its normal course, and Chelsea and I were inseparable except for the time Chelsea spent with Emily.

There is a note in the margin on this manuscript from Carlo on this page. It reads, *"Max just laid down. Watch the digression! Love – C".*

I know Carlo, but there is a lot of ground to cover and in the course of writing this memoir, it has become both therapeutic and cathartic for me, so too bad on Max. He can edit it out later.

Chelsea became a legend in the neighborhood. Everyone knew her and knew what a fabulous temperament she had. I would walk her and people I did not know would greet her. I paid very careful attention to Chelsea during these times, as I was trying to categorize people by the reaction "feelings" I would receive from Chelsea.

Early in my high school days, I learned to play the piano. I have the Beatles to thank for this. One day I heard *Let It Be* on the radio and knew I had to learn how to play it. We had an old piano in the basement of my parent's house, and once I showed interest, my parents had it fixed up, tuned, and I would play it nightly. I got very good, very fast. Chelsea would always lie on the old couch next to the piano while I played, for she seemed to enjoy the music. To this day, I still play frequently. Sarah loves my piano playing, but I fear I do not play for her enough. I will fix that soon.

There are hundreds of Chelsea anecdotes to share. and I will choose a few of them for this memoir, but know this: There were probably many more in the version I submitted to Carlo and Max for review, but I bet Max edited a few of them out. He can be a little jealous sometimes.

One of the best Chelsea stories actually made the local paper in Nyagg. Chelsea and I were walking a good distance from my house near a small park that featured swings, a mini-carousel (the metal kind), and several other playthings for youngsters. As usual, Chelsea was off-leash, dutifully keeping slightly ahead of me and to my left. It was almost dark, and no one appeared to be in the small recreation haven. As we reached about the halfway point of the park, I heard what sounded like a stifled sob and other sounds I could not identify. Chelsea heard it too, and stopped. Two sentries in the late spring evening, we both stood statue still and stared into the gathering gloom of the playground.

Without warning or preamble, Chelsea bolted at full speed into the park. I called after her, which did not slow her down. I took off in a full run right behind her. By the trees at the back of the park, hidden by the gathering shadows and the myriad tree trunks, were a man and a girl. The man was standing stock still, the girl standing with her back to a tree, and she appeared to be crying. Chelsea had stopped about four feet away from the man and had her front paws lowered and was baring her teeth. As I caught up, I heard a menacing growl emanate from Chelsea's muzzle followed by a sharp bark.

I began to apologize to the pair as I approached, but something stopped me. Something was wrong. The man backed off slowly, moving away from Chelsea, towards the thickening trees that bordered the park. He turned, and ran. Chelsea stood up, stared after him, looked back to see me, and then settled down on the ground on her belly.

The girl, who was about thirteen or fourteen, burst into a loud cry and wrapped herself around me. Chelsea arose, tail wagging, and stood next to us. I was not sure what to do, so I stood there for a moment, feeling my shirt dampening from tears and sobs.

I gently pushed the girl back, and asked, "Are you okay?"

The girl nodded, tearfully, and kneeled down next to Chelsea and started thanking her profusely. For what, I still did not understand.

"You are such a hero! You are the best! Thank you so much! Brave, brave dog!" She hugged Chelsea about the neck and Chelsea stood there looking off into the distance.

I felt pride coming from Chelsea. I felt something else too, which I cannot to this day properly quantify, but let us call it "good." Chelsea felt good. I was still baffled.

The girl straightened up, looked at me, and said, unsteadily, "Can you please walk me home?"

Not having any idea what was going on, I agreed to do so. Chelsea and I walked alongside the unknown young lady, and before long, we found ourselves approaching a large Victorian house about four or five blocks from my parents' house.

The girl went inside, and Chelsea and I stopped halfway up the walk, unsure of what to do. Well, I was unsure. I am certain Chelsea knew exactly what was going on.

A moment or two later, a large man and a dainty woman burst through the front door of the house with the crying girl in tow.

The man looked at me, at Chelsea, down the block, up the block, and seemed on the verge of breaking something. The woman had the girl's hands held in hers, and together the three approached us. Chelsea sat.

"Son, can you tell me what happened?" the man began, looking down at me. He seemed tense, anxious, and upset.

"Hello sir, I'm Mark. This is Chelsea." I said, pointing at her. "We were walking past the park when my dog burst away from me and headed into the park..."

I gave him a quick rundown of what I remembered, and the girl sobbed and nodded through my narrative. The man said nothing to me and turned and went into the house. The girl fell into the arms of the woman, who I assumed at that point was her mother, and began to cry once again.

The man returned about three minutes later while I stood there in absolute uncertainty. He said to no one in particular, "The police will be here shortly, let's all go on the porch and sit down."

Police? I was still unsure what was going on. Was I going to be arrested?

The man gave me little choice as he moved past me, put his arm around my back, and led me up to the large porch at the front of the house. Chelsea followed dutifully, and I suppose it was the calm, unworried countenance I sensed from Chelsea that kept me from panicking or asking questions. I just followed.

Only minute or two later, a Nyagg police cruiser pulled into the driveway, and a young police officer approached us.

"Hi folks, you the ones that called?" he asked as he made his way onto the porch and removed his hat.

The man rose, "Yes sir, thanks for coming so quickly. My daughter has a something to report. Honey?" he looked at the girl, who I now knew was his daughter, and I noticed she looked much more composed than she had a few moments earlier.

I stood transfixed as she told this young police officer of walking home past the park when a man grabbed her, brought her to the trees behind the park, and told her the things he was going to do to her. He also had threatened to kill her and her family if she made a noise. Wow. I am so oblivious sometimes.

Her narrative included a very accurate account of Chelsea's approach followed by mine. Her story concluded with us walking her home, her telling her parents, at which point the father chimed in and mentioned his call to the police department. I stood with my mouth open.

The police officer looked at me, smiled, and said, "Does that sound about right to you son?"

Still a bit in shock, I said, "Yes, sir."

The police officer took my name (and Chelsea's) and I asked if I could use the phone to call home since I was overdue and did not want my parents to worry. The police officer asked where I lived, and when I told him, he asked me to hold off and informed me he would take me home in a moment.

The officer informed the parents and the girl that a detective would be by in less than an hour to take a full report of the incident, and thanked them for their cooperation. He admonished the father not to take any steps on his own, and asked the girl if she wanted to go for medical treatment. She replied in the negative.

Just as we were about to walk away, she came over, hugged Chelsea one more time, and kissed me on the cheek. I blushed, which made her mother laugh despite her anguish, and I followed the police officer to his car. As I got in, the girl's father lowered his head in what I took to be a nod of appreciation and a salute all in one.

Chelsea hopped into the police car without hesitation, I followed, and I was driven home by Nyagg's finest. My father was in the driveway when we approached, and I can only imagine the thoughts that went through his mind as he saw the black and white car approach with perky ears showing through the windshield from the back seat.

The rest is local history. Chelsea received a medal from the town council (Emily is in the picture with her, not me) and my name appeared in the paper with her. The paper inaccurately printed my name as Chelsea's owner, which Emily ensured was corrected through repeated letters to the newspaper. I never found out if the bad guy was apprehended, and I never heard from the girl or her family again. Come to think of it, the whole incident sometimes feels like it happened to someone else, I was so behind the curve the whole time.

Another memorable day, I heard Chelsea barking loudly from our backyard. We usually left the back door of our house open, and it was not until later in life, meeting lots of other dogs and dog owners, that I realized how special Chelsea was in this aspect as well. We never even had the thought of her running away – she was ours and we were hers, she would never go anywhere.

I went into the backyard in response to the barking, and found Chelsea lying down near the back fence. A few feet away, a cat was in the midst of giving birth, with three wriggling little ones already out and another on the way. Something was wrong. The cat seemed in pain and distress, which I could clearly feel as I approached.

Looking more closely, I noticed half a kitten outside the mother cat, and I could only assume the other half was still inside. The mother cat looked completely drained. She was lying on her side and breathing very heavily.

I had no idea what to do, but instinct and my empathy took over. Chelsea lay down next to me with her head on the ground very close to the back of the mother cat. I tentatively reached down, and touched the half-born kitten. The mother cat made no indication this was a problem, and I moved closer.

I was a bit more forceful this time, and gently surrounded the half-born kitten with my hand, and pulled. It felt very strange, but somehow I knew I was doing the right thing. I felt the little thing move a bit, so I pulled with a bit more strength. The little kitten exited the mother cat's body completely now, but was not breathing. I held her in front of her mother, but the poor Queen was simply too exhausted to do anything about it. The umbilical was still attached, and the kitten had yet to breathe. Chelsea rose, stuck her face between my hand and the mother cat, and began to intensely lick the breathless kitten repeatedly.

I will never forget what happened next. All of a sudden, the tiny ball of fur opened his mouth, and gasped his first full breath of air in this world. He resembled a swimmer emerging from a long dive. Chelsea continued to clean off the newborn, while its mother looked on impassively, exhausted.

Once I was certain the kitten was breathing normally, I laid him down next to his mother and his siblings. I noticed the umbilical still attached but had no idea what to do about it. I remember thinking the mother cat would deal with it when she was strong enough.

I stood, and Chelsea stood alongside me looking up at me. I said, "Great work, Dr. Chelsea!" and I swear she smiled. At least I remember it that way.

We went in the house and reported the incident to my mother and Emily, who both went out to see the new additions to our backyard. I remember that sometime shortly thereafter my father had planned to bring the mother and the four kittens to the shelter, probably afraid of adding another five mouths to the household if they were allowed to linger too long and we were allowed to grow too attached. He never made it, as he was intercepted by Mrs. Katz, who took in all five cats. They lived with the Katzes for as long as I can remember, and Chelsea would play with all five of them constantly. Mrs. Katz noted many times that the cats were not truly "outside" cats, that the only place they would venture from their house was to our house. It was not unusual for me to come home and see a cat or two lounging on the couch watching television with one of my parents and Chelsea. I still think about that to this day. In fact, I can tell you the names of all of them: The mother cat the Katzes named Venus, and the kittens were Yoda, Fred, Matilda, and Molly. Memories.

I cannot tell you much more about Chelsea and the next few years. As I look back on them, they are a blur of happy memories, growing pains, learning, and happy times. I cannot empathize with those who had bad childhoods; I am wise enough to know I was very, very lucky. My parents were wonderful, my home was wonderful, and Chelsea was a soul made of solid gold.

I left for college the fall before I turned 19. The previous December, Chelsea died at the age of 10. I was dating Stefania at the time, and she never understood why I was morbid for an extended period of time after Chelsea died. That put a wedge in our relationship, tender as it was. There was no warning that Chelsea was ill. Although she had slowed a bit the previous two years, she was still energetic, always loving, and always brilliant. I have quickly jumped the years to arrive at this juncture as it is still painful for me to think about, and the only way I could accurately put it down here on paper is to simply spit it out and get it over with. There is no way to explain Chelsea any further, except to say she was the best creature I have ever known, human or otherwise. She will live in my memory forever.

***

19 – When The World Is Running Down

The night my Jeep's tires were slashed, ring in my pocket – I did NOT give Sarah the ring. It was not completely my fault. Okay, okay, take it easy. When I got home, Sarah was in the middle of an intense phone conversation with her mother. Apparently, her father had not come home the night before, and to this point, her mother still had not heard from him. This may seem extreme to you, but for him it was not all that unusual. Even so, whenever it happened, Sarah's mother broke down and called Sarah to piece her back together. It made me angry that Lou treated his wife that way, but it was truly none of my business. Sarah stayed on the phone for hours, so I went into my office to secrete the ring and do some paperwork. By the time I emerged, hours later, Sarah was still on the phone. I smiled, she smiled back apologetically, and I sauntered up the stairs to go to sleep. I do not remember Sarah coming to bed.

Next morning broke bright and sunny, and Sarah was off to work before I arose. I had office hours later in the day, so I had the morning to myself. I meandered into the office in my sweatpants and socks, since the coffeemaker in there was quicker and easier than the one we kept in the kitchen. My Jeep was towed via flatbed to the local repair shop in town, and I had arranged to have four new tires installed and balanced, and was expecting a call that the Jeep would be ready for pickup any time now.

I enjoyed my morning coffee, showered and dressed, and looked at my watch. I had some errands to run, and the call from the repair shop came, so I called a taxi, which took me into town to my now new-footed Jeep.

I mentioned once before in this story that when my world seemed upside down, I could turn to my old friend Carlo to have it straightened out.

After picking up the Jeep, I headed to Carlo's almost by instinct. With the few errands completed and still a few hours before my first patient of the day, I found myself entering the parkway that led to only one place as far as I was concerned: Carlo's.

I always had a treat for Max with me when I visited my old friend, and today was no different. As a veterinarian, my mailbox is inundated with sample "healthy" pet treats on a daily basis. Some of these make it into my office, others are too ridiculous to do anything with but practice my basketball skills towards the large trash bin by the side of the house. When I remember, I take a few and toss them into the glove compartment. Hey, you never know.

Max loved a particular brand that resembled little pigs in little blankets, and I happened to have a few upon inspection of the contents of the glove box. Lucky Max. Lucky me.

Except for the few planned barbecues and family get-togethers at Carlo's to which Sarah and I were always invited, none of my visits to Carlo is announced or planned. As if aware of some cosmic mentoring responsibility, Carlo always seems to be home when I come calling, puttering around his garden or enjoying the panoramic view of the Atlantic Ocean from his back porch. Today would probably be no different.

As I meandered through the local streets of his town, I thought about the strange events of the past few days, and I had that nagging feeling that they were somehow connected. I suppose this feeling was my main purpose for seeking Carlo out; he was a detective by trade, albeit retired, but Carlo was always able to see between the lines and sense the underlying heart of things. It is what, I believe, made him so good at his job. He would listen to a scenario of mine, fix his mouth with that telling amused smile, and in one sentence put the whole thing into perspective. I was hoping against hope he could do the same today, for I was sorely in need of some logic and grounding. I had a momentary panic that perhaps my luck would run out finding Carlo both home and available, but his familiar figure was obvious on the front lawn of his house as I approached. He turned, that enigmatic smile already in place, and gave me a brief wave. He walked toward the car and said, "Don't put it in the driveway today, I'm having something delivered." I nodded and continued past the driveway, putting my truck against the curb at the far side of his pristine driveway.

Max heard my car door slam, and came bounding from the side of the house, tongue wagging, and knelt down in his inimitable style at my feet. Like a courtier bowing at the feet of royalty, Max peered up with me with his sharp smile in place and tail wagging a mile a minute.

Yes, I am an animal professional, but I am also an animal-lover, and I engage in silly banter with pets I know, just as you would.

"Hey Maxy!" I said as I knelt down to one knee and rubbed his head enthusiastically. Max rose to all four legs and nuzzled his face against my shoulder, an affectionate gesture that he has done since he was a puppy. It always solicits an "awww" from whatever female of my species happens to be nearby.

Max and I continued our greeting while Carlo wordlessly made his way towards the wrap-around porch fronting his white beachfront home. Carlo was a smart investor, and a frugal man. It was nice to see his efforts pay off. His house was beautiful.

I walked with a prancing Max up the three steps of the porch and settled on the cushioned swing hanging from two pristine silver chains. Max jumped up beside me and grinned. As I always do when petting a dog, I felt for anything unusual. Glands felt right. I picked up the side of his grinning mouth and examined perfect white teeth. Check. I also ran my hand over the top of his head, feeling for anything unusual on the skin. Smooth as a baby's bottom. This is a habit I do not remember specifically developing; it just sort of became part of my modus operandi. A hazard of my trade, I suppose. There have been times when I have performed this little impromptu inspection on dogs in the park, or on dogs that surprise their owners by insisting on saying hello to me when we happen to pass one another. Rarely, but sometimes, there is a cause for concern and I usually pass it off with a question for the owner rather than a bold statement of my expertise. People do not always respond well to the latter.

I have an intimate knowledge of dog breeds, and can usually

pick apart the parentage of a dog I see going back two or three generations. I always enjoy this endeavor, and many times, I surprise owners by informing them that the adorable cur they thought was a purebred "Majestic Emperor-Regal-Hound" from exotic Myanmar (for which they paid a fortune) is actually the product of a Spaniel that *somehow* hooked up with a Rottweiler. Fun, fun, fun. Dogs do not care about breed names. Dog is dog to them.

Carlo emerged from the house with a small tray loaded with two steaming cups, and a plate with those little Belgian seashell chocolates on it. I love those things almost as much as Mallomars. I had an uncle that would bring them to every family dinner when I was a child, and they always trigger that same emotional remembrance we were discussing back at the lawnmower and grapevines. I smiled and reached for a cup and a chocolate.

"My friend," Carlo began with his enigmatic smile, "it is always a joy and an honor when you show up at my door. To what do I owe the pleasure?"

Carlo has a manner that is hard to describe. I will try, but even in this written work that I have toiled with for what seems like centuries, I realize I still cannot completely and accurately convey the countenance of this man. For example, take the line he spoke when he greeted me. Let me try to give you an accurate sound-picture of how it was delivered. Where I have emphasized and left space, take a one second pause before continuing: "it is *always (pausepausepause)* a joy and an *honor (pausepausepause)* when you show up at my door. To *what (pausepausepause)* do I owe the pleasure?" Get the idea?

I once had a silly thought while on vacation in Niagara Falls. Sarah and I had taken the trite tour through Madam Tassaud's Wax Museum, and while staring at an incredibly lifelike wax duplication of Captain Kirk (William Shatner, actually) the thought struck me that Carlo would be almost impossible for the master wax molders to duplicate. His expressions were too deep, his soul too loud to be captured in permanent repose. Some people's aura or soul is too complex to be frozen in time. On the other hand, perhaps, there is much more to the human being than simply its physical manifestation. Something would be missing from the wax statue of Carlo, if they were to make one, I am sure. Captain Kirk was dead-on accurate.

Carlo looked at me with endless patience. His mouth formed into his famous half-smile, and he waited while I gathered myself.

"I'm not sure what's up, but something is bothering me."

Carlo laughed easily, saying "Well, that sounds like about five billion people's description of daily life, go on." His smile widened.

Carlo has a way of disarming me. Although I am a professional, in my mid-thirties, self-confident and outgoing, Carlo makes me feel like the shy kid on the bus that has rolled up paper thrown at him constantly and sits there with a silly smile, happy for the attention.

I sighed heavily. "I'm not sure how to explain it any better, which is part of the issue in and of itself." I took another chocolate. "For weeks now, I have had this feeling at the back of my thoughts, never clear or demanding, just nagging in its nature. Last night, it hit me so hard I lost my bearings, and had to sit at the top of the stairs for a bit. "

Carlo took on a bit more serious pose now, and leaned back into his chair and crossed his right leg over his left.

I continued. "It was, and is, like a wisp of smoke. If I concentrate on it and try to grab it, it's gone."

Carlo leaned a bit toward me.

"What kind of feeling is it? Good? Bad? Painful? Joyous?" he asked.

Right to the heart of it. I love this guy.

Looking back into his eyes, I started, "It's not a good feeling. It's not positive. It's almost haunting. Foreboding. Dark." I realized as I said these words, this was the clearest grip on the feeling I had experienced to this point. "It almost feels like a big 'wrongness', if you get my drift."

Carlo leaned forward, then back again, and glancing at Max who stared back at him, he said, "I see. Let's see if we can find the source, or the root. When did it begin?"

I stopped for a second and realized I had not thought of this most obvious element either. When did this feeling manifest itself? Was it the day outside *Reflections* with the Great Dane? Was it before that? I clearly remember the dinner at Sarah's parents with Drake and the gummy squirrel, and I do not recall having any of this "heaviness," as I have begun to call it, that day.

"I think it began one day when I walked up to *Reflections* because I was pissed off at Sarah and Stefania."

"How could one possibly be pissed off at the lovely, shy, timorous Stefania?" Carlo asked in a mocking tone.

I smiled at his comment, and put my head back down in thought.

"Yes, Carlo, it was that day. I remember it clearly now." I retold the incident with the Great Dane outside of the bar, the follow up visit back at my office, and the comments made by Cindy, the girl whose name I probably should not remember. The phone call! I had completely forgotten about the phone call.

"Crap, I'm so dense sometimes!" I blurted out as the realization that I had nailed the day this feeling began swam through me like a river otter. I explained to Carlo about the mysterious phone call with the warning. At this, his manner changed. His old detective hat came back on fully. He did not like that.

"That changes things a bit, my dear friend. That means someone has singled you out, or marked you, as we used to say in the trade, and I do not like that one bit."

I knew it was about to get worse. "Oh yeah, "I began, nonchalantly, "then there was the pickup truck outside my office door."

I relayed all of the detail of that incident as well.

Carlo's manner changed. No longer with a smile on his face, he rose and headed into the house. Max and I shared a look as if to ask each other "should we follow?" and it was clear neither of us knew.

Carlo emerged from the house and stood before me. "Here is the number of an old colleague of mine." I started to rise and protest, but Carlo would hear none of it. "You WILL call him, and you WILL tell him I asked you to do so. That alone will be a message to him that this is not some nut-job calling with a paranoid delusion."

Carlo had nailed it again. My fear was that calling a detective to report a prank phone call and a random driveway visit would have me headed off to the loony bin.

Carlo continued, "Do this tonight. It should be on record that these things occurred. You were targeted, and should anything take place, I want it on the record."

The sound of that made my blood run cold. What was I getting into? Then, I got mad. I was not getting into anything! I had nothing to do with this happening. I received the phone call. I saw the truck in my driveway. Yes, I was receiving the dark, foreboding feelings also. Suddenly I wished for a story about being rescued by forty men lined up against a wall, it seemed so much more innocuous than the turn my path was taking. Little did I know how right I was.

***

20 - I Should Really Learn To Go Straight Home

After my visit to Carlo's, I headed back to my office. Almost to the exit for Nyagg, I suddenly found myself continuing one more exit on the Long Island Expressway. Not sure why, I drove, turning north at the next exit which would lead me parallel to my normal route home into Great Neck, the town immediately to the west of Nyagg.

As I approached Great Neck, I veered off in a northeasterly direction, taking a seldom-used road that cuts between Great Neck and Nyagg. Why I was on this road I did not know, but it felt – necessary? That was the right word.

I was becoming frustrated. My life was such a simple, lovely affair just a short time ago. I then berated myself for my internal whining. "Man up" I told myself. Within seconds, my despair returned, and I indulged it. Why me? What the hell am I doing here?

I had the brief thought that perhaps I wanted to pass Grove Street, the street where Cindy had mentioned her and her wonderful boyfriend had rented an apartment. I was pretty sure Grove was up on the northwestern corner of Nyagg, near the water, but that did not feel right. Something else was pulling me here.

I had a brief dismissal of all of this detouring and sensing as nonsense. Nothing is more frustrating than arguing with yourself. Give me a tabby cat who hisses when he sees a needle any day. That would be a walk in the park compared to this uncertainty.

I drove on. I waited for something to happen.

In familiar on the large scale but unfamiliar on the small-scale backwoods, I continued to drive, unaware of what was navigating me in this direction. Then it hit. The fact that something hit at all was a tremendous relief to me. Something HAD drawn me in this direction – and that helped me overcome the fear that I was slowly going insane.

I was forced to pull over on the side of the narrow lane and gather myself. Waves were crashing over me. They were mixed, anxious, and negative. This was the source of the wrongness...I was sure if it. But, where was I?

The waves felt similar to the waves from the day we met Chelsea, but there were many differences, and the overall tone of the waves was most certainly more urgent, and more negative. It seemed like whining. Complaining. Distress.

I exited the Jeep and stood on the side of the road, looking north. I could see Long Island Sound, and noticed what looked like an abandoned wooden structure standing about seventy or eighty feet from the water line. There was also a house about two hundred yards east of the building, with modern trappings and an opulent look about it. I glanced around and noticed other houses as well through the trees, all a healthy distance from this old building. I studied some of them, but I was sure that the old wooden building was the source of the waves, but that made no sense. My attention kept creeping back to the old, solitary building. I searched my memory for any indication of this place, but nothing emerged. I did not think I had ever seen the place before.

I closed my eyes, focused, and tried to discern the myriad feelings I was receiving. There were simply too many. I caught bits of fear, bits of anguish, and bits of anger. Nothing was clear.

A moment or two later, a local police cruiser pulled up behind my Jeep, and an older police officer stepped out.

"Everything all right sir?" He asked, surprisingly kindly.

"Yes, yes sir." I must have replied a bit unsteadily, for he began studying my eyes, I suppose looking for signs of intoxication.

"I'm fine, officer, just had a sudden headache hit, and I thought stopping and getting some air was the best thing to do."

He hesitated a moment, probably debating whether to interrogate me further or simply drive off.

"Do you need an ambulance? Anything I can do?"

I replied anxiously, "No, no sir, nothing like that. I'll be fine in a minute. I'm a veterinarian from Nyagg, on a house call (I lied), and as I said, just felt a bit uneasy there for a second."

He seemed to relax at that explanation, which I suppose was supported by my DVM license plate and clean-cut appearance.

Suddenly, an idea struck. "Sir?" I asked. "Do you know anything about that building over there?" I pointed at the dilapidated wooden structure that I was now sure was the source of a large amount of animal emotion.

"Sure, sure," he replied, smiling now. "That's the old Horton Mill. Used to be quite the operation years ago. They made musical instruments there for a while, mostly guitars I think. Used to make paper products years back, which is why it is called a mill. Old George Horton used to own the place, but he retired and moved south decades ago. Helluva guitar player, that George. Have no idea who has the property now, probably the town. Why do you ask?"

"Just curious, I suppose." I replied, as casually as I could. "I've been up this way a lot, and I do not think I ever noticed it before."

"Well, most people just drive right by, it's been abandoned for some time now. It has a dock that reaches out into the Sound, but I don't think anyone's used that for years either." He placed his hands on his hips, and continued. "Well, sir, you enjoy the day, and take it easy. Nice to have met you." He tipped his cap with the index finger and thumb of his right hand.

With that, he turned and returned to his car. I returned to the driver's seat of the Jeep, and stared at the mill for a while. I do not know why or how I knew, but I would be back here soon. And that did not bode well in my heart or my head. But I would be back. I was sure of it. By the way, wasn't that the nicest cop ever? Wow.

***

21 – This Is Interesting, Wait Until Carlo Hears About This

After my unplanned visit to the narrow lane and my discovery of the old mill emanating dark feelings, I was back at my office in a matter of minutes. I had the normal run of patients, checked on a few details with Gina, and started to unwind looking forward to a nice, long anticipated and busily booked evening with Sarah. We had yet to have the conversation about THE Craig, my sleeping in the office, and we had not yet fully explored Cindy and my meeting at the bar. Oh yeah, and there was the matter of a ring.

Before exiting my office and heading into the house, I had a thought. I went to my files, and looked. Yep, there it was, just where I thought I had left it. Remember when I had borrowed my grandfather's camera to take pictures of mean-guy's house? I had actually done so, and managed to get several pictures of the Walrus (aka mean-guy) and his devil offspring, Craig. Something tugged at me, and I searched through the photos. Why I had saved these, I did not know. Now I was very glad I had.

He was much younger, meaner looking, and shorter. However, there was no doubt any longer. The boy in the photos and the man that had given Cindy the one-fingered salute at Heitner's were the same person. There was no mistaking it. The world is much too small. It then dawned on me – how did I miss this before? THE Craig was this man also, I was sure of it. Oh, to live a Walrus-offspring free life. I suppose that was not my destiny. Now, I had fuel for my discussion with Sarah. If this Craig in the photos and at Heitner's was in fact THE Craig, I had lots to say.

Cindy was now part of the puzzle as well. She had mentioned something about Pennsylvania, but also that her boyfriend, who I now knew to be Craig, had kicked her out of their apartment –

where was it? Yes, on Grove, she had said. Things started to click in my mind. Grove was about six blocks from the mill that I had stopped near just before. This was getting complex, intricate, and frightening at the same time. What relationship, if any, did Craig have to all of this? I did not know, but intended to find out. I distinctly thought at this point too that someone owed me four new tires. Was it possible that the wave of feelings that had hit me on the road near Nyagg was from Craig, and not from a group of animals? In my experience, I had never had that happen before, but Craig was unique in my life. He was what author Carlos Castaneda referred to as a "petit tyrant." That one person in everyone's life that causes grief. Think about it, isn't there always one? In every job, there is one person you wish did not work there. In every social situation, there is the one person who makes you annoyed at his or her presence. I used to enjoy Castaneda's books immensely, and despite him turning out to be a complete fraud, I still gained much perspective and vision from his works.

I walked into the house, planning to wait for Sarah to come home and deal with the ends of my life that had been neglected for a few days. I would not.

Sitting at our kitchen table was a very upset Sarah, and an angry looking Sophie, Sarah's mother.

I stopped suddenly, quite surprised at seeing the two of them here – why was Sarah home?

I smiled, and said, "Hi! Wow, you're home." I noticed Sarah did not look happy at all, and suddenly I was very worried. Was it her something with her father? Remember, last I had heard, he was still missing in action.

Sarah had an envelope in front of her open on the table. I could not see anything else.

Sophie spoke first. "Hello" she said, and never before have I heard the word said with such syrupy sarcasm. What was up?

"Hi Sophie, I…" I began, but got no farther.

"Not expecting us to be here? Perhaps expecting someone else?" Sophie said in an unkind tone. What the heck was this?

I stammered a second, and tried to reply, but was cut off by Sarah talking directly to her mother.

"Mom," she said firmly, "I'll handle this. Be quiet." Sophie made a wave as if to say 'alright' and looked back at me.

I moved towards Sarah and slowed as I approached the table. I had never seen this look in her eyes before, and it was hurting.

"Honey, what…" I began.

"Can you explain these?" was all she said.

She did not give me a chance to, as she rose, took her mother's hand, and walked out the front door.

The photos were black and white, a bit fuzzy, but there was no mistaking the image of me sitting at the counter in Heitner's with Cindy wrapped around my back in an obvious embrace. "Fuck."

I thought. What else could possibly happen? Innocent as I knew I was of any wrongdoing, I started out the door after Sarah and her mother, but they were pulling out of the driveway as I reached the porch. "Fuck."

I quickly grabbed my cell phone, and pushed speed-dial 2, which was Sarah (speed dial one was reserved for voicemail, NOT Stefania or anyone else, you troublemaker). The call immediately went to voicemail, indicating that Sarah had turned her phone off. "Fuck," I thought for the third time in as many minutes.

I went back into the kitchen, and noticed for the first time another photo had been included with the first. This one showed a smiling Dr. Canis and a smiling Cindy standing in front of *Reflections*, but the picture had been professionally altered. It was in black and white, and it appeared to be taken at nighttime. That never happened. Also, the picture was carefully cropped so Spirit the Great Dane was not in the frame. Someone was setting me up. I had a feeling who it was. However, I had no idea why. On top of that thought, I now had the terrible suspicion that Cindy was in on it. What the heck was going on? If that were true, Cindy was one heck of an actress.

I called Carlo, which was very unusual for me. Usually, I dealt with Carlo in person. I relayed all this to him, and he was silent for a long time. Finally, he said, "Come over."

I spent the afternoon at Carlo's, but did not feel better for the trip. I was nervous now, as too much was happening at once. Carlo listened with his regular meticulous attention, but could offer no immediate solution or even opinion. He drank it all in, and told me he would think on it.

Repeatedly through the day, I called Sarah, but she never answered. I left messages detailing my devotion and loyalty to her, indicated that it was a setup, but I had to admit it was a good one. As if things were not interesting enough, as I pulled into my driveway, I spotted Stefania's car sitting in front of my house. Great, just what I needed.

***

22 – I Wonder If She Knocked This Time

Stefania was in the kitchen when I walked in, and looked up at me without starting or making any indication of the strangeness of me finding her at my kitchen table. Actually, she was seated on one of the raised stools at the kitchen island. Next to her were an empty glass, and a half-empty bottle of Absolut vodka.

"Stef? You okay?" I asked, tentatively.

Stefania nodded in the negative, and I made the connection in my mind that her eyes looked like a bloodhound's – red and droopy. She had obviously been drinking for a while.

I stood, not sure how to proceed or what to do, and waited. After a time, Stefania looked up at me, and in uncharacteristic somber tones, said, "Men suck." At this, she burst into a full-blown cry.

As you know, Stefania and I have a history. As anyone who has ever had a history with another person will tell you, the connection is never entirely broken. I felt badly about Stefania's condition and obvious distress, but I had bigger problems. Nevertheless, I walked around the kitchen island and took Stefania in my arms in a comforting hug.

The Stefania I knew twenty-four hours ago would have pushed me away and called me something rude, so I immediately knew something was very wrong. I also knew, by default, that Stefania and Sarah had not spoken; otherwise, I would have been attacked by Stefania immediately. When I first spotted the car in the driveway, I had the thought that Stefania was in the house ready to bludgeon me to death to defend Sarah's honor regarding the pictures of me with Cindy. Obviously, that was not the case.

Stefania was quite drunk, and she stood unsteadily as she

disentangled herself from my embrace. She held me at arm's length, and tried to speak. She failed.

She reached back for the Absolut bottle, and began to raise it. I intercepted it, and she screamed at me. "I WILL DRINK AS MUCH AS I FUCKING WANT TO!!! WHY DO YOU MEN ALWAYS HAVE TO BE IN CONTROL??? WHY DO MEN ALWAYS TRY TO MANIPULATE??? WHAT THE FUCK IS WRONG WITH ALL OF YOU???" She followed this tirade up with a relapse of tears, and took a healthy, nasty pull of the now three-quarters empty bottle of vodka. I do not know how anyone can drink that stuff straight.

"What happened, Stef?" I asked, not sure if I wanted to know.

"That jerk-off...he...he was so nice, then we went at it, then he told me he had a wife back in Pennsylvania and he, sorry, (she burped rather loudly at this point – nice) and that... that... he just wanted a 'taste' of me again." She cried again, and looked absolutely miserable.

"He just used me, Mark." She broke down again, and fell back into my arms. Yikes. I need this, sure I did. However, truly, I did care for her, and through extension, she was Sarah's best friend, so comfort her I did.

"He just got what he wanted, had a fling for a few nights, and told me he had just used me. Just like that. He was laughing."

I had no idea who the heck she was talking about, but said nothing. Stefania was not known for the best discretion when it came to men. Well, except for pursuing me way back when of course.

"But I don't know how the fuck I got here!" She laughed in an almost insane manner after saying this, and she looked truly crazy for a moment. It was frightening. Was she serious? Did she not know how she came to be at my house? Did she not drive here? I was confused.

She tried to walk away from me, but was in no condition to successfully do so. Unsure of what was occurring, I took her by the elbow, and led her into the den, where we had a large, comfortable couch.

"Come on, Stef; let's get you horizontal, okay?"

She smiled wickedly at this, and moved in close to me, putting her alcohol smelling face very close to mine.

"You always liked getting me that way, didn't you, big boy." She said in a teasing, sultry voice. She suddenly grabbed my crotch and gave a quick squeeze. I tried to ignore it. That was not easy.

"Yes, hon, you were the best. Now come on, let's get you down." See what a good boy I am?

I led her to the couch, where she promptly collapsed and within seconds emitted snores that could have awakened the dead. Ok, one down.

I tried to decide if leaving Stefania on the couch was the prudent thing to do, so I resolved to sit with her a bit to make sure she was okay. Assuming she had consumed all of the vodka in the bottle, (I did not remember how much was in there before or if it was in fact a new bottle) I wanted to make sure she would continue to do that ever-important thing – breathe.

Once I was content Stefania would live long enough to nurse a heck of a headache, I went into the kitchen realizing I was famished. There was a leftover cold chicken on a plate, and that would do just fine. I brought it, a napkin, a can of Diet Coke and my cell phone into the den and sat on the chair across from Stefania. I ate. Cold chicken is awesome.

I dialed Sarah a few more times, and left a message about the state of her best friend and where she could be found. I hoped against hope that perhaps this would bring her home so I could explain about the pictures and we could talk.

In our lives, there are moments that can only be described as "watershed". We do not always know when we are in the midst of watershed moments, as we tend to react as we do to all things in our life as our character defines. Sometimes the significance of an event is lost on us until later reflection. It is one of the reasons you are reading this memoir. Max needed it to be on paper, and in retrospect, so did I. I had no idea if this was a watershed moment or not at the time, but I would soon find out.

Stefania continued to snore, and at about eleven that night, giving up on her regaining consciousness, I brought a blanket from the hall closet and covered her with it. I looked down at her for a moment, and her beauty caught me by surprise. She was truly a lovely woman. I smiled thinking about some of the times we had shared, and I remembered that she was never much of a drinker. Whatever had precipitated this incident must have been pretty serious. I was divided. On one hand, I was insanely curious to hear about it – on the other, I could see no good coming from me doing so. If only Sarah were here, this would not be an issue.

Confident that Stefania would live through the night, I went upstairs to call Sarah one more time, and to try to get some sleep. I had no idea if I had office hours in the morning (which I did not) and was too tired to check. I knew I would awaken about seven, as I always did, and left the bedroom door open so I could hear Stefania if she woke up during the night and needed assistance. If I did have a patient in the morning, it would be no earlier than 9:30, as that was the start of my business day, barring emergency.

I undressed, laid down, and tried to slow my mind enough to get a grip on everything that was going on. I left my light sweatpants on, since if a sudden call from Stefania precipitated my running down the stairs to her I preferred to do so mostly covered. How did my life become such a mess so quickly? Last week I was fixing a gummy squirrel. This week, I bought an engagement ring for a girl who will not talk to me, had my tires slashed outside a milkshake shop, was set up as a cheater to ruin my relationship with my girlfriend, was harassed both by a vehicular ghost and one on the telephone, felt waves of something "bad" near an old abandoned mill on a road I had never travelled before – and – worst of all – Milo the goldfish had died. Okay, that was not the worst, but I was trying to make myself feel better. Too bad I did not wait until morning to make this list, as there was about to be one more thing to add.

***

23 – Oh No

It must have been about three, or three-thirty. I could not see the clock on the other side of the bed, but as I was in a stupor from waking in the middle of the night, I did not immediately seek the reason I could not see the clock. I also had no idea why I was awake. Something had stirred me.

I heard something or someone on the stairs. I stayed motionless in bed, lying on my back, and listened.

I heard the bedroom door open, and saw the familiar shape of Sarah's head outlined against the scant light coming from the hallway.

As I have said numerous times before, Sarah is a better person than I am. Throughout our relationship, we have enjoyed the good and the bad, but disproportionately the good. We have travelled, we have dined, we have watched movie after movie together, we have driven, and we have loved.

There is something extra special about this relationship. There is an indescribable closeness and depth to my feelings for Sarah, something I never experienced with any other woman. I have not had many relationships, but I have had a few, and none of them approached the depth and quality of my relationship with Sarah.

From the time we first met, there was a chemistry. We met much by chance at *Maria's*, which is an upscale Mediterranean restaurant/catering establishment in Bayside, not too far from Nyagg. I was there with a few other veterinarians seeking food and libation after we had completed a day's worth of lectures from an eminent veterinarian who had visited a nearby college, SUNY Old Westbury, to deliver a speech and seminar on the latest prosthetic devices available for dogs.

Sarah was attending the retirement party for one of the

teachers in her school who had joked about having Abraham Lincoln as one of her first students. Taking a break from her coworkers, Sarah came along side me at the bar as I was awaiting a refill of my red wine.

Our eyes met, held, and I smiled. Normally shy with women, I was struck by the simple elegance and beauty of Sarah's face, and I said, "Hi there." Smooth, huh?

Sarah looked at me, smiled back, and said, "Hello."

The bartender, a young man named Saki, whom I knew, came over and took Sarah's drink order. Sarah had no idea what she wanted. She explained, "Oh, I don't know, I just had to get away from cackling old ladies and bad jokes for a while. I'll take what he's having" she said, pointing at my glass.

I turned to Saki and said, "It's battery acid with a pinch of cayenne pepper, remember?"

Saki laughed, and so did Sarah. She fixed me with a look that I have seen a thousand times since then, and said, "Oh, really? Sounds good. Make mine a double."

Saki brought her a wine to match mine, and Sarah and I laughed and talked and chatted. Neither of us returned to our respective groups, and we ended up closing the place. We drank lightly, for we were too busy talking and learning about one another. I was fascinated by her face, her wit, and her smile. I suppose she saw something in me too. I distinctly remember how we laughed and laughed. I told you I was funny.

After we were kicked out of *Maria's*, I made a bold move. I said to Sarah, "Hey. We both had a few. Want to walk with me for a while?" I had no idea where she lived, if she had driven there, or anything else for that matter except for the fact that I was smitten with this charming, beautiful girl.

"Sure. Where to?" she asked, innocently.

"I have no idea." I replied.

"That's where I was headed! What a coincidence!"

Off we went. We walked for a long while, and then stopped on a dock overlooking Long Island Sound. My imagination got the best of me, and I could have sworn I saw a green light reflected in Sarah's eyes as I looked at her. The light was not from across the bay, but right there, in her eyes. Literary geek that I was, that was it. This woman had to be mine.

I leaned in confidently and kissed Sarah. The kiss lasted a long, long, long time. It was then followed by another, and another, and another.

These kisses were different. They were not overtly sexual, they were more sensual. They affected my entire person. I will never forget that first kiss as long as I live. Or the forty kisses that followed.

Sarah and I had walked back to *Maria's*, and laughed as we noticed our vehicles happened to be the only ones left in the lot, and also happened to be parked right next to one another. She had a Ford Explorer, and I had my trusty Jeep. The two vehicles appeared to be chatting much as their owners were. Fully sober at this point, we exchanged numbers, and went our separate ways. That night, and the next, was the longest time Sarah I and have ever spent apart since that day we met. It took me a day to call, as I still could not believe it was real, but when I did, the first thing Sarah said was, "What took you so long?"

The shape of the head outlined in the light of the hall was a comfort and a relief to me. Sarah had come home. I suddenly remembered Stefania downstairs, and rose up a bit on the pillow.

"Honey? Hi. I'm so happy you're home."

Sarah said nothing, and did not move.

"Where's Stefania?" said a cool voice, chilling me from across the room. I was right. Telling her Stefania was here via her voicemail motivated her to at least come back to the house. Smart.

"She was on the couch… she's not there?" I asked, surprised. I thought I would certainly hear Stefania or at least her car if she had awakened in the night and left. Only a few hours from her passing out, I had the fleeting thought that even a few hours would not have been enough to return her to driving condition.

A dim light went on from the switch that Sarah had thrown next to our bedroom door. I looked to my left, and I saw something I have seen before – and I suddenly realized how completed screwed I was. Next to me, not two feet away, was the very nice and very naked female butt of Sarah's best friend, Stefania.

As this is not a story like *The Godfather*, let me assure you the rest of Stefania was there as well, and there was no blood. Nor was there a horse's head.

I stared, probably a bit too long, and my mouth hung open as I looked back at Sarah. Stefania was lying next to me, completely naked, above the covers, and was snoring softly.

"Holy fuck, Mark, holy, holy fuck. I can't fucking believe you. OR her. FUCK YOU!" she screamed and tore down the stairs. I heard her cry, which broke my heart. I swear I actually felt my heart crack. Holy fuck was right. I had one thought. "Fuck." However, that word, which usually can cover anything, did not cover this.

I jumped up, said "fuck fuck fuck" to try to get the word to resonate with its usual power, and spun around in the bedroom not sure what to do. I covered Stefania with a sheet, and then headed downstairs at a half-run. I heard Sarah's car screech out of the driveway. I was in serious pain. I sat down heavily on the bottom step, and put my head in my hands.

How the heck had Stefania moved from the couch to my bed? Why did I not hear anything? What the heck had happened? I shook my head, and felt nothing. I had the brief thought that perhaps I had been drugged, but my clear head and lack of headache ruled that out. I simply had slept through her coming into my bed. Wait a second. Why on earth would Stefania, who was Sarah's best friend and at best had little use for me for the past few years suddenly decide to strip naked and climb into bed with me? It made no sense.

I sat a bit longer, and thought a bit longer. Only one possibility came to mind. Someone had done this. Someone had brought Stefania into my bed and left her there for Sarah to find. No, that was too outlandish to be true.

As I have said before, I am a literary geek, and one of my favorite authors has always been Sir Arthur Conan Doyle. His Sherlock Holmes came back to me in a flash – *When you eliminate the impossible, whatever remains, no matter how improbable, must be the truth.* Amen, Sir Arthur. Someone – probably related to the tire slashing and the pickup truck and the phone calls – was trying to ruin my life. Actually, he or she was trying to ruin my relationship with Sarah, which to me was the same thing. Someone was doing a hell of a job. It was the only explanation for Stefania's magical levitation from couch to bedroom. Someone had moved her there, and done so with skill and stealth to not wake me in the process. Where was Dr. Watson when I needed him?

Suddenly nervous and feeling violated that someone had been in the house; I went to try to wake Stefania to see if she remembered anything. I was rewarded with muttered curses and gibberish, so that idea would have to wait. This probably meant she was oblivious to how she had gotten there herself. Great. Now what the heck was I supposed to do?

The only thing I could think of was to call Carlo. I did, and he said he was on his way over, and to call the police. I really did not want to do that, but I also did not want to deny Carlo's order. I could imagine the call. "Yes, um, hi, there's a beautiful naked woman in my bed who wasn't there before, you could come investigate?" They were surely going to lock me up.

I defied the order to call the police for the time being, and went downstairs. That is when it hit me – Carlo was worried someone was still in the house! I froze, and listened. Man, I could really be stupid sometimes. It dawned on me, however, that if there truly was an intrusion (which there must have been otherwise how else could Stefania be upstairs?) the culprit was surely long gone.

I noticed then the door to my office was open. That made the hair on the back of my neck stand up, for I never left it open, and I know for a fact if Gina were last in the office she would have ensured it was closed and locked.

Warily, I moved towards my office door, trying not to make a sound.

When I was at the threshold of my office door, I saw no light, heard no movement, but smelled something unusual. It smelled like alcohol. Not the drinking kind, the rubbing kind. I had a large supply of alcohol in my surgery room, but it was kept in a drum and carefully sealed. I used it quite frequently, but had purchased a drum years ago, and probably still had two-thirds of the liquid in there, maybe forty gallons or so. I listened again, and heard nothing. I crept backwards slowly, turned, and tiptoed to the front of the house. In the closet by the front door, I grabbed my six iron out of my golf bag. Always funny, (I keep telling you that I am hysterical) I put that club back and took the seven, remembering I never hit the six iron that well. Man, I am crazy sometimes.

Armed with my Ping Weapon of Doom, I crept back towards the office. I opened the door slowly, and turned the lights on in the waiting room. There was something wet on the floor. I moved into the room, and felt moisture on my feet. Pissed off now, I went further into the office and turned on all of the lights from the master switch by Gina's desk. The entire floor was soaked with what I was now certain were at least forty gallons of rubbing alcohol. The drum of alcohol was lying on its side, still dripping slowly. My couch was drenched, the computers on Gina's desk were dripping, and every wall surface showed splashing and dripping alcohol. Someone had tried to trash my office, succeeded, and did so quietly so as not to alert anyone in the house. I would have to shut down my practice for a while and have this cleaned up. I knew, somehow, that was the motivation here. Things were starting to add up. I was angry now, and decided it was time for all this to stop.

I heard a car in the driveway, and assumed it was Carlo, but I was not so sure that I put the golf club away. I waited. Carlo was about to be a bit surprised at the countenance he met when he came in the house.

***

24 – Hey Hot Stuff, Remember Me?

Next morning, I planned to drive to the police station in Nyagg to file a report, but never made it. Carlo and I had spent what was left of the night talking, and after listening to the entire tale, he decided that I was certainly correct someone was out to cause me problems. It was not his contention that the idea was to disrupt my life; he felt it was more serious than that. I cannot tell you how I knew, but I knew he was wrong. If someone wanted to hurt me, I am easy to get to. I have a pretty standard routine, and oftentimes I am alone in my office. Carlo and I shared a laugh when he suggested he go upstairs at about five AM and verify that Stefania was, in fact, naked (you know, fact checking). He did not.

That was the only levity the early morning had in store for a while, as my situation started to weigh on me. I went into my office again to survey the damage, and see if I could read the schedule to determine if I had anyone due in this morning.

Carlo and Stefania were at the kitchen table a bit later when I came out from my office. It was a good sign that Stefania navigated the stairs and the house to the kitchen without assistance. That is how bad she looked last night. I made a mental note to call Gina as soon as the sun was fully up, so as not to wake her earlier than I needed to.

Stefania looked awful. Carlo, as always, looked bright and completely together. I greeted Max (who Carlo had brought with him last night) and went to get a bowl to put down some food for him. I always had a healthy supply of dog food in my office – oh crap – no, Max, I'm sorry, I don't, everything is covered in alcohol. I stood up, sighed, and said, "Normally I would have a ton of food for Maxie here, but…"

Carlo nodded, smiled, and said, "I brought some. Just in case. In my bag."

I went to Carlo's bag, which was on the kitchen counter and removed a Tupperware container filled with dog food. Next to it, in the bag, was Carlo's Walther PPKS in its nifty leather belt holster, a handgun he had worn while on active police duty. He had, in fact, come prepared.

Max sat patiently as I filled a bowl with the kibble, and another with fresh, cold water. I patted him on the head a bit, and he sneezed. "Yeah, Maxie, the fumes are getting to me too." The smell of alcohol was hard to miss. I had opened all the windows in the office to help air it out, but I would need professional help to clean up.

The normally loquacious Stefania had yet to make a sound, and looked depressed. This worried me. "Stef, you okay?"

Her only reply was, "Sarah doesn't like it when you call me Stef, Mark." She was wearing one of Sarah's robes that I had bought Sarah one Valentine's Day, and that made my heart hurt a bit more.

I put my head down, took a deep breath, and said, "I need coffee. Stefania, dear, do you know how to work Sarah's coffee contraption? I usually use the one in my office."

Carlo rose, and said, "Ah ah ah, I've got it, you two sit. I'll take care of it." Max chewed on.

Stefania put her head in her hands, and spoke. There was a serious tone in her voice that I did not ever remember hearing before. It was a combination of contrition, regret, and sorrow. She spoke to both of us, actually, as through the years, Carlo had met her several times and the two always enjoyed each other's company. In fact, Stefania and her "man of the month" are usually invited with Sarah and me to Carlo's barbecues and dinners. She usually attends.

"Oh my God, I'm such an idiot." She seemed on the verge of tears, but did not actually cry. She wiped her nose on the robe, and continued.

"I cannot believe what happened last night, Mark, I'm so sorry."

"Stefania, nothing happened last night."

"What do you mean?" She seemed genuinely confused.

"Stefania, dear, nothing happened last night between the two of us. Nothing."

"Mark, come on, I mean, I was totally trashed. I woke up naked in your bed. Something happened. Did you come and get me or something? After the creep told me to beat it?" I had no idea what she was talking about. Did I go and get her? What?

I looked at Carlo and he helpfully shrugged his shoulders and smiled. This one is on you, kid.

"Stefania, some strange things are going on, and I assure you, lovely as you are, and as much will always treasure you, nothing happened last night."

She looked at me with a mixture of disbef and shock.

"Really?" she asked.

"Really." I replied.

With that, she brightened a bit. Within a second or two, her smile faded, and she looked confused and annoyed again.

"Then what the heck…" she began, but tossed her head back and looked at the ceiling. "Holy crap, I'm remembering things."

The coffee maker chimed in at this point, ringing three times to let us know its work had been completed. Carlo, without asking for location, deftly opened the correct cupboard and pulled three white mugs down and placed them on the kitchen island where Stefania and I were now seated.

Carlo retrieved milk from the fridge, and the three of us sat there listening to the sound of a spoon circle rapidly in a porcelain mug.

I think Carlo's detective genes kicked in at this point, and he asked Stefania pointedly, "Stefania dear, what do you remember?"

Stefania sipped her coffee, and with a sudden "ow" from the heat of the cup, started to talk.

"Two nights ago, I met an old boyfriend."

"Craig." I interjected.

Stefania looked at me, and seemed surprised.

"Yes, how did you know?" she asked me.

Carlo shot me a look and I looked down at my coffee.

"It *was* Craig, this guy that I dated my last year of high school and for part of the year after. It was right after you and I broke up." She said this directly to me, but Carlo treated it as if she had answered his question. He prodded her to continue.

"I used to be crazy for this guy. He wasn't that awesome looking, but he was charming as hell and I loved to be around him." Strangely, I felt a pang of jealousy at this. I told you the connections are never truly broken with those from our past.

Stefania continued. "Last week, I saw him at Heitner's, but he didn't see me." She suddenly turned to me, and said rapidly, "remember the morning I came over and Sarah and I sat and talked and you went out?" This came out in machine-gun fashion.

"Yes, Stef, I remember. Go on."

She fell silent at the mention of Sarah's name, and neither Carlo nor I said anything either. I suddenly jumped up, and said, "Shit, Sarah, I have to call her."

Carlo put his arm on my shoulder, and said, "No, Mark, that can wait a little bit. Let's hear what else Stefania has to tell us. You may have something new to tell Sarah that will help."

His power is hard to refuse, and I put my phone away and sat back down. Stefania continued her narrative.

"I ran into him again at the bookstore in Manhasset two days later. I was ready to rip him a new one, but he smiled and we chatted, and one thing led to another..." she trailed off at this.

Carlo, gently but firmly, said, "What one thing led to what other thing?"

Stefania looked miserable at this point, but continued.

"We kinda hooked up."

"Can you be a bit more specific?" Carlo asked, the smile gone from his face, but still maintaining his gentle manner.

Stefania seemed to make a decision at this point, and went on. "Mark, you know I love Sarah, and I love you too, and I'm so sorry this all happened, and now I'm thinking it was somehow my fault." She broke into tears.

I put my arm around her shoulder, and said, "No, no, Stefania, nothing's your fault. We just need to find out what happened. It may be really important. Take a minute." Carlo looked at me approvingly and went to fetch the box of tissues from the kitchen table and gave them to Stefania.

"Thanks" she said through muffled sniffles.

We waited.

I drained my coffee, looked at Max who was contentedly lying down under the kitchen table, and waited some more. I sensed nothing from Max.

"We went out to dinner after we met at the bookstore, and the next thing you know we were getting a room at the Fox Hollow, over on Jericho." Stefania continued.

"I know the place," Carlo said gently, "go on."

"Well, damn, I'm not going to paint a full picture here, but you know, we hooked up."

She took a deep breath, a sip of coffee, and resumed her tale.

"The next morning, he was gone, and I was like, 'crap.' I guess I still cared for the guy. But then, he comes walking in about ten minutes later with breakfast. It was sweet."

"The breakfast?" I broke in, and the three of us laughed, which diffused the tension just a bit. Max looked up at me, and had I known then what I know now – his look probably meant, "Don't put that joke in the book." Wow, Max, really?

Stefania went on to tell us how she had then spent the day with Craig, who informed her he was back in town to visit his parents and was running a very successful car lot in Allentown, Pennsylvania. I knew this was all bullshit, but did not say anything yet. I knew about Cindy, about the place on Grove, and about some other aspects of Craig as well.

She told us they spent the next night together, at the Fox Hollow as well, which, as it turns out, was last night. That is when the narrative stopped.

Carlo asked, "So, last night, you dined at the Fox Hollow, went back to the room with Craig, and that's all you remember?"

She seemed to be as lost in all this as we were.

"Yes, I mean, I have no idea how I got here? What the heck?"

Carlo said, "Let's make sure we have the dates right. What day did you first see Craig at the bookstore in Manhasset." Wow, no notepad or anything, this guy was good.

"That was Wednesday, the day before yesterday. It is Friday, right?"

"Yes, hon, it is. Ok, good. Then, Thursday, yesterday, you had the breakfast in the room, spent the day together, and last night you remember going back to the room at the Fox Hollow with this Craig again, is that it?" I liked the way Carlo said "this Craig" but I did not say anything.

"Yes, Carlo, that's right. The next thing I know, I woke up in Mark's bed, well, Mark and Sarah's bed, with my birthday suit on. You didnt look, did you Mark?"

"Do you know how your car got here?" he asked, again – gently.

"My car is here? Holy shit, no. I have no idea. My car was in the lot at the Fox Hollow. I parked it there myself. What the heck?"

Carlo thought a moment, and we left Stefania's rhetorical question unanswered. No one spoke for a long while. I arose, refilled my coffee cup, and sat back down. I topped off Stefania's as well, but Carlo waved me off as I motioned towards his.

Stefania seemed to be coming fully around now, and said, "Where the fuck are my clothes?"

Carlo, still not completely satisfied, said, "We'll worry about that later. Tell me if you remember anything else, anything at all."

"No Carlo, I'm sorry, that's it. Last thing I know we were drinking in the room, and…shit, that's it. The bastard must have put something in my drinks back at the room. Scumbag. But why? It's not like I was playing hard to get or anything." She smiled at this, and I felt her normal self starting to emerge, which was a good thing.

We all smiled at that comment, yet Carlo had his detective face on, and I knew he was adding things up in his head.

"Stefania, I think you should go to the doctor and be looked at, and I also think you should then return here and stay with Mark. Neither of you should be alone for a while. I have some people to talk to." With that, he rose, and spoke to Max. "Max, I'm going to leave you to watch over Mark and Stefania for a while, that okay?"

Max came to his feet, looked at Carlo and me, and laid back down.

"Good boy, Max, I'll be back for you soon," said Carlo, and he headed out the door. He stopped in the hallway and said to me, "Mark, you are not to go anywhere without letting someone know. You can tell me if you wish. Do not go out alone, and do not go far. Stay close to home, and stay in touch. I will call you later. Take care of Max. He should be walked every four hours. " With that, he was gone. Only Carlo would feel the need to tell a veterinarian when to walk a dog. I hoped someday I would have that kind of self-confidence.

I looked at Stefania, and she looked at me. We had no idea what the heck to do next.

***

25 – I Go Out Anyway

I took Max out into the backyard so I could think. He wandered about, inspecting everything, and looked up at me repeatedly as if he was trying to figure out just what I was trying to figure out.

Stefania raided Sarah's closet and drawers and appeared in the backyard looking much more like herself. Actually, she looked more like Sarah. Her color was back in her face, and she looked fully awake.

"My keys were in the ignition. This is so weird" Stefania said as she sat down on one of the Adirondack chairs Sarah and I kept in the yard. The vision of Stefania sitting there, in Sarah's chair, in Sarah's clothes, was surreal for me. It also reaffirmed something I already knew. I was in love with Sarah. Many things that happened last night reaffirmed that fact of which I was never in doubt. Seeing Stefania naked made me feel guilty, not aroused. The anger about my office was patent, but it was anger at my pleasant household arrangement being violated – the peace and joy I enjoyed on a daily basis with Sarah – not about the equipment or the temporary interruption of my practice. Shit, my practice. I never called Gina.

"Be right back, Stef, I have to call my assistant." I explained and shot into the house, Max at my heels.

I called Gina and explained the situation. She insisted on coming to the office to see for herself, and handle the cleanup detail. I am lucky to have such wonderful people in my life. Truly, I am. I thanked her, hung up, and returned to the backyard.

Max was looking up at me intently, and it dawned on me that Carlo had probably trained Max not to soil his own backyard, and Max was most likely respecting the same rules at my house.

I went inside in search of a leash, and fortunately, the few I had hanging in my office closet were free of alcohol adulteration.

I went back to the backyard to tell Stefania of my plans to walk Max, but she stood.

"Carlo said you can't go anywhere alone. I'm coming with you."

"I have Maxie, Stef, it'll be fine."

Stefania looked at me, parked her arms on her hips, tilted her head to the side in a stance very familiar to me from our time together, and said, "Mark. Let me explain something to you. Men do nothing but fuck everything up. For once, don't argue, just say, 'ok', then shut the fuck up, and listen. For once." Her tone was imploring.

I felt anger rise in me, but realized it was misplaced. Stefania was not the one pissing me off, it was the whole darn situation.

"Fine. Let's go." I said this with no malice in my voice, simply resignation.

Stefania and Max followed me as I locked up the house and the office, but left the office windows open. "Nothing left to mess up in there" I said to no one in particular.

The mad trio walked out onto Florida Lane, into the brightening sunshine, and by habit and nostalgia, started away from Bambi Lane, the source of so much angst in my youth.

We walked silently for a long time, and Max promptly completed his business on a lawn a few houses down from mine. I picked it up, and we continued in silence.

Stefania broke the silence. Surprise, surprise. Man, was I in a pissy mood.

"Mark," she began, "what the heck is going on? Where's Sarah? Why hasn't she called? I left her like a million messages."

I had already figured out that Stefania did not know about my confrontation with Sarah and her mother Sophie at the kitchen table about the photos – and I guess it was time to fill her in. I did.

"Holy shit, are you banging this chick?" she asked, incredulously, with her normal reserve and tasteful choice of language.

I was getting frustrated and angry, but knew that launching on Stefania would only make things worse. I stopped, Max stopped, and Stefania stopped.

"Stefania," I began. "Let me fill you in on a couple of things. First of all, I love Sarah with all my heart and would never do anything to hurt her. Nothing. Ever. We clear on that?"

Stefania raised her eyebrows in response to my tone, but said nothing.

"Second, this woman in the photos was a setup. I'm almost positive of it. Someone is trying to ruin my life, or piss me off, or is seeking revenge for something I know nothing about, or do not remember."

At this, Stefania's face took on a more serious look, and her angst seemed to wane.

"Third, somehow you are involved, Craig is involved, whoever the fuck he is, and something is going on that is making my world completely crazy."

As we were near the park where Chelsea had rescued the girl all those years ago, I moved to a bench and sat down heavily. Max investigated the flowers that were across from it, and then settled down facing me on the patch of grass nearby. He was content to watch the few butterflies that decided to dance for him at that moment, and I put my face in my hands.

Stefania sat next to me and said nothing for a long while.

"Mark." She began, with tenderness and kindness in her voice. "You are the best guy I know, really. You always have been. I know you love Sarah, and I swear to God I can't believe it but sometimes I am jealous of her, you're so in love with her. I know how wonderful you can be when you give your heart. I really do."

I was moved by this. I felt affection for Stefania that I suppose has always been there. It felt good. The sexual aspect was gone, and that was okay. Despite her beauty and how desirous she truly was, I felt no desire to jump her bones – but I knew I wanted her as my friend as long as I lived. I would happily pay to repair slammed doors for a long time – she was worth it.

I looked at Stefania, and I think that in my eyes she saw all of this. She smiled, and was gentler than I ever remember her being. It was nice.

"Stefania, what the hell do I do? I mean, my practice is shut down for a while unless I am going to open up a clinic to clean boo-boos for the neighborhood kids, the best woman in the world is gone, convinced I slept with some blonde stranger and her best friend, and someone is really trying to mess with me."

"What do you mean her best friend? What? How does she know about that?"

I realized that Stefania did not know that Sarah was at the bedroom threshold and saw us in bed together. Oh hell. I spilled.

"Oh man, now I'm in it all the way. Let's find out what the fuck is going on." She rose, and started pacing rapidly, in true Stefania style. Max got up, and watched her intently.

She went on. "Whoever is doing this just messed with the wrong bitch. Let's find out what this is all about. Come on." She grabbed my hand and led me back towards the house, but I had no idea what we would do from there. Max followed dutifully, and he seemed energized.

***

26 - I Have To See (Feel) It Again

I spent the next twenty minutes taking care of business. When Stefania, Max and I returned to the house, Gina was in the office with her mouth formed into what looked like a permanent 'O'. I hugged her quickly, told her it was going to be all right, and asked her to go home, take the week, and investigate companies that would clean this up. I also asked her to retrieve what she could from the patient list and call everyone to postpone appointments. Furthermore, so as not to worry patient's parents, I told her to tell everyone I had been asked to consult on an extremely difficult case, which would have me busy for a while. We discussed which doctors to refer the more immediate patients to, and settled on simply postponing well check-ups and routine matters. Hopefully, Milo's replacement would last at least a week.

To this point, Gina really had no idea that anything was amiss with Sarah or any other aspect of my life, so she was understandably shaken. I offered no explanation other than that someone was being mischievous, and I tried to play it down so as not to worry her too much. She did not completely believe me, as she knows me too well after the few years she has served as my 'right hand man.' I think she also realized that I would tell her when and if the time was right, so she left it alone and accepted my explanation for now.

Stefania stood stoically by while I briefed Gina, and Max went to clean out the remnants of his much earlier breakfast. I realized at that point I was very hungry, which I took as a good sign, and thought about what my next move would be.

In my garage, I have something very special. I bought it a few years ago, and only use it very rarely. Usually, it is a special occasion with Sarah, and by doing so, I truly enjoy this little indulgence that much more. My indulgence is a four-year-old BMW convertible. It stays in the garage for most of the year, but I ensure I drive it at least once a month to keep it in shape.

When I opened the garage, I paused. Seeing the car brought back memories of buying it that were so rich and full that I felt a wave of loss over my present situation with Sarah.

I had purchased the car off-lease, one year old, with very few miles on it – and I had purchased it online. I arranged the pickup of the car as a surprise trip for Sarah. It was right around her spring vacation from school, and I knew we had no commitments at home. I like to think of myself as a romantic, and that trip convinced me I was.

I told Sarah I wanted to take her away on a mysterious trip involving multiple forms of transportation, and said no more. Early on a Monday morning, we were picked up by a stretch limousine and driven to Kennedy airport. I had asked her to pack for warm weather and for a few days – but other than that, she had no idea what was in store. I loved the fact that she accepted that and went along with a smile and a sense of adventure.

We flew to Fort Lauderdale, which was about ten or twelve miles from the owner of the car's house. With a certified check in my wallet, license plates secreted in my carry-on bag, we took a taxi from the airport and I gave the driver the address where we wanted to go. The taxi driver was a garrulous fellow, and kept asking what brought us down to his sunny state. I kept saying in my head, "Stop asking questions," but after telling him it was a surprise for the lovely lady next to me, he actually did stop asking. Thank you. Sarah kept looking at me the entire time with an inquisitive smile, but said nothing.

We arrived at a private house in Tamarac, not far from the airport. In the driveway, shiny, bright, clean and inviting, was my purchase. The owner was a genial fellow, business was transacted quickly (he was expecting me) and after a struggle with a rusty screwdriver and two New York license plates, Sarah and I hit the road. Oh, wait, there's more.

I had sent some extra money and asked the owner if he would be kind enough to buy some Hershey bars (Sarah's favorite) and stash them in the glove compartment. Two or three miles from the house, I told Sarah to check in there – and her smile and laughter were more than enough to make my efforts worthwhile. See what a sap I can be?

We took a full three days to drive home, stopping here and there, including one memorable day and night in Hershey, Pennsylvania. The car was a convertible as I mentioned, and we were driving with the top down when something very memorable and 'sweet' happened.

As we drove slowly down Cocoa Avenue in Hershey looking for a restaurant, I suddenly stopped and pulled over. I did not have to say a word. We happened to be next to the factory where Hershey makes its world famous cocoa – and the scent – oh my, the scent – was washing over Cocoa Avenue and right into the topless car with two rapt people sitting in it. We must have sat there for twenty minutes breathing in the sweet, incredible scent of cocoa. It was truly an amazing experience. To this day when someone uses the cliché "stop and smell the roses," I always reply with, "No, stop and smell the cocoa, it's better." They don't get it. Their loss.

All the reminiscing about that trip held me steadfast as I looked at the car. Memories. Thick, rich, incredible memories. I snapped back to the here and now.

My logic in taking the BMW was three-fold. One, the car was not well known in town, or by anyone for that matter, so if someone were out there waiting for me to appear it may throw him or her off the trail for a while. Two – I had not run the car in more than five weeks, so it was time. Three – I loved driving the thing.

I said to both Stefania and Max at the same time, "Let's go."

Stefania said nothing, I felt a bit of excitement from Max, and off we went. The back seats in the car are leather, and Stefania and I chuckled a bit as Max tried to gain good footing in the back seat. The little things.

I did not discuss my intended destination, but I most certainly had one in mind. I felt a bit empowered now. I had Carlo doing whatever it was Carlo was doing on my behalf, and I had a pissed off pistol of a girl riding shotgun. I think I would rather take Stefania into a bar fight with me than many of my male friends. I also had Max, who I knew could be counted on in myriad ways. I wanted my Sarah back, and I wanted my life back.

I headed northwest, the BMW whining sweetly as we took turns a bit faster than I normally would in my Jeep. Stefania said nothing, and I could tell Max was enjoying the ride once he parked his butt in the corner and could get some leverage. I would have taken the top down, as the weather was perfect, but that would have ruined the whole incognito effect, would it not have? I was content to cruise along with the windows completely open and the convertuble top up.

Passing two diners along the way, which made Stefania look my way questioningly, I continued towards Grove, the street of destiny.

I slowed as we approached Grove, and then I spotted it. Bingo. Sitting in the driveway of a nondescript house towards the middle of the block was a pickup truck with tinted windows. It looked remarkably like the one that had droned outside my office window a few days back. Wow, that seemed like a year ago.

Stefania turned to me and said, "What?"

"Do you know that truck?" I asked as we cruised by at about fifteen miles an hour. I did not want to call unwanted attention to us, but at the same time I wanted a good look and to get the plate number. Guess what? Pennsylvania plates. Check.

As we were passing in front of the house next to the one with the pickup, I saw in my side view mirror a man exit the pickup truck house and head towards the truck. I sped up surreptitiously, and we turned on the adjacent street and stopped.

Unsure of what to do, I waited. "Stefania." My tone must have sounded serious and stern at the same time, for she looked at me and waited.

"I think that truck belongs to Craig, and I think that somehow he is the key to all this."

Stefania's head whipped around at this, and I cautioned her. "Just stay put, please, don't do anything rash. I want to see if it is Craig, and if it is where he is going."

Her face had such a look of anger and determination I was impressed. She stoically returned her gaze forward, and waited with me. Max looked around, and I felt curiosity from him, but no warning or danger signs which I was especially looking for. James Bond has nothing on me when there is a canine nearby.

Sure enough, the pickup whizzed by behind us on Grove, heading north. I waited a full thirty seconds, then backed up into a 'K' turn onto Grove, and followed.

I lost sight of the truck for a minute, but then spotted it turning onto Christopher Way, which ran north towards Long Island Sound. There was not a lot of traffic here at all, so I would need to keep a discreet distance so as not to be spotted. My cell phone rang. Damn. I hit the Bluetooth button on the car dash, which would place the call through the car's system, and I could remain driving hands free. I did not look to see who the caller was.

"Dr. Canis" I said without thinking.

"Hello there, Dr. Canis. This is retired detective Carlo. Where are you?"

"Hi Carlo." I looked at Stefania. She shook her head 'no'. I nodded. "Stef, Max and I went out to grab a bite. Took the Bimmer. We're near the house, just had to get out for a bit."

"Ok" was the reply that did not sound convinced. "Just be sure not to do anything foolish, I'm pushing some old buttons trying to see what I can find out. Stay smart." With that, he disconnected.

Stefania and I looked at each other, and said nothing.

Following at a discreet distance once more, I spotted the pickup truck where I knew it was going to be. I just knew it. It was parked in front of the old Horton Mill, where I had sensed the trouble and met the old police officer who gave me the mill's history.

This was good in that from the side of the road I could observe the mill at a decent distance without being spotted. Stefania asked, "Why are we stopping here? What is that place?"

I replied, "I don't know, Stef, but I know that is Craig, and I was here last week and felt something."

Stefania knew about my affinity with animals, but not the full extent of it. She simply thought of me as a very talented veterinarian (she had said so in weak moments in the past) but did not know how powerful, overwhelming and specific these feelings could be.

We sat, and watched. Max began to whine, which was very unusual for him. I tried to pin down the feelings he had, but got a jumble of things I could not identify. Slowly, I realized there was more. Much more.

It hit me like a tsunami. Coinciding with the large barn-sized door of the mill opening in the midday sun, I was hit with a ton of animal emotion. Wow, holy cow, was this strong. Stefania noticed my change in aspect, and put her arm on mine.

"Are you okay, Mark? What is it?"

I shushed her, and watched. She turned back to watch the mill as well. Max's whining increased.

"It's okay, Maxie, take it easy. It's okay."

For the first time in my life, I was in full control of a wave of animal emotion. I felt like a ship captain navigating a storm with a well-know and trusty schooner beneath my feet while a thunderstorm raged overhead. I could see, feel, hear, and sense everything coming at me, and I was maintaining my head. Another watershed moment.

In everyone's life, there are remembrances of certain times that stick out, as we have discussed before. Some are more poignant than others are. Ask anyone born before 1950 where he or she was on November 22, 1963. You will get a specific answer. Ask anyone born before 1980 where he or she was when the white Bronco was speeding down a California freeway followed by half the police in Los Angeles and a plethora of news helicopters. You will get an address and a time. Ask anyone born after 1990 where he or she was on a bright, sunny, clear day in New York, or anywhere else for that matter, September 11, 2001. You will most certainly get a descriptive response. In fact, sometimes it even goes deeper. I can tell you that on September *10*, 2001, I was with a large group of colleagues on a fishing boat that we had chartered out of Captree Boat Basin near Fire Island. About twenty of us had chartered the boat as we tried to do every summer, and we had a terrific paradoxical time. Think about the paradox – a group of men (and two women) who dedicate their lives to helping animals – out there trying to catch aquatic animals for sport and maybe food. Strange, right? That's life. I never would have remembered that date if it were not for the heartbreaking conflagrations of the next day.

All of this rushed through my head as I continued to watch the mill. Nothing was happening. I took the opportunity to put my arm on Stefania's shoulder and say, "Stef, I am very glad that you are with me, and I am doubly glad that you are my friend. I am eternally grateful that you are Sarah's too, since I may need a heck of a lot of help fixing that."

She replied, "I don't know how much help I'm gonna be there, Mark, remember, she thinks I betrayed her too." She seemed very sad about that. I had the thought that Stefania was deeper than I had ever realized. It was a nice thought.

Good point, though. It dawned on me, though, that women tend to trust other women more than they trust men no matter what the circumstances. My swearing on a stack of whatever prayer book struck my fancy over and over again would not carry the same weight with Sarah as would Stefania corroborating my story. It is just how it is.

Okay, at the risk of having this memoir heaved across the room a dozen times over, dear reader, let me tell you that I, Mark Canis, veterinarian extraordinaire and otherwise regular guy, have figured out women. Yes, that's right. I have the secret. I know it all. Want to know?

I am not even going to make you wait for my aforementioned philosophy tome to tell you. I am going to share it with you right now.

This now qualifies as a watershed moment for you. I assume, since you are reading this book, that this is not the first book you have read. A safe assumption. But, you should most definitely prepare for the next paragraphs, since nowhere before has the secret to men completely understanding women ever appeared in such a pithy manner in written form before. Ok, I should probably stop talking now and just tell you. In addition to being a romantic, I tend to have a flair for the dramatic. You know that already, don't you? Okay, okay, here it is:

Women- those wonderful, soft, beautiful, understanding, forgiving (one hopes) gentle, kind, adoring creatures that we fight wars about – make everything in a man's life exponentially bigger.

Follow me for a minute. You will get it, I promise.

Give a woman one tiny, microscopic sperm cell, and she will make you a baby, millions of times larger than the cell you gave her.

Give a woman a house, no matter the size, and she will give you a home, larger in scope, beauty and depth than one could possibly imagine.

Give a woman a smile, a genuine smile, and she will give you her heart.

Give a woman crap – and you – my friend – will get back a world of shit.

Got it? You do not need to thank me, just buy my philosophy book when I publish it, okay? I may need the income after the alcohol based trashing of my practice.

Back to the here and now once more. Stefania saw it first. "Mark?" she inquired, causing me to end my philosophical musing and concentrate fast. I was still inundated by emotion, but it had waned significantly in the recent minutes.

"What is it, Stef?" I asked, piqued.

"What's that?" she asked as she pointed towards the Sound.

Moving slowly in the Long Island Sound, just north of the old mill, was what appeared to be a sizable watercraft of indeterminate type. We watched as it approached, and could hear the sound of powerful motors wind down as it made its approach towards shore.

We could not see anything further, as the combination of trees, the mill itself, and the angle we were watching from colluded to block our view. Something was up at the old mill though, and I felt the intensity of the animal emotions rise once again.

Not content to simply sit where we were, I realized there was nothing further I could do with Stefania and Max with me, so I started the car and swung around on the narrow road to head back home.

Stefania looked at me. "That's it?"

"For now, Stef, for now. Let's go back to the house and see if we can get a hold of Sarah, Carlo, Gina, and get something to eat. Okay?"

She smiled. "Okay." I sensed from her a relinquishing of

command that in a million years I never thought I would see from Stefania. I felt a sudden resurgence of affection for her, and patted her knee. She stuck her tongue out at me in a move reminiscent of Sarah, and my heart ached a little. We headed back to Nyagg, back to my ranch/office, and onward towards whatever was coming next.

***

27 - What's That On Your Shoulder?

Lest you fear I have completely abandoned anecdotes from the past building you up to the present state of me, Mark Canis, let me regress once again.

It was my third year of college. Looking back on the situation, I can laugh about it now, but at the time, there were moments when it was more difficult than funny. Time has a way of washing our memories, leaving only the good and fading shadows of the difficult.

Crossing campus one spring morning, I felt something coming from an animal I could not pin down – but it was strong and urgent, yet tiny at the same time. That makes no sense, but if you stay with me, I think you will understand.

By this point in my life, animals sought me out regularly, which was a blessing and a pain in the butt, depending on when and where I was. I always tried to help in some way. It can be heartbreaking when I cannot.

On this particular morning, my seeker turned out to be a young bird- an owl to be more precise. Not exactly a baby, but a very young owl. At the time I had no idea of the species (I later discovered he was an Elf Owl, abundant in this part of the country) but he was struggling on the ground near a pond on campus, obviously in distress. He was attempting to move towards me, away from the pond, so I knew he was seeking me out.

I put down my book bag and headed carefully over to him. He had a broken wing, creased right across the middle, which looked like it may have been run over by a bicycle tire, but he was too small for that to have been the culprit. The poor thing was in rough shape. I looked around and saw no other creatures, human or otherwise. He was tiny, no bigger than a guinea pig for lack of a better size reference.

This was pre-internet, for if it were the modern era, I could have taken a photo of the owl and found out immediately what species he was, what he ate, how old this particular little guy probably was, and what his natural habitat was. There was this place called the library on campus, but I shuddered at the idea of navigating its maze of shelves to research a particular species. I knew a little bit about owls, but certainly not enough to care for this guy without research. I had no idea what to do. I knew he was in distress, and that was enough.

I brought him to the science building of my college, but the guard at the entrance would not let me in, quoting some code about undocumented animals and so forth. Red tape is the same wherever you go.

I gave up trying and brought the little fellow, who I had named Oscar, to my dorm.

I was very lucky that year that I had pulled a single room in my dormitory. Every suite in that particular dorm had three rooms – two doubles and a single. Single rooms were distributed by lottery, and I had gotten lucky. It was the first time I truly lived on my own, and I enjoyed the ability to shut out the rest of the world thanks to a large wooden door, whenever I wanted to. I now had a roommate.

Oscar was calm, gentle, and incredibly cute. I set him up in a shoebox I had stuffed away in my closet, and after reading some about owls in general in a reference manual one of my suitemates had (he was an Environmental Science major, whatever the heck that is), I stuffed some cotton socks in the box to make Oscar a nice home. I read that owls liked to perch, so I borrowed a drumstick from another student who lived down the hall (we heard him practicing constantly), cut two holes in the shoebox, and made a perch. Oscar popped onto it immediately, looked at me, and let out the most adorable little hoot you have ever heard. He seemed to be happy. I felt it.

I had planned to become a veterinarian all my life, and was studying to do so in college at the time, and it was Oscar who really gave me the full gamut of responsibility for the first time. I spent most of the next day reading about owls, and learned as much as I could. After educating myself to his anatomy and structure, I built a splint for his broken wing from some popsicle sticks and thread. He sat impassively as I tended to his wing, looking up at me with those incredibly round eyes as I worked.

As if he understood, as soon as I finished, he flapped the wing tentatively. I immediately sensed affection from him, which was simply endearing. He flapped the wing repeatedly, and hopped happily on his new drumstick perch in his makeshift owl condominium.

Now, to feed him. I read that this species of owl dined on insects. I had the thought of going into town in search of a pet store that sold crickets or the like, but the girl I was dating at the time (who absolutely crooned over Oscar) gave me a better idea.

This owl's main diet consisted of moths. How does one gather moths? Easy. We went to the campus center where the annoyingly bright lights of the student center were low enough to reach, and saw our answer flitting to and fro immediately. Jumping and grabbing, like two kids reaching for helium balloons, we gathered about a dozen of the little flying creatures and secured them in a jar we had brought along. Yes, Mark Canis, mighty flying creature hunter. Next stop, pterodactyls.

What a laugh it was when we returned to my dorm room. How does one get a flightless owl to eat moths? I tried to hand him one, but that did not work out too well. Apparently, he wanted to catch them himself, but he was not strong enough to fly yet. Again, my female friend had the answer. We brought the jar to Oscar, and he deftly stuck his beak in and caught a few moths. Three were all he needed, and he hooted happily to indicate he was done. I brought him water in a glass, which he drank easily and immediately by pecking at it with his tiny beak. I left the glass on the table near his box should he want some more.

I became incredibly adept at catching moths. I also learned to ignore the strange looks from other students on campus. Hey, it's research, go away.

After two weeks, Oscar grew a bit and took to riding around everywhere on my shoulder. I would put Oscar on his perch when

I needed a break, and he would immediately start hooting until I returned close enough that he could make a broken-wing aided jump back to my shoulder. Oh boy.

Oscar would not leave my shoulder. If I tried to remove him, I was rewarded with a nip on my ear (ow!) or on the hand that tried to remove him. Nope, my shoulder was his new home. The only break he gave me was when I laid down in bed.

Going to classes with a juvenile Elf Owl on my shoulder made me quite the celebrity on campus for a while. Oscar enjoyed Calculus 202, Etymology 201, and he audited some Spanish classes as well. I have to tell you – if you are looking to meet chicks, walking around with an adorable Elf Owl on your shoulder is a definite winner. It beats a toy poodle any day.

I tell you all this for a few reasons. First, to point out that animals seek me when they need help, which I started to think may be why I sensed such strong feelings coming from the Horton Mill. If that were true, then a very large group of animals was in trouble. I had no idea beyond that what it could mean. Second, it is a cute story, so there. Third, I am trying to understand why all this has happened, and in the course of doing so, went back in my mind to see if I had done some cosmic wrong at some point that caused my Karma to need balancing. I could not find anything. If nothing else, this whole situation has made me feel good about myself. I joke that I am a nice guy, but feeling inside that it is true is warming to the soul.

By the way, after my third year of college, I donated Oscar (with his permission of course) to a zoo near my college. I would visit him monthly, and it was always a bittersweet reunion. For years after I graduated I received letters from the ornithologists at the zoo updating me on what they called "our most popular attraction." Another permanent attachment of a memory. Every time I see an eclipse of moths about a light, I think of Oscar.

***

28 – What Next? Which First?

There were three things in my life that needed immediate attention. In order of importance, they were: Find Sarah, explain, and pray she would understand. Actually, I was praying at this point simply for the opportunity to make her understand. Then – figure out how the mill, the harassment I have endured, my office vandalism and other fun occurrences were related. I knew Craig and his pickup truck were obviously the key, but had no idea how to proceed. Finally, find something to eat, because I was really, really, really hungry.

Stefania and Max went into the house, and I, in a blatant act of subterfuge, went out the office door and back to my car without saying a word. I think I heard something like, "Mark, you bastard! Come back!" as I pulled away. I did not want anyone with me for this next errand, despite the warnings from Carlo not to go out alone. Sorry, Stefania, but you are only second most important on my female list.

I drove directly to Sarah's parents' house, which was not far. I was hoping Sarah would be there, but I felt inside that was a hopeless endeavor. I also knew, without knowing, that I would not find her in her classroom at the elementary school two towns over where she taught. I just knew.

The shiny Cadillac I had met at the Japanese restaurant was not in evidence, which I thought was good, since it meant I did not have to deal with Lou immediately, only Sophie. Sophie would be easier, despite her attitude at the kitchen table about the photos.

I parked outside and walked to the front door. I knocked heavily and waited. I saw the curtain in the living room move, but I missed the face. The front door opened, and Sarah's mother, Sophie, stood there.

"What do you want? You have some set, showing up here.

What's the matter, ran out of tramps so soon?" Sophie could be very cold when she wanted to be. I had never thought this trait had been passed on to her daughter until I heard Sarah's voice at the bedroom door the night before when she spied Stefania and me in our bed.

I deflated. Full of vim and vigor on the way over, I simply emotionally melted. I had no angst or strength, although on the way over I had worked myself into a quick frenzy practicing what I would say at this juncture. It all failed me.

"Sophie, I..." I stammered, and was rewarded with a heavy oak door slamming in my face. I woke up.

"Sophie, dammit," I yelled, not caring who in the neighborhood heard me, "Let me in; I need to talk to you. Please!"

Nothing.

"You know me, Sophie, and you know I love your daughter. Come on!"

Why hadn't I thought to bring the ring along to show her? Where the heck did I put the ring anyway? In all that has happened, I did not remember where it was. Great.

I stood for about five or six minutes, shouting into a closed front door. I did not hear the man approach from behind me.

"Well, look who it is. Mr. Perfect..." spoke Lou, Sarah's father, who had apparently come home and walked up undetected by me to this point. I looked and saw the Cadillac at the rear of my peripheral vision. I will give Caddy credit for this much, that car sure is quiet.

"I think you should probably go, Mark, before I say something or do something we will both regret." Lou said this with darkness in his tone that I knew was always lurking below the surface, but had never heard before.

"Lou. This is all bullshit. I never did anything, and it's all a setup. You have to believe me." I sounded more desperate than I had intended to.

"Save it, Mark. My daughter is a mess, and if you think I am going to let you (he moved closer to me so he could poke his index finger in my chest at the word 'you') make it worse, you don't know me that well. Why don't you take a long walk?"

He brushed past me, intentionally jarring me on his way by, and went into the house. I turned, deflated, and started walking back to my car. My cell phone rang. I practically tore my pocket grabbing for it, hoping to see that familiar and ever-so-welcome word "SARAH" pop up on the screen. It was not. It was Emily, my sister.

***

29 – Take A Few Home With You, C'mon

I know you are anxious to find out what happened. I know you are reading this and saying, "C'mon Mark, we heard about the owl, now tell us the whole story happening today – and get on with it!"

You are probably right that I should do so. This is my memoir though, so you have to write your own if you want to dictate the order. So there. If you are reading this chapter, though, it means it survived the literary axe of Max, and hence is important or at least interesting enough that you can take a moment out from the action to hear about Emily again. Remember my sister?

Emily and I were never remarkably close over the past decade and a half, but we have kept in touch. Emily joined the family business, and is teaching school on Long Island. She teaches elementary, and loves it.

She married a man that she had dated once in high school and then did not see for ten years. A chance meeting very similar to the one Sarah and I enjoyed reunited the two still single people and sparks flew anew. Within months, they announced their plans to wed.

I like her husband; he is a really nice guy, although his sports team affiliations are the opposite of mine. I often joke that I am not surprised by that, anyone who would marry my sister has suspect judgment to begin with. Ha ha.

One week last summer, Emily called and invited Sarah and me to come out for a weekend barbecue. Emily was the mother of two at this point, a boy and a girl, and we had not seen them for a long while. I was excited and pleased by the invitation, and we readily accepted.

Sarah and I took the BMW and headed out east. It was not a long drive, about forty minutes, and we soon found ourselves navigating a four-lane road with every conceivable fast food store lining the way. Strip mall here, McDonald's there, Long Island is rapidly becoming very redundant. Same scene, different town. It has changed remarkably from what I remember growing up.

I remember when I was much younger, maybe five or six, my parents would drive us into Queens every Sunday for dinner at my grandparent's (mom's parents) who lived in the house with the grapevines and the metal mower. I loved these trips, as I loved my grandparents, and no one could beat grandma's cooking. I always left full to the gills.

What prompted this memory was my reference to the way Long Island, and I am sure towns across America, has (have) changed in the short span of my lifetime. What I specifically remember – coming home after dinner at grandma and grandpa's, usually about 9:30 or 10:00 on a Sunday evening – and encountering NO traffic at all on the Long Island Expressway, the major east-west thoroughfare which splits Long Island. It was downright spooky sometimes. I would stare out the window, my sister Emily safely strapped in a car-seat beside me, and watch for the occasional car that would be coming the other way, or pass us on either side. They were few and far between.

Today, one can find a traffic jam at any point on this very same road at three in the morning on a Wednesday. I always ask, "Where are all these people going?" It truly is a dramatic change from my youth, and I cannot get over it every time I experience it. Life is never static.

To Emily's again, we arrived a few moments later and pulled into the driveway in front of her well-maintained mini-mansion. Emily's husband is an accountant, and they make a nice living together. We exited the car, popped the trunk to grab the presents we had brought for my sister, her husband and my niece and nephew, and headed towards the house.

As we walked, we were attacked by two very wet children who came flying from the side of the house. "Uncle MARK! UNCLE MARK! AUNT SARAH! YAYYYY!!!" shouted the voices of both my sister's kids.

We were engulfed in moist hugs, and laughed aloud. Jordyn, the girl, was about seven, and Jacob was about five. Shame on me for not knowing exactly how old they were.

My niece was extremely excited. "Uncle Mark, you HAVE to see what we have in the backyard! COME ON!!!" With this, she grabbed my arm and practically dragged me towards the side of the house. Sarah laughed, and went in the front door from which my sister Emily had appeared. I heard them exchange enthusiastic greetings as I was dragged to the backyard.

"HURRY! HURRY UNCLE MARK!!! WAIT 'TILL YOU SEE!!!" screeched Jordyn, still dragging my staggering form with her. "THEY'RE SO CUTE!" Uh-oh.

Jordyn led me towards the shed that was in the backyard. Exaggeratingly staggering as I went along with Jordyn, I waved to my sister's husband and two people I did not recognize who were enjoying cocktails on the back patio. "Save some for me..." I said in a trailing voice when I noticed they were holding cocktails raised in a toast. Jacob seemed content to return to some other boys in the pool, who I assumed were the neighbor's kids.

Jordyn and I stopped next to the shed, and before I even had a chance to sense anything, I saw a large box lying on the ground. Inside the box was some sight. At least six or seven kittens were bouncing around a prone mother cat. All of them were black as pitch, and looked to be about four to six weeks old.

"My, my, what do we have here?" I asked, kneeling down near the box.

"Uncle Mark, you have to give them all checkups! They're new! They were just born!" Jordyn obviously had her mother's energy, which never waned.

So much for a nice, quiet visit to my sister's, huh? How does one say no to a swimming pool wet niece that one has not seen in far too long? Right, you cannot.

"Ok, Jordyn, I'll look them all over. Can I go get a drink first?"

She appeared to think about this, and her answer was priceless. "No. You cannot work on the kittens if you're drunk. You'll have to wait." Everyone on the patio, who was listening, laughed at this. So did I.

I picked up the still moist Jordyn, and carried her towards the porch. "Ok, ok, Jordyn, I'll take it easy until I have looked at the kitties. I promise."

She accepted this, and I put her down on the patio and greeted Stan, my sister's husband, and was introduced to Mel and Arlene, two neighbors of my sister's they had become friendly with. They seemed like very nice people.

Sarah and Emily appeared magically from the large double-doors of the house, and Emily came over to give me a kiss.

"Drafted into duty, huh bro?"

I sighed, smiled, and said, "Yep. You knew she would do so. Thanks for the heads up." Emily's reply was her tongue sticking out at me, which made me laugh and feel nostalgic at the same time.

We spent a pleasant few minutes chatting, Stan brought me a drink and told his daughter it was just soda (which it was not) and we caught up a bit. Emily had always loved Sarah, and so did everyone else once they got to chatting.

Jordyn was staring at me the whole time, so after a few minutes, I waved her over to me, and we went out front to get my medical bag from the car. Uh-oh, wrong car, no medical bag. Oh boy.

I explained my predicament to Jordyn, and she took it very well. She said that she was sure I was a good enough "veteran" to look at the kittens without all that "fancy stuff." I laughed.

"Veterinarian, Jordyn. Veterans are people who have fought in wars." She tried to say it, and after a few cute tries, we agreed "vet" would work.

We marched back into the yard, I shrugged my shoulders at Sarah, and we approached the kittens.

As I approached, I tried to feel anything such as fear or wariness coming from the mother cat, but there was none. Apparently, she was well fed at this location, was used to my sister and her family, and had no issues with her kittens being handled by the occupants of the backyard.

The mother cat rose and walked over to Jordyn as she approached, leaving me alone with the wiggling box. I sat down and tipped the box on its side, which had the effect of freeing the kittens to go wherever they liked. They liked me.

I giggled like a small child as seven, yes; seven small black wiggling kittens began to climb on my shoes and on my pants and bite at my shoelaces. They all looked about the same size, except for one, which was a tad smaller and had less developed fur but still appeared healthy. They were adorable. Mother cat returned to see what was up, and brushed against me in an affectionate manner. I stroked her head, looked her over quickly, and called her a "slut" under my breath. Good luck getting child support, mom.

I replaced the kittens in the box, and made my way back to the patio announcing that all of the critters were healthy as far as I could tell. Jordyn tilted her head to the side, in a move reminiscent of most of the women in my life, Sarah, Stefania, and Emily (do they teach that move at woman school???) and said, "Even Joey? He's the little one."

"Yes, Jordyn, even Joey. He's the 'runt' of the litter, but he's fine too."

Jordyn looked at her father, and he explained what a runt was. Since Emily was actually an inch taller than I was, he used me as the example of the runt of the Canis family. One point for Stan. But his teams still suck.

The inevitable question came at last, from Arlene, the neighbor on the patio, who asked, "What are you going to do with all of them?"

My sister's smile was evil. Pure evil.

"Oh, Mark will take them back with him. He's a veterinarian, as I'm sure you know by now, and he'll find homes for them."

Thanks, sis. Her smile was all I needed to see. She had this planned out all along.

Life was good for Mark Canis at this particular juncture, and I suppose my happiness with Sarah, being with family, and being full of three fake soda drinks from Stan had me in a good mood. Remember to stop and smell the cocoa. Indulge those you love. Swallow some crap every once in a while, it will be worth it in the end.

Emily probably expected a fight, but got none. "Sure, I'll find them homes. No problem."

It was worth it to see Emily's face drop into an expression of disbelief. I squeezed my face into a grimaced smile and poked it out at her. I felt twelve years old again.

Two weeks later, I had found homes for the kittens as promised. Sarah was helpful in this, asking around her school and spreading the word. I threw in a free year of check-ups for the kittens as an incentive, which was a brilliant double-sided stroke. Not only would it help move the kittens, but also it would allow me to give updates on them to Jordyn. I felt like a good uncle.

Now that you are caught up on Emily and her life, let us get back to the here and now, and the mill. I promise it will be worth the diversion.

***

30 – I Know, I Know

Driving back to my house after my impromptu visit to Sarah's parents, I knew Stefania was going to be very angry, but I was prepared to deal with that. She was flexible enough to understand why I had to go to Sarah's parents', and I hoped I could calm her down easily and quickly.

Who I was not prepared for was Carlo. He was standing, hands on hips, on my front steps as I pulled in. Max was next to him.

"So (pausepausepause), perhaps I was not clear (pausepausepause) in my earlier statement. Let me reiterate." He did not sound happy.

"Carlo," I started, but I was cut off.

"No. I do not want to hear it." He moved into my personal space, putting his face a few inches from mine, and gripped my right shoulder firmly with his left hand.

"This is no joke. You do not seem to understand. There are bad guys out there, and you are on their radar. If you pull anything like that again, I am going to break both your kneecaps so I can hear the clink of your crutches to locate you. Are we clear?" He said this with no humor whatsoever. I noticed he had also taken the step of attaching his Walther PPKS to his belt in its leather holster.

Fully chastised, I managed, "Yes, sir. I got it."

He released my shoulder and I went into the house. He and Max followed me, and we all sat down at the kitchen island again, which seems to have become the center of operations for our little group.

Stefania looked miffed, but said nothing. I breathed out a sigh, and looked at her.

"How did it go?" she asked, as if my sojourn was easily discerned.

"Not well." was all I said.

She put her arm around my shoulder, and leaned her head against my arm. "It'll be okay, Mark, it'll be okay. It'll all work out."

I wish I shared her enthusiasm and optimism, but I could not, not now. We sat in silence for a time.

"Any luck with anything, Carlo?" I asked, more to break the silence in the room than out of any hope he had found something concrete out.

"Mark, to be honest, it has been difficult to generate any sympathy for our situation." I was touched by the fact that this rock of a man, my friend, referred to these hardships as "our" situation.

"You chose not to report the damage to your office, so be it. I would have done so immediately, but you do not seem to be concerned about that. You chose not to report the truck in your driveway, or the phone call urging you to take a vacation. I am at a loss as to what it will take for you to properly advise law enforcement."

He had an excellent point. I had respect for the police, but I simply could not see what could be done in this situation. I knew who was behind those things, but did not have a modicum of proof. What difference would it make to report it? I had no insurance claim to make on the office, my insurance would not cover it, nor would it be covered by my homeowner's insurance policy. I was stuck there.

I thought about the damage to the office. What possible motivation could someone have for making my office unusable? I thought about Craig's pickup truck (I assumed it was his at this point) in my driveway. What was the point of that? I thought about the phone call. Does anyone really think that a phone call like that will make someone else jump on a plane? None of it made any sense, unless...

Unless the idea was to get me out of the way. That was the only reasoning that fit the facts as I had them. Someone wanted me to disappear, but not in the permanent sense. Why? I asked

Carlo.

"No, I am afraid that is an amateur assessment of all of this. I do not agree that is the motivation here, I'm sorry." He said this firmly, without hesitation. Again, I had the strongest feeling that this time he was wrong.

Carlo rose, reissued his "watch over them" command to Max, and started towards the front door.

"Don't make me come back this way, Mark. Be smart." He said without turning around. I heard the front door close.

Stefania stared at me for a long time. I started to apologize to her, but she waved it off.

"Oh, please, Mark, I would have done the same thing. Forget it." Thank you, Stefania.

I said to her, "Want to order in? I'm starving." With everything going on, and nothing being solved, I still had not managed to find something to eat.

Stefania suddenly had a thought. I saw it physically hit her. "Hey", she said. "Let's go find that Cindy chick. I have some questions for that bitch." Ok, a plan. Why not? Maybe she would have food, too.

***

31 – Spirit Plus

Tulipwood Lane was just around the block from Florida Lane. Instead of driving there, Stefania, Max and I decided to walk. Well, I decided, and they went along with it.

I leashed Max, tried to leash Stefania, which earned me a look of mixed disgust and mirth, and we headed out.

I secured the house again, except for the office windows, but felt naked without a weapon. I suppose this is what it was like to live in the old West. Hat? Check. Spurs? Check. Gun belt? Check. Except I had no gun belt.

To arrive at Tulipwood Lane, we had to pass the old Walrus-Craig house. I watched Stefania for any reaction as we did, but none was forthcoming. I remembered then that by the time Stefania and Craig had hooked up back in high school, Walrus and Craig had already moved to Douglaston. The house was meaningless to her. It would never be to me. Another family lived there now, and the house looked bright and cheery, but those memories of the fence, the barking dog, and pock-faced Walrus would stay with me forever.

Tulipwood Lane is a road much like many others in suburbs throughout this great country of ours. Middle-class to upper-middle-class in component, the houses were comfortably sized, the lawns well cared for, and a mixture of middle to upper quality vehicles gleamed in driveways from the midday sun. Almost, but not quite bucolic, it was nevertheless peaceful, and quiet. A few kids rode bikes around the streets, which were still devoid of enough traffic to make that hazardous. I had a sudden surge of affection for my hometown. I had lived here all my life with the exception of my years of college and veterinary school, and I decided I liked it. I also decided that after I married Sarah we would stay here, have children here, and give them the same safe, loving childhood I had been provided with. I had become very decisive in the past few days, hadn't I? I sometimes wonder how it is Sarah grew up so warm and loving with her crazy father and enigmatic mother. She did, though; there is no doubt about that. Sarah's parents had raised a wonderful person, despite anything negative I may think of them. Give credit when it is due.

I noticed a jetliner overhead, and briefly had the fleeting, horrible thought that Sarah was on it, off to some exotic destination to start a new life without me. Stop doing that, Mark; it will not help the situation or your mood. I breathed heavily, sighed, and flexed my shoulders.

"Okay, Mark?" Stefania asked, and I nodded. Max looked up at me as well, then returned to his panting exploration of the new sights and sounds of a neighborhood unfamiliar to him.

I stopped, and looked. I was almost certain this was the address of old Mrs. Sullivan and the Chihuahuas, although I had never actually been here on a house call. I remembered the house number from her visits – it had a mnemonic attachment – it was number sixty-nine. Juvenile as that connection may be, it was helpful now as I was certain we were at the correct address.

I nodded at Stefania, and the trio made its way up the driveway. I noticed a whitewashed wooden staircase on the side of the house leading to a door on the second level. I assumed this was Cindy's apartment and its associated entrance.

I debated our best approach. Should we call on Mrs. Sullivan? Or, should we just knock on Cindy's door? I had no idea. I am not good at this stuff.

Stefania said nothing as we began our climb up the stairs. Max had no trouble navigating them, and soundlessly followed us to the landing at the top.

The wood was worn and the paint chipped in places, but the staircase seemed otherwise well maintained. The door to the apartment had two panes of stacked glass with a wooden rod between them, and a sheer white curtain filtered our view from the outside. I knocked.

There was no answer. Actually, let me qualify. There was no human answer. There was a series of barks however, and the barks were not friendly in aspect. Spirit, the Great Dane, I assumed.

"Spirit? Hi baby, hi sweet girl, hi!" I shouted through the glass, and tried the doorknob. It was unlocked.

Never in my life has an animal done anything to me except love me. I have never been bitten (well, except my ear by Oscar the owl when I tried to remove him from my shoulder), I have never been scratched; I have simply never had a bad experience.

Years ago, I travelled to a convention in Tempe, Arizona for some veterinary event of which I do not recall the details. While there, I met up with some other doctors about my age, and we decided to stay a few extra days and play some golf. It was winter, so the idea of enjoying eighty-degree weather and a golf course in February appealed to us. We all hailed from cold climates.

We rented clubs, carts, and bought "Superstition Springs" golf shirts (that was the name of the course we had chosen) and headed out to the links.

Tempe is just outside of Phoenix, and it is an interesting place. It has all the modern trappings of home - strip malls, hotels, restaurants and many people, but it feels different. It feels like desert. Cacti are evident everywhere you go, and the dirt and grass just feel different. I am not sure if I am explaining that properly, but hopefully you understand what I mean. It felt foreign.

We were enjoying our round of golf, when Steve, one of the doctors in our group, did something strange. Paul and I were sharing a golf-cart, and we were cruising up the fairway to hit our next shots. Steve was standing stock-still at the side of a mound of tall grass and cacti off to the side of the fairway. His arms were halfway up his body, and he looked so comical Paul and I started to laugh.

"Hey Steve, you okay?" Paul called with laughter in his voice. Steve did not move, and did not say anything. Curious now, we parked the cart about twenty feet away and started walking towards him. He made the tiniest movement with his right hand, which was facing us, waving just the fingers in a gesture that clearly meant, "Don't come over here."

Steve was staring at a five or six foot rattlesnake that was staring right back at him. I heard the rattle first, turned to Paul, and said, "Oh, shit. Was that what I think it was?"

Paul turned a bit ashen, and said, "Yeah, I think so. What the fuck do we do?"

The fourth member of our group, a gentleman from Detroit named Carl, made his way to us out of curiosity. He stood next to the cart and asked, "What's up?"

The rattlesnake indicated its unhappiness with the situation again, just to make sure Carl knew as well. The rattle of a *Viperidae Crotalinae* was unmistakable.

"Oh crap." he said. I guess they are more polite with language in Detroit.

Here were four seasoned veterinary professionals, and not one of us had any clue what to do when encountering a pissed-off rattlesnake in the wild. Great.

I figured, bravely, I had the best chance of extracting Steve from his predicament. I also thought, correctly I would like to add, that if the worst case scenario presented itself and Steve were bitten by the snake, we were in the right zip code for it to happen. I would bet they even had anti-venom in the pro-shop. You will not find that at the Bethpage Black Golf Course on Long Island.

I slowly approached Steve, and his waving of his hand became more frantic.

"Relax Steve, just stay still, and let me take a look." Steve looked grey in the afternoon sun. He was terrified.

I made my way over, and stood just behind him and to his right. The snake was large, and there was no question it was upset. Sitting a few feet behind the snake was the wayward golf ball that must have brought Steve over here in the first place. I sent out calming feelings as best I could toward the serpent, but that just felt silly and had no discernable effect. However, the snake reacted to my arrival in a most unusual way. He lowered his rattle, and immediately slithered slowly and quietly over to me. He meandered across my shoes, one at a time, which had the effect of freezing me as if I was poured from cement. He then circled around the back of my legs, ignored Steve, and moved off without further incident into the brush.

Steve and I stood stock still for another minute. Steve looked at me, breathed for the first time in a while, and said, "How did you do that?"

"Do what?" I asked.

"Calm him down and make him leave?"

"I don't know, I didn't, I just came over to see what I could do."

"Well, whatever it was, you saved my life." My reply to this was clever, I am proud of it.

"Great. Then you can buy drinks after the round since dead men don't need money anyway – we'll spend it all."

We laughed, and without further ado, backed away from the brush and reassembled at the one golf cart.

Carl asked, "Want to just hit the bar?" I like the way they think in Detroit.

We all laughed and relaxed, agreeing instantly that golf was suddenly overrated. We headed straight for the clubhouse.

No creature has ever done me harm. Rattlesnakes, wild dogs, nasty cats, I seemed to be immune from their darker, nastier sides. This comes in very handy in my profession. I am not sure why this is, but I do not question it.

With a quick recollection of the rattlesnake, I opened the door. Spirit growled menacingly, but made no move. I greeted her by name.

"Hi, Spirit, honey, it's me, Dr. Canis, remember me?" I put as much sugar and high-notes as I could in my question.

Spirit hesitated from moving forward, whined, and settled down on the floor. She rose again immediately when she spotted Max, but by that time I was next to her and had hold of her collar.

"It's okay, baby, he's my friend. It's okay. Shhh, shhh." She settled down again immediately.

Spirit began to nuzzle my leg, and I looked her over quickly. She did not seem well, something was wrong. I looked quickly at the kitchen area that was immediately off the entrance, and noticed her food and water bowls were empty. Perhaps that was the problem.

I asked Stefania to check the cabinets and refill Spirit's bowls, and Spirit's tail began to wag in earnest as Stefania did so. When the bowl of water was refilled and replaced, Spirit spent a good thirty seconds sloppily slurping water. Where was Cindy?

I felt a bit nervous all of a sudden, as if something in this apartment was going to jump out and take a swing at me. Max did not seem upset or on point, and this I took as a good sign.

Max followed me towards the back of the apartment. I know that Carlo at this point would have told me to leave and call the police. I had already established my track record of ignoring this sage advice, and continued to do so.

As I reached the bedroom in the back of the dwelling, I was greeting by the sight of the second naked woman in just a few days who was not my girlfriend. Lucky me.

I moved quickly to Cindy, and called to Stefania. Max moved toward the bed and started sniffing at Cindy's body, which, thankfully, was warm and breathing. She looked asleep.

I could see no sign of injury, and I pulled the sheet that had gathered on the side of the bed over Cindy and stood straight up again.

"Oh shit," started Stefania, "is she…"

"No, just out like a light." I lifted her arm and felt for a pulse. It was strong and regular.

I sat on the side of the bed and gently tapped Cindy's cheek with the side of my hand to see if I could wake her. Nothing.

"Fucking Craig again, I bet, Mark" said Stefania, which was exactly what I was thinking. I remembered I had told Stefania about the connection with Craig and this unknown soul from Pennsylvania, and I looked at her.

"He's a real piece of work, isn't he?" I asked, rhetorically.

Spirit had joined us in the bedroom now, and she whined as she spied the prone form of her owner.

"It's okay, Spirit honey, she's just sleeping." Spirit settled down and for the first time took an interest in investigating Max a bit better. Max impassively tolerated this, although his head swiveled at the larger creature as she moved around him.

Both dogs laid down simultaneously and looked at me. Stefania did as well. Looked, that is. She remained upright.

A moment later, we heard a noise from the front of the apartment. I did not remember if we had closed the front door after entering, but I was pretty sure we had. Someone had just opened it.

A second went by, and suddenly THE Craig appeared at the bedroom door, looking startled.

Stefania needed no invitation, and started towards him. Max and Spirit both rose and started barking.

"You mother-..." Stefania began, but Craig turned and ran the way he had come. All of us followed.

Craig made quick work of the stairs, said nothing, and hopped into the monster of a pickup truck that by now was all so familiar. I took the opportunity I had waited longer than twenty years for.

"That's right, dumbshit, run! Run back to mommy, you fucking wimp!" I only hope he heard me before he slammed the door and skidded away in a screech of tires and rubber.

Wow, that felt good. Stefania looked at me as if I was nuts.

"Shouldn't we follow him?" she asked, incredulously.

"And do what, Stef?"

The logic of this penetrated her angered brain, and she slumped.

"You're right. I don't know. But what was he doing here?"

"I don't know that either," I replied, and went to the kitchen to check if Spirit still had water remaining. She did not, so I refilled the bowl from the faucet above the sink.

I could not fathom leaving the apartment before I knew Cindy was okay, but I also did not want to linger here any more than I needed to. I turned to Stefania.

"Stef, see if you can get her up. I'll make coffee." She nodded and started back towards the bedroom.

Spirit looked up at me (over at me actually, she was a big dog) and I asked her, "Where does mommy keep the coffee, big girl?" I received no reply. I did not expect one. For some reason, at that moment, I had the poignant thought that Chelsea would have immediately led me to the proper cabinet.

I found instant coffee, which would have to do, but no milk or sugar. I abandoned the coffee idea when I had another one. I would call for some food (I was still starving!) and ask for some milk and sugar to be included. I never got to that step.

Stefania returned in a moment with a shaky, bad-hair-day Cindy next to her. Stefania was helping her walk as Cindy looked unsteady and not completely awake.

"Doctor, um, hi..." she began, and looked extremely confused. "What are you doing here?"

I looked at Cindy and tried to use my super-spy skills (you know, the ones I do not have?) to detect if there was any malice or evil in Cindy's countenance. That was a wasted exercise.

"Hi, Cindy, come, sit down." Stefania and I led her to a chair near the small table in the kitchen area, and she sat heavily.

"Wow, I feel horrible." Cindy breathed, and everyone in the room except the dogs had a momentary moment of empathy.

"Do you remember anything, Cindy?" I asked. I suppose I figured that was what Carlo would have said were he here. I suddenly wished he were. Hey! That's an idea. No, he would be pissed I did not tell him where I was going. No! He said 'don't go out alone' – and I did not, I had Stefania and Max with me.

I fished my cell phone out of my pocket and hit Carlo's number. Voicemail. I decided against leaving him a message, and hung up. He would see the missed call eventually, and call me back.

"What day is it?" Cindy asked.

"Friday, hon." Replied Stefania.

"Whoa. Shit. That's messed up."

"What is, Cindy?" I asked.

"I came home from work Wednesday, had a few drinks, and went to bed. Seems like I missed Thursday completely." She let out a weak laugh at this.

Wednesday, Wednesday. What happened Wednesday? Stefania was "hooking up" with THE Craig at the Fox Hollow; I was looking at a floating goldfish. That seemed like years ago.

It occurred to me that Craig had some reason for needing Cindy out of the frame for the time being. I had no idea what that could be. I tried to find out.

Cindy then acknowledged Spirit, which she had to this point not done, and Spirit happily smooched and cuddled with her best friend.

I then felt something that I had missed to this point. I knew that feeling, and I knew it could not have possibly been coming from Max.

I spoke. "Cindy. Is there any way, any possibility that you know of, that Spirit is pregnant?

"My gosh, I don't know, Doc."

"Mark, Cindy, call me Mark. We're friends." I do not know why I said that, but I was rewarded with a warm smile from Cindy. Stefania looked at me with a raised eyebrow, but said nothing.

"I don't think so, no, she has never been out of my sight."

Not until yesterday, which Cindy had spent unconscious. An idea was forming in my brain, but I was not sure exactly what it was.

I knew Spirit was pregnant, I could feel it. However, she was not pregnant when she was in my office previously. What did that have to do with anything? I had no idea.

"Cindy, do you want to go to the hospital or something? Are you going to be alright?" I asked, with as much concern in my voice as I could muster.

I surveyed the scene in front of me, and again marveled at the changes the past few days had wrought upon my normally prosaic existence.

I was standing in the kitchen of a stranger with a huge, newly (I was sure) pregnant Great Dane at my side, my girlfriend's best friend with me, and a girl I barely knew answering questions from me wearing nothing but a sheet. And Maxie, cannot forget good ol' Maxie. He was there too. I longed for my plain old life back.

We left Cindy with little explanation of our appearance, some cash to order in food (she had none), and left Spirit with a full bowl of food. I told Cindy to discard the remaining meds I had given her for Spirit for treatment of the abscess, as they were not good for a pregnant bitch. I do not know why I used that word just now, except that in a memoir that is full of dog stories you would think I would have found a way to work it in before now, it is such a powerful word. Especially with Stefania around, right? Hey, whose side are you on? If Stefania knew I had just had that thought, she would have smacked me. Please do not tell her.

***

32 – Back Home Again, Still Hungry

Unsure of what our next move should be, Stefania, Max and I left Cindy's and headed back to my place. I looked for my car, and then remembered we had walked. That turned out to be a good thing, as I am sure Craig would not have come into the apartment had he seen an unfamiliar car in the driveway. Why was he there? What was he after? I did not know.

I was confident, now, that he was definitely a bad guy in this whole scenario, whatever it was. Cindy, Spirit, Craig's dumping of Cindy and subsequent drugging of her (I was sure about that too) and his reconnection with Stefania were all related somehow. Carlo had not yet reasoned why, so I had almost no chance of doing so. Carlo did not have this latest intelligence though, and I planned to give it to him as soon as I heard back from him. I pulled my phone out of my pocket to see if I had missed a call from him, or hoping beyond hope one from Sarah, but the screen told me I had missed no calls. Damn.

We walked silently, back past Walrus house, and went inside my place. It felt wrong without Sarah there. I guess Stefania knew what I was thinking, for she kissed me on the cheek, gave my arm an affectionate squeeze, and said "Don't worry Mark, she'll be back." I liked her more and more every minute.

I went into the den and poured myself a small drink. I knew that it would not sit well on an empty stomach, but felt like having one anyway.

I was never a big drinker, even in college, and the warming effects of the brandy were immediate. I felt a bit swimmy in the head, and sat down heavily on the comfortable reclining chair (that Sarah had purchased) and tried to clear my head and think.

I had no idea where Stefania was, she had probably gone upstairs to change or use the bathroom.

Max padded in and laid down in front of my chair. "You're a

good boy, Maxie" I said for no other reason than that it occurred to me to say at that point. He looked up at me, and returned his head to the floor.

Something about that mill was at the heart of all this. The abandoned Horton Mill, on Long Island Sound, former workplace of George Horton and his magic guitars – was instrumental (ha ha, get it?) in the changes in my life recently. However, I had no idea how, nor did anyone else. Damn, I'm hungry, I thought again, but moved on from that thought as I had for the past day or so. This was too intense. I made a decision. I would do something about this tonight, with or without the blessing, cooperation or agreement of the others in my party. I am sorry, Carlo, I know you will be angry, but I have to get myself back to that mill and get to the bottom of this. Somehow, I knew that was the first step on the path to getting my life back. I just wish I knew how, or why.

***

33 – This Place Is Kinda Cool

The memoir you are holding was compiled on a laptop computer. I wonder how Shakespeare, Chaucer, Fitzgerald, and even early DeMille did it without these handy devices.

Spell check, research, corrections, movements, replacements. I do not truly understand how anyone could compile anything worth reading (let alone be a masterpiece) on paper with a pen. However, they had. Amazing.

I bring this up because as I came to this part of this memoir, I did the following search on an internet search engine, and was rewarded with this information, paraphrased below.

138 million per week
19.7 million per day
84% of Americans

Curious? I was too, which is why I searched how many people shop at Wal-Mart. Yes, that is what those numbers represent. I, until today, was not counted among those in the numbers above. I had never been to America's favorite store as of yet. That was about to change for two reasons I could think of. One, it was open twenty-four hours, and the plan I had in mind would need to be commenced well after dark. Two, I was relatively certain the store would carry exactly what I had decided I needed for my mission.

It was late now, Carlo had not called back (nor had Sarah replied to either Stefania or me) and I anxiously waited for the hours to pass. Stefania came in at one point, looked at my far off expression, and silently went elsewhere in the house. I heard the television in the kitchen go on, and I heard the distinct sound of Max's food bowl being placed on the kitchen tile. Thank you,

Stefania.

At about ten PM, Stefania and Max came in and stood by the doorway to the room from which I had not emerged. I looked at both of them.

"We ate, aren't you starving?" asked Stefania.

"Yes, I am" I replied, breaking from my distant revelry, "but I don't feel like having anything right now. Does that make sense?"

Stefania said, "I guess so. If you change your mind, I made you a sandwich and it's in the fridge." She had certainly changed over the past few days. Wow. "Max needs a walk, come with us."

I rose wordlessly and followed Stefania and Max out the front door. I locked it, and we walked down the eerily quiet Florida Lane.

Max immediately took care of business, and turned around and headed back towards the house without either of us prompting him. His white fur was almost invisible in the dark night, but his eyes were alert and looked at me as if asking what was going on. "I don't know, Max, I just don't." I answered his unspoken question.

I looked at Stefania, and realized I loved this girl very much. I did not love her the same way I loved Sarah, although I had to a lesser extent some time ago, it was more of an affection and appreciation. She returned my solid look but said nothing.

"Stefania. I love you." I kissed her hard on the cheek, and she had the hint of a tear in her eye.

"I love you too, Mark. I really do." She half-smiled and I looked down. I knew she knew what I had meant; I did not have to qualify my statement with anything trite like, "I don't want to bang you or anything, you know…" She got it.

"And I love you too, Maxie-Waxie!" I leaned over and put a kiss on his white head and rubbed his ears. Stefania let out a wet laugh and the tension of the moment was broken. I took Stefania's hand and led her back to my house.

Stefania had elected to sleep upstairs in my and Sarah's bed, but I remained downstairs in the den. I had hoped it would work out that way. Max kept Stefania company. That worked in my favor too.

Stefania had not said anything about my Jeep, which I had

moved a few houses down the block earlier in the day once I had decided on a course of action. So far, my plan was holding up. It was not that I did not want Stefania along, or even that I thought she would not be an asset, she probably would be, but I just did not want to involve her in something that could very possibly be dangerous.

My nervous energy had me wide-awake, and I decided the time was nigh.

I went into my office, and left again through the open window at the front of the house.

I walked to my Jeep, armed with my keys, cell phone, my American Express card, and a plan, and drove off to make my first ever trip to a Wal-Mart.

The Wal-Mart closest to my house is actually quite a distance away, in a town called Valley Stream on the south shore of Long Island. At that hour there was a bit of traffic on the roads, but not too much. I made the fourteen mile drive in about twenty minutes.

I parked my Jeep, and went inside.

The place is huge. I mean, I have been in some big stores in my life, but this one you could land an airplane in.

There was a scattering of shoppers throughout the place, but for the most part, it was empty. I headed to the men's department, and quickly found what I was looking for.

I looked at the shelves while I was walking, and made a note to explore this place further one day, it seemed to have many things at prices that seemed good. I had the quick question in my mind as to whether or not Sarah had ever been here, I did not know.

I paid for my purchase - a pair of black sweatpants, a black t-shirt, and a black wool hat. The cashier probably thought I was planning to rob a liquor store, and that is the sort of look she gave me, but I just smiled and handed her my secret American Express card.

I exited the store, and returned to my Jeep. I opened the back gate, and climbed inside with my shopping bag.

I do not know if you have ever tried to change clothing in a SUV, but it is not easy. Despite the roomy environs of the Jeep's cargo compartment, I hit my head a few times and did a strange horizontal dance to get my jeans off and put on the newly purchased sweatpants.

Attired in my new garb, I climbed over the rear seat and into the front seat. I then went back again, as Mr. Super-Spy had left his keys in his jeans. Off to an excellent start.

You, dear reader, already know where I am going. Some of you may be yelling, "Don't! Idiot, call Carlo! Call a cop!" and you are most definitely wiser than I am. I was miserable, though, missing Sarah and lamenting I may never see her again, and I felt taking this action might resolve that and all the other issues, although I had no idea how. I simply knew I had to do something. I was still hungry, too.

I went back into the cargo compartment AGAIN, to retrieve my cell phone. Some spy I was. A thought gripped me. Later, you will discover how important this thought was. I typed a text on my cellphone, but did not hit send. I returned to the main menu, which had the effect of saving the text as a draft for easy sending later. The only thing I had to do was ensure I remembered to send it.

Twenty-five minutes later, I arrived at the spot where the pleasant old police officer had explained to me the history of the Horton Mill. Leaving the Jeep on the side of the road, I made my way down the rocky approach towards the dilapidated building, hoping I would see Sarah, Stefania, Emily, Jordyn, Jacob, Stan, and everyone else in the world once again.

***

34 – I Digress Once More

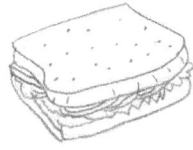

I have no idea if Max, my editor, will leave this short chapter in the final manuscript. If you are reading it, he did. If not, you would never know about it anyway.

Back to my childhood for a moment.

No, I am just kidding. I am just as anxious as you are to read the climax of the story, so no more musings, no more flashbacks, and no more digression. Turn the page and find out what happened. In my honor, if you feel like it, grab a sandwich before you do.

***

35 - I Should Have Backup, But What Could Happen?

I felt like a super-spy again. Dressed all in black, I froze in place for a few minutes, listening, feeling, and looking around. I had a moment of panic when my internal voice said, "What the heck are you doing? Get the hell out of here you moron, you're no cop." I told him to shut up so no one would hear us.

I had slowly, meticulously, and soundlessly made my way from the parked Jeep to approximately twenty feet from the Horton Mill. It was probably about midnight, but I was not sure. My silent egress from my house was apparently successful, as I figured were it not I would have received a million calls from Stefania already. Max, as far as I knew, did not own a cell phone.

In a way, my internal voice was right telling me to get the hell out. I had no weapon (I had even forgotten to bring my trusty seven-iron), had no idea what was going on inside the mill, how many people would be in there, or what to do once I was inside. I did not really know why I was here except I needed to be. I had remembered to send the text though, and that made me feel better. I had not, to this point, received a reply.

I sensed calm from the mill. I also sensed myriad waves of canine "existence." There must be many dogs in there, which still made no sense, but I was certainly feeling them. At the moment, I felt calm.

I crept slowly, approaching the mill from the east side, since the moon was on the west side, and my super-spy instincts told me I would be harder to spot approaching from that side. Again, that panicky feeling. "Get out of here." The internal voice said again. I shushed it again.

Moving again, I kicked something, and it made a loud snap. It was a thick branch, but the result of the sudden snapping sound confirmed my earlier thought.

At once – barking began. Mixed barking. Shrill barking. Overlapping barking. My goodness, it sounded like a concert of hundreds of canine voices. I staggered from the wariness that accompanied the barks, and fell right on my butt a few feet back. Holy crap.

I worked hard to keep the feelings channeled and not be overwhelmed by them. It was not easy. I had never felt anything this strong - not at the dolphin pool, not at the animal shelter, not at the bad pet store. This was on a scale I had never encountered before. The suddenness from the calmness to the wary, nervous barking was incredibly quick and incredibly powerful.

I heard a man's voice. "Shaddup, you stupid mutts. Shut up!" screamed the voice, but the barking did not subside. The voice did not seem immediately familiar, but then again it was masked partly by hundreds of barks. Yes, hundreds.

After what seemed like an hour but was probably only two or three minutes, the barking started to subside. With it, the wariness and nervousness I felt waned in concert. I continued to sit, but shimmied on my butt to a nearby bush to give myself cover were the door to open. It did not open.

After another two or three minute hour, I rose once again and moved to the large door of the mill. There was a window about seven feet off the ground, but I had no means to reach it. I would have to approach the door, and hope I could reconnoiter what, who, and how many I would be up against if I was actually brave enough to go inside.

The concept of the "petty tyrant" came back to mind. I sat back down behind a bush just west of the big door. I breathed deeply and took a minute to compose myself. Why on earth did this place exist? Why me? I have never been annoyed about my gift of animal empathy, but I was starting to feel a little cheated out of my normal, uneventful, simple glorious life. I made vows to myself at this point.

I promised myself that if I emerged from this situation whole and intact, I would never take another minute of my life for granted. I vowed I would, should I be able to convince Sarah of the setup and my innocence, kiss her face every time I could, squeeze her until she kicked me, and love her harder and better than I had before this all happened.

I vowed to be nicer and more attentive to Stefania, and make a concerted effort to be friendlier to her "men of the month" when we would go out on double dates. I would buy her presents for her birthday, and buy things she liked for the house. She was my friend, and I did not let her know how much that meant to me for the past few years, I was blinded by my fear of irritating Sarah. I should have known better. If Stefania could tell how much I loved Sarah to the point she was even a little jealous of it, then Sarah must also know.

I vowed to visit Carlo more often, and not just when I was in trouble. I vowed to ensure I had a bucket-full of dog treats for Max with me whenever I did. I vowed to invite them both to my house more often, which I had been remiss in doing for the past few years just out of the natural attrition that happens to us all too often.

I vowed to visit my parents more often. They were happily enjoying Florida, travelling frequently, and living the good life they had earned for themselves. I did not see them enough, for I suddenly realized they would not be around forever.

I vowed to visit Emily and Stan more as well. Since my trip out there last summer and the kittens, I had not even spoken to her. Darn it, she has children, they are my blood, and I barely know them. I vowed to fix that.

While I was doing all of this vowing, things were calm again in the mill. I heard nothing except the occasional stray bark. No movement, no other sound.

Finally, I vowed to get that ring around Sarah's finger as soon as humanly possible. Once it was there, I would use Crazy Glue if I had to to make sure it never came off. How I longed to have that opportunity.

Suddenly, there was movement. The door, which was only a few feet away from me, swung open. Apparently, it was on metal hinges as it made a squeaky, rusty sound as it moved. Thank goodness, I was behind a bush and wearing black. I hoped the scant light coming from inside the mill would not display me, and

I silently stuck my tongue out at my internal voice – so far, my spy tactics were holding up. Take that, voice. It did not reply.

I heard a car start, and thought if I had noticed one parked outside the mill on my approach. I had not, so this was a bit strange. Then I realized it was not a car, but a boat. I am not an avid sailor, but I have been fishing enough times to recognize the unmistakable sound of powerful inboard boat engines warming up. I heard multiple voices now. Some were speaking Spanish. As I can speak Spanish pretty well, I listened intently to the voices to hear what they were saying but could not make out the content. I did hear the words "vamos" and "rapido" but living in New York as long as I have would have translated those for me.

Another door, this one on the water side of the mill, slid open with a creak. I heard men grunting, and then more barking. This was not as loud or as numerous as the first set I had heard, but it was certainly many canines.

After four or five minutes, I heard the door slide closed. The boat powered up, the voices faded, and the sound of the engines clearly indicated the boat was moving out into the Sound. From my vantage point, I could not see the water, so I started to move parallel to the mill to get a look. I peeked around the corner of the mill, nervous that someone would be there, but there was no one in sight. I was too late to get much detail, but I clearly saw the boat Stefania had pointed out to me the day we sat watching the mill cruising steadily away from the dock. I saw three heads on the boat and what looked like a dozen or so square crates about three feet across stacked on the deck everywhere there was free space. Strange. Smuggling? Drugs? Weapons? The third choice seemed the most likely. That would explain the barking – guard dogs, but then there seemed too many barks for that to be the case. I needed to get inside and take a look.

I waited again (I was becoming a really patient guy) for about ten minutes. I heard no movement or sounds from the mill, so I returned along the wall I had approached from, the east wall. The door was noisy and large, but I needed to move it just a little to get inside. The internal voice came back – "…bring a flashlight? Genius?" Shit.

When it comes to spying, I suppose I have a lot to learn. Not thirty seconds after I realized I had left the flashlight in the car, something even less spy-like happened. My cell phone rang. It did not vibrate, did not wiggle, it did not tap me on the shoulder – no, it rang loud and clear. I had forgotten to turn it to silent. Ok James Bond, you win.

I quickly jabbed my hand in my pocket to silence the beast, but its ringing woke up the myriad dogs in the mill from their silence. I never looked to see whom the call was from. I should have, it would have given me a large clue to who I was dealing with. I would have also seen a terse reply to my text. But no, I did not look. Hundreds of barks began again, and the waves came back. Wow.

With stealth abandoned, I simply walked to the large door and pulled it open. I tried to see something, anything, but it was dark inside the mill. It also felt large. It stank. The scent of animal waste was terrible. I covered my face with my sleeve and tried to see. Slowly, my night vision kicked in, but it was still too dark and gloomy to make anything out. An idea struck me. I took my phone out, and without looking at the history, I brought up the main menu where I had a flashlight thingy I had downloaded once. I hoped it worked, and I hoped it was bright. It was.

Suddenly the huge ceiling was revealed to me in the harsh light of the flash bulb LED of my cell phone. I moved the light downward, and noticed a bank of switches on a wooden post in the middle of the room about fifteen feet away from me. I could sense nervous animals all around me, and tried to radiate calm and "good" feelings. It must have partly worked, for the barking calmed, and finally stopped. I heard panting, lots of panting.

I had said, way back in Chapter 1, that my life could be measured in pants. These were the pants I was talking about. My life could certainly be measured in the pants of the myriad creatures I have met, enjoyed, treated, and known in my life. Lots and lots of pants. Happy pants, excited pants, labored pants, worried pants, painful pants – I have witnessed them all.

I walked to the post with the light switches, and decided that I had given my position away already - if someone was still here and wanted to hurt me, it would be easy. Truthfully, I was tired of all this sneaking around and spy stuff anyway. Time to light things up. I stopped just before I threw the switch and listened. I heard no one, and I told myself that all of the human "users" of the mill, whoever they were, had departed on the boat and that I was alone with a few dogs that barked like maniacs. That made me feel better, but I suppose it was such a stupid and careless thought the inner warning voice could not even bring itself to comment. I threw the switches.

***

36 – People Can Really Suck Sometimes

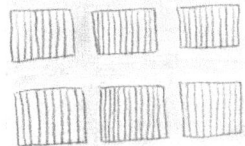

The ceiling is what I noticed first. Strung from wires that stretched in every direction, bare light bulbs illuminated the entire inside of the roomy mill's main room. I noticed faded murals on the walls. There were music notes, guitars, people, and drum kits drawn expertly with what appeared to be chalk, or perhaps paint. However, that was not what held my attention for long.

Against every wall, stacked three high, forming aisles throughout the space, were cages. Cages everywhere.

I walked a few feet over to one of them. Inside was a Standard Poodle, lying on her side. She was in bad shape. I knew it was a she, since there were four little poodles inside the cage with her. Three were nursing, but not the one towards the edge of the cage. That one was dead.

I felt fear and recoil from her, and I sent her calming thoughts. Suddenly some of the nearby cages burst into song. Well, barking. I closed my eyes. What the heck was this? Inside a nearby cage was what I recognized as a Bichon Frise, also with a litter of puppies.

I walked, my mouth wide open, and surveyed. Everywhere there were dogs. Shepards. Collies. More poodles. Basenjis. Dogs in tiny cages, puppies with most of them, except for one row towards the back that held only single occupants. I felt eyes on me, hundreds and hundreds of hungry, lost eyes.

The conditions in the cages were deplorable. There was feces everywhere, and the smell of urine and unwashed bodies was almost unbearable. I had to get outside and get some air, so I burst towards the open door. Without thinking, I opened the door completely then crossed the floor between more rows of cages – blocking out what I was feeling from the occupants – and opened the other set of doors on the north side of the mill. A breeze went through the room, and the dogs that started to bark again fell silent once more.

I could not stand to look at anymore. I figured it all out very, very quickly.

I had read about puppy mills. I knew of their existence. I know that people take advantage of other species on our planet for their own gain, but seeing it on this scale and in this manner was almost overwhelming. I got angry. Very angry. I tried to do a quick inventory – but that would be pointless. Still, I estimated there were more than one hundred and fifty cages, which meant probably close to five hundred or so dogs. Unbelievable. I did some more mental math. Poodles, like the ones I had seen in the first cage I examined, could sell for upwards of six or seven hundred dollars each, possibly more. Even if they were not purebred or pedigree, I am sure anyone who ran an operation like this could generate paperwork to make such claims. My mental math zoomed. This room could be holding more than a quarter of a million dollars in dogs. Maybe more, depending on the breeds.

I gathered myself, and without thinking turned to head back to the door on the east side, planning on running back to my Jeep and calling everyone from the ASPCA to the National Guard to come and meet me at this horrible, horrible place. I would also call a pizza place, as I still had not managed to feed myself. Only I would think of food at a time like this.

I turned, and the last thing I remember was thinking "fuck" before I hit the ground. A two by four piece of lumber made contact with my head, obviously wielded by a human I had not seen or heard during my exploration, and I went down hard. I might have also heard my internal voice say, "Told ya!" But, maybe I dreamt that.

***

37 – Not The Ending I Expected

Next thing I knew, I found myself floating. I was looking down at my house in Nyagg. This was strange. I felt that months had passed since my visit to the old, abandoned Horton Mill, source of all my misery, but I was not sure. Suddenly, I was standing at my front door. I stopped. Perhaps my head injury was still bothering me; I had a quick memory of doctors warning me about that. "Moments of dementia or extreme vertigo" was the warning I had been issued. I guess this is what they meant.

I walked in the front door. The boxes were all neatly stacked, awaiting the arrival of the moving van, and the house felt empty and weird. Something was definitely still wrong with my head.

Next thing I knew I was upstairs, staring at the empty room. I do not remember climbing the stairs. So many wonderful memories in this room. Sarah's bedroom that I shared with her that she had decorated so beautifully. All gone. All over.

I could not clearly remember anything. Everything I looked at seemed to fade away unless I viewed it with my peripheral vision. I did not feel well at all.

My next connected thought was again of Sarah. She was gone. I had no idea where. Lou and Sophie were gone as well. Their house was gone. I do not know how I knew this, but I knew it.

Stefania was gone too. I am not sure where, or how I knew that either. Perhaps I really was missing chunks of memory as the doctors had stated could be the case. As I could feel animals and their emotions all my life, I could now feel my friends, my family, and my loved ones as well. All gone. Still shaky, I wondered if the feelings I had were memories I could not retain and recall correctly, or if I was truly too damaged to function correctly and these things had just happened yesterday, or even this morning. I had no idea what time it was. None.

Quite simply, I had fucked up. I had not trusted those around me enough, and I had plunged headfirst (literally) into a situation way beyond my scope or ability. Now I would have to deal with the consequences alone. I did not care about anything anymore. Everything I had was lost, and gone.

I do not know how I knew, but I knew Sarah was far away, and that I would never see her again. She was the love of my life – and as trite as that may sound – there is a reason it is a cliché. I had the love of my life, and I was not strong enough, was not smart enough. I had lost her.

I had lost my practice, my house, and my friends. Carlo. My next thought. I did not remember anything about my dealings with him, just that I knew I was no longer welcome at his home. That made me incredibly sad. I would never see Max again. These feelings and memories were so painful I began to weep. For a moment, I forgot completely where I was. I looked up. Yes, that is familiar. This is my parent's house. The house I used to live in before I tore it down and built my new one.

Wait a second. How could that be?

Then, it dawned on me. Relief so thick and rich I could swim in it washed over me. Thank you, thank you, and thank you.

I was dreaming.

As soon as that realization hit, I woke up with a start. Wow, that seemed so real. I was now energized to make sure nothing I had just seen could ever possibly come to pass. What a wakeup call! I felt invincible now. I was also incredibly pissed off, and had one hell of a headache. I still had one big problem though: Unfortunately, I had no idea where I was or why I was lying on my back at the moment. This life thing is certainly not as easy as it looks in the movies. Slowly, it came back to me.

***

38 – Guess Who?

My head was still killing me. That was real, and I was fully awake now. I mean, I did not have the kind of headache that I get when I have a bit too much to drink the night before – no – this was the kind that made me wonder how the human body was constructed. Nothing should hurt this much. The pain was mixed with the relief I now felt that I had dreamed the most awful path my life could have taken, and I had not yet destroyed everything I had worked so hard for. I was rip-roaring mad now.

I looked up and for a moment and again had no idea where I was. I felt pressure on my chest, and saw a ceiling beam (or what my non-carpenter mind thought was such) lying across my chest. I felt pressure, but my mind was slowly clearing, and I was calm. The mill. I remember.

One of my best features, if you will permit me, is extreme equanimity in the face of unusual situations. This was serving me well here, as I did not panic. I slowly took stock. I flexed my feet, yes; they were still there and still connected. My arms felt okay as well. This beam that lay across my chest was a bit of a problem, for as I breathed I felt it pressing against me harder. Where the heck had that come from?

My headache eased as I forcibly relaxed and breathed regularly and deeply. I tried to shimmy back a bit, but I could not move. The beam had me pinned. I looked from side to side, but could see nothing of interest or value. I felt, though. I felt a mix of emotions powerfully washing over me. I felt the urge to simply relax and let the emotions take me, but a warning bell sounded somewhere inside my mind and derailed this train of thought. I forced myself to relax again and tried to decipher the emotions.

Slowly, surely, the feelings began to take shape. As I was attempting to mentally label them, I felt light and warmth from behind my head.

The emotions hitting me started to sort. Fear. Pain. Uncertainty. Curiosity. Power. They were strong, and they were numerous. Some were mine, and some were emanating from outside of me. I felt something brush my head, and I leaned back as far as I could. A large Rottweiler was nudging me and licking my forehead where I was bleeding a bit. I stretched as far as I could, trying to make eye contact with the canine.

"Hey, there, winner." I said aloud, and the Rottweiler turned his head to the side as if trying to understand me. He moved to my side now, and I had a good view of the beautiful, muscular dog. He was a mottled brown and black, with a wet muzzle. Panting heavily, he lay down next to my and seemed to be waiting for something.

I tried to move my thoughts to him, but it was to no avail. As I have said before, I never truly had the ability to directly communicate with an animal, I am just able to hint through feeling, as you have witnessed me attempt on many occasions. With all the dogs in the room, although that felt like a much smaller number now, sending a clear, understandable message was simply not going to happen.

Suddenly I heard a low growl, and turned the other way. Two more Rottweilers were standing on the other side of me, looking at the Rot that was now lying next to my right side. I had a brief vision of a dogfight occurring with me as the ring. Not a good thing.

The Rot to my right looked directly into my eyes, and I started to speak to him.

"Hey, boy, pretty boy, you think you can move this?" I moved my chin toward the beam that had me pinned, wondering if he had any idea what the heck I was talking about. He simply glanced at me with big, black eyes. So much for all of the episodes of Lassie I had watched as a kid.

I was bordering on panic now, as I felt the heat growing in my body. My anger was stifling, almost as much as the large piece of wood someone had placed or had fallen on my chest, essentially immobilizing me. I needed to figure out a way to get this stupid beam off me, or I would end up as a permanent part of the decaying floor in this dilapidated mill.

Suddenly, a sound came from behind me and my left. The dogs, as one unit, turned and headed silently to the direction of the sound. I heard a voice, charmingly and affectionately greeting each dog by name. I could not hear the voice clearly, but something about the voice gave me chills. It could not be.

I heard footsteps approach. I closed my eyes, hoping against hope that who I thought I heard was not who was approaching me at this very moment. For the last few minutes, I had been desperately hoping for another human being to appear and lift this beam from my chest. All at once, I felt that hope drain out from me. I was reeling. If this was who I thought it was, my whole world was shaken to its core. It could not be.

Betrayal. Probably the most awful thing one human being can do to another. When a person does it to his country, it is called treason. When a person recruits others to do it to his country, it is called sedition – the most serious crime one can commit. More serious than rape, more serious than murder in the eyes of the law. I felt betrayed. My body shook. My heart ached. I ached for me, for the dogs in the room, and if this person was who I was now sure it was – I ached for Sarah.

It was.

I opened my eyes, strained back to see behind me, and stared right into the amused eyes of the man I had hoped someday would be my father-in-law.

"Hello, Lou." was all I could manage.

***

39 – Does He Really Expect Me To Feel Bad For Him?

"Mark, Mark, Mark." His voice sounded amused, like his eyes had seemed, and he sat in a wooden chair I had not noticed until now. The three Rottweilers sat around him. He looked like an ancient king, surrounded by his loyal hellhounds ready to do his bidding.

I had no idea what to say. None.

"You know, Mark, it's a shame, it really is. Sarah has told Sophie and me about you, so, so much about you. She loves you very much. Such a shame." He seemed genuinely sad.

"What's a shame, Lou?" My voice sounded calm, which was quite an achievement for me. My mind was racing, my head was throbbing, breathing was difficult with this piece of wood on me, and a man who up until five minutes ago I did not really care for but tolerated for obvious reasons appeared in a position that could only mean one thing: He was behind all of it.

Lou was behind the acts Craig had perpetrated, and now I knew it was Craig for sure once and for all. Hadn't I already reasoned that out? I think so. Lou and Craig had known each other. Remember, Sarah and Craig had dated? They must have met, all those years ago, and recognized some con-man kinship in each other. The pieces were starting to fall into place.

"This" was Lou's reply. I could not see his face clearly, but I felt that he was smiling, but experiencing mixed emotions. He went on, "the worst part of this whole thing is that my daughter really will miss you." I did not like the finality or the past tense in that statement. "She really, really loves you, Mark."

"And I love her, Lou. Let's figure a way out of this, huh?"

"That's already figured Mark, I'm sorry."

"What do you mean?"

I had the sudden thought that in movies, you should always

keep the bad guy talking and have him explain everything to you so you would have time to be rescued. However, no one knew I was here, despite my super-spy text message. I had no idea if it even been received. The thoughts of myriad movies in which this happened were so clear and so sudden I almost laughed aloud as they came to me. With absolutely nothing to lose and no other plan, I tried to get Lou to speak.

"Tell me, Lou, why? Why all this? What's the end game?"

"Mark. I like you, I really do," he replied, but there was now coldness in his voice that was not there a few minutes ago. "But unfortunately, things have gotten out of hand to the point that I have no choice. Too much is at stake."

"Too much what, Lou?" I was losing my confidence.

"Too much money, too much trouble. I cannot come out of this clean with you around Mark, it's just not possible. Sarah will heal, we all will, and she'll be okay eventually."

I was angry now. I had the fleeting thought that a man like this might respect strength in the face of danger, so I tried that tactic.

"You're just a pussy, Lou. If you're going to do something to me, just fucking do it then. You don't have the balls. Pussy."

I waited. He chuckled. Not what I was hoping for. Plan B, anyone?

"Nice try, Mark, nice. But you see, you are the only loose end. The dogs, most of them, are off to where they need to be. I have the cash, the promise of the rest of it from that load of dogs, (I guess he nodded towards the boat, but I could not see it) and when this place is burned to the ground, they will find you – the brave, selfless vet, crushed to death by a falling beam trying to rescue the screaming dogs. At least you'll go out a hero."

It all made sense now. Every last piece. Except for one.

"Why, Lou?"

"Money, Mark. Sophie doesn't know, and of course Sarah doesn't know – but I have been broke for almost a year. Lost everything on that stupid Hong Kong deal." I had no clue what he was talking about but said nothing.

"I needed cash, and this 'opportunity' came along." I put the single quotes around 'opportunity' because he said it with a dripping sarcasm. He knew it was a crime, but did not have the guts to say it.

"Why involve me? What was the point of that?"

"That day at our house, Mark, the day you did something or other with that squirrel and freaked out that Drake kid. Sophie and I asked Sarah about all of that, and she told us about your 'specialness' as she called it. At first, I thought it was a lot of bullshit, but I did some checking. I got your files from veterinary college. I read about that girl you and your dog saved when you were a kid. I read about some stupid owl you walked around with in college. Actually, Craig did. That useless fuck was at least useful for that. Gotta love the internet."

This may seem strange to you, but at that moment I felt one thing and one thing only – pride. You know what? I have done a lot of good in this world. Silly as it may seem, there are myriad lives out there that are better and were better because of me. I made people happy, and I made animals happy. There was a squirrel out there with a clean face thanks to me. There were thousands more I could never remember. I was good. As quickly as those thoughts came, another one did- I was eulogizing myself. Fuck.

"I'm sorry Mark, I never meant for anyone to get hurt, but now there is really no choice. I'm fixed now – I have the cash I need, and I have set up this little network, which is incredibly easy. I have a new place in mind to move it to, and it'll grow, and people pay incredible money for these dogs. I'm set. You're my only problem now."

"Lou, those dogs were miserable. Sick. Unhappy."

"Yeah, yeah Mr. Bleeding Heart" he began, "in the new place it won't be so bad. But you can't think about it that way. Do you think about the cow when you bite into a filet mignon? Nah, didn't think so. It's all a means to an end, my man, and this is easy."

I had the fleeting thought of trying to use my empathy to turn the three Rottweilers against Lou. That was a dream as much as my floating over my house was earlier. No way. I did not see a way out.

"Listen, Mark, just so you know, I'm sorry about all this" Lou said, and really did sound contrite. How wonderful, now I feel better. Fuck you, Lou.

Nothing more was said for a few minutes. I heard Lou walking around, and I heard the sound of something splashing. The distinct smell of kerosene assaulted my nose. He was setting the place up to burn, me along with it.

"Lou, please" I implored, not wanting to think about becoming a roasted veterinarian. That was a painful way to die, I was sure.

"Ah, relax lightweight. I'll knock ya out before I light it. I'm not the devil."

No, of course not. You're a friggin' boy scout.

I had no idea what time it was, but it appeared to still be dark outside as I saw no sunlight coming through the walls or ceiling of the mill.

"You still have some time, kid, I have to get this last load of pups out, and that will take a while. Relax. It'll be done soon."

Lou walked out, but the dogs did not. They came back over to me, and settled around me. I sensed nothing from them, but perhaps my inner panic was blocking out any feelings from getting through. Not that it would have made a difference anyway.

***

40 – Pause, Then Paws, Then More Pauses

I remained still (not that I had much of a choice), and thought. I played back everything in my mind and I decided, with some comfort, that I had done everything I could have. Sometimes, you are just destined for a harsh end.

Some people in this world believe that our destinies are pre-ordained before we are born. Others feel our fates lie completely within the choices we make in life. At this point in mine, which I knew was probably going to end shortly; I had no answers as to which group had it right. I had the thought just then as well, that I would never get to write that philosophy book I had threatened you with a few times. That made me sad.

Not sure how much time had passed, I heard footsteps returning. They sounded like Lou's.

"Ok, kid, everything's set." Lou's voice came from the same position it had before, from behind me and slightly to my left. The dogs looked at him, but stayed next to me.

I tried one last-ditch move. "Lou," I started, "I bought a ring, you know."

Silence for a moment.

"And?" he said, but I could hear some hesitation in his tone. Hope for me, maybe?

"I just thought you should know. I would have made Sarah very, very happy." I was immensely sad again.

Apparently, Lou was not in the mood to go down this emotional path any longer, for he said, "Yeah, well, I hope it's a good expensive ring. I'll find it at your place and get a good price for it. Sorry." So much for that.

True to movie form, Lou said something next that served as a great cue for the other person that I did not know was in the room. Text messages are the greatest things on the planet, did you know that?

Lou said, "Mark, this won't hurt. It's chloroform. Just breathe."

A voice came from behind him, silent until then.

"I'm sorry Lou, (pausepausepause) but I'm going to have to ask you not to do that." The greatest man in the world. Carlo. The greatest person on the fucking planet spoke those words in his imitable, confident tone.

Lou spun, and looked.

What he saw, I found out later, was a recently cleaned and polished Walther PPKS staring at him from about ten feet away. It was in the hand of retired detective Carlo Rockman.

"If you would be so kind, (pausepausepause), please place the rag you are holding on the floor and step slowly away from Doctor Canis."

"I know you," started Lou, "you're that cop that's always hanging around my kid and this jerkoff. Well, too late, everything's already done."

Movement. From the other side of the room. Carlo had this one figured already too.

"Ah ah ah," said Carlo, with the same tone he had used at my house to stop Stefania from getting up to make coffee. "That will be far enough, Craig, I presume. By the time you reach me, your boss here will be full of holes, and you will be next. Stop." Craig stopped.

When the next James Bond movie is made, if they do not cast Carlo in it, the producers will be leaving millions of untapped dollars at the box office.

Carlo called Craig to him, and Craig's face twisted into a scowl that was reminiscent of the face he wore on my front porch with his walrus of a father next to him when he had come to apologize for beating me up at the bus stop.

"Craig, if you will be so kind, (pausepausepause) gently remove the piece of wood that is pinning my young friend here. There are many officers of the law enroute to this location presently, and I do not feel it necessary to add assault and battery to the already impressive list of charges the two of you are going to face."

Craig looked at Lou for direction, but got none. He leaned over me, put his legs on either side of me, and our eyes met.

"Fuck you, asshole." came out of my mouth immediately. I could feel Carlo smile although I could not see him do so.

Craig said nothing, and pulled mightily on the beam. He was a strong man, and it crashed heavily past my feet, freeing me.

At once, the remaining dogs in the mill began barking, startled by the sound of the crashing wood, and Lou tried to hush them. No one said anything for a few minutes and the barking subsided.

I rose, unsteadily, and moved towards Carlo. The Rottweilers, which had up to this point been lying beside me, all stood and looked between Lou and me. They had not moved when the wood crashed down. They simply watched. Carlo's eyes darted from the dogs to Lou to Craig, but he said nothing. He was most likely computing who or what to shoot first if he had to. This guy missed nothing.

"You okay?" he asked me without moving anything but his lips.

"Yeah." I replied. I was feeling better by the second. I was still incredibly hungry though.

Carlo intoned, "Do you have any weapons, Lou?"

"No." Came the reply.

"Check." Carlo said to me.

I did. I roughly patted down Lou, and then Craig. I shook my head in the negative at Carlo. I felt like super-spy again.

"Why don't we all have a seat," said Carlo, "and discuss our options." I did not know what Carlo meant by this, but I knew he did, so I said nothing.

I love my father very much, have always respected him and enjoyed him, and I have learned an incredible amount of wisdom from him. However, at this moment, Carlo Rockman was the greatest man on the planet. That is no reflection on you, dad, simply a statement of admiration and debt to Mr. Rockman.

Carlo pulled over the wooden chair, and sat down, his Walther still trained on Lou. I looked around, and saw more chairs like the wooden one, and brought another over. I sat down next to him.

"Mark, my dear friend, find another two chairs for our friends here." It was a command, and I obeyed. I learned, if nothing else this night, that no command from Carlo should ever go unheeded. I wondered what Stefania was doing, but quickly dismissed the thought. I stayed longer on the thought of what Sarah was doing. Where was Sarah?

My attention back on the present, I brought the two chairs over to Lou and Craig, accidentally landing the leg of the second chair on Craig's foot with all the strength I could muster. He glared at me, but said nothing.

"Sorry." I said with amusement.

Carlo smiled, and time passed. I suddenly remembered an anecdote Carlo had told me a few years earlier. While he was a detective, he spent a brief amount of time with the sexual crimes unit. He detailed how on one particular night, he and his partner brought in a suspected rapist for questioning. Carlo and his partner had practically witnessed the rape, so they knew the accused was most certainly guilty. Rape is a particularly galling crime, especially to a man like Carlo. He relayed to me that, under the guise of needing to "view the evidence", he had the suspect pull down his pants and place his private parts on his desk. Then, from somewhere completely unknown, a dictionary came down on the "evidence" as hard as a human hand could move it. The devastated accused, when he regained his senses twenty or thirty minutes later, would have an abject apology offered and the explanation that there was a possible misspelling of a word in the report and the dictionary had simply slipped. Sorry! I love that story.

"Now, then" Carlo finally began as if pausing to let me relay the "evidence" anecdote, "What to do about all of this."

Lou must have had a thought at this point, and said, "There are no cops coming, are there?"

Carlo confidently replied, "Not at the moment, no, but they are on notice. When I call them, they will be here in a matter of minutes. I have informed the local authorities of the situation, but failed to give them a location. I am sure they are as anxious as you are to see this situation resolved."

I thought to myself, "Checkmate, assholes."

Lou spoke next. "So, what are you going to do?"

Carlo hesitated, but I knew better. He had this whole thing figured out.

"Well," he began, "there needs to be a reckoning, if you will.

Someone must pay for what has happened here, and happened to my young friend. You will make that reckoning happen, Lou, in the following ways."

Lou said nothing, but looked frightened.

"First of all, whatever money you have gleaned from this little endeavor, you will turn over to my young friend Mark here for the repair of his office, his pain and suffering, and because it will be very expensive to see these animals are properly cared for. Secondly, you will call your daughter, and explain to her that it was in fact you who set up Mark here."

"That's not going to happen." Lou said, quickly and firmly.

"Fine." Said Carlo. "I had hoped to avoid completely destroying the life of the father of my friend's future wife here, but I see you will give me no choice." He rose, and took out his phone.

"Wait!" shouted Lou. "Tell me the rest."

Carlo sat back down and put his phone away.

"Okay. You will make the aforementioned call (pausepausepause) so that my friend may return to the life he has so carefully built for himself. Your daughter will (pausepausepause) no doubt be disappointed, but I doubt she will be that surprised. I am certain she knows what a louse you truly are, and will be doubly angry with you for wreaking havoc with Mark here, but you can deal with that if and when you get the opportunity. That's a fine girl you raised, sir, although I'm not sure how you managed that."

Lou said nothing. He put his head down. Craig looked confused, the dumb shit.

"Your friend Craig here will take the legal fall. I will see to that. You, Lou, will leave Nyagg, with or without your wife, who I understand is a pleasant woman, and you will never return. Agreed?"

He gave Lou no time to think about it, and shortly said again, "Agreed?"

Lou nodded his head.

"Let me hear you say it."

"Agreed, agreed." Said Lou, but I wondered at the wisdom of this move.

Craig, dumb shit that he was, then said, "Wait? What does he mean?" He said this to Lou.

"It was all your doing, moron. Shut the fuck up." Lou said quickly to Craig.

Craig still looked confused, and I laughed. How this man had talked Stefania into bed recently – and worse – how he had talked Sarah into dating him all those years ago were mysteries I could not fathom.

Lou spoke again. "What now?"

Carlo answered. "You will find my car about one hundred and twenty feet south of this location." He was so fucking cool. "You will find the keys in the ignition, and you will take it and return to your home. You will inform your wife of your transgressions, if you wish, or you may pack your things and leave. If you do leave, sign over that garish Cadillac you recently purchased to her before you go so she will not be left wanting." Man, he really thought of everything.

"If your wife is willing to go with you," Carlo continued, "have her follow you to my house in the Cadillac so you can return my vehicle to me. The address is in the GPS unit, already queued. Do not concern yourself with gasoline consumption." If you do not love Carlo as much as I do at this point, there is something wrong with you.

Carlo spoke again, "I do not expect to hear from you for at least a year. Then, and only then, may you contact your daughter if she is reunited with Mark. If she is not, then it is not my concern, only that I never see you around here again. Clear?" Wait a minute, Carlo, had you not worked out Sarah returning to me yet? Too much to ask, I suppose.

Lou said nothing. He looked at me, and I think I saw remorse in his eyes. Carlo had not detailed the return of the money, but I was absolutely certain it would be done. I smiled to myself again, for I knew Lou would skim a bit off the top so he could survive to find his next scam. No matter. I did not care about the money, I cared about his daughter.

Carlo held his cell phone out in front of him, towards Lou. You will find your daughter's cell number queued. Hit speaker, and make the call. Lou took the phone.

Lou did as instructed, and I waited.

I felt a lump in my throat as I heard Sarah's voicemail greeting echo off the walls of the mill.

Lou began to talk. He greeted his daughter, and then apologized. He paused, gathered himself, and then explained how he had lost everything in a bad deal with some merchants in Hong Kong. He explained how he loved her and her mother and her sisters very much, but that he was in real trouble.

He went on to explain that he had contacted Craig, whose number he had, to see if anything promising lay down in his 'neck of the woods' as he put it.

Lou looked up at Carlo, who nodded, then continued to dictate into the phone.

He explained about the dogs, about the mill, and about me. He said the puppy mill was Craig's idea, and since Craig said nothing, I assumed this was true.

He apologized more, and then the real good stuff came. He explained how he had set me up. He explained that after the Drake incident and their conversation he was fearful I would detect the profitable puppy mill operation. He explained how he had tried to set me up to take a fall, but that I was too clean and did nothing wrong. Thanks, Lou.

He continued to talk about sending Craig to – he paused – stop me from being able to detect the mill, but never meant to hurt me. He explained Craig involving Cindy, and that she had been manipulated towards Craig's and his ends. Well played, that part.

He finally admitted to having Craig drug Stefania, and place her in my bed in a last ditch attempt to remove Sarah from me. That part had been chillingly effective as well. He told her he loved her, said he was sorry again, and that he and mom were leaving, and hung up the phone and would be in touch. He handed it back to Carlo.

At that pristine moment, my cell phone rang, and Carlo looked at me. "Go ahead," he said.

It was Stefania. I breathed.

Before I could say a word to Stefania, I heard Carlo say, "You may go now, Lou. Good riddance." Lou walked out the east door of the mill.

I walked a short distance towards some of the cages, and took the call. I had a hard time getting Stefania off the phone with my quick explanation, but I managed to do so. I promised her all would be made clear in a little while.

I returned to Carlo's side, and my eyes must have said, "What now?"

Carlo moved so quickly I barely saw him start. He crossed the ten feet to Craig with such speed it startled Rottweilers, the Craig, and me.

He smacked Craig soundly across the mouth with his pistol, and Craig fell to the floor. The Rottweilers started barking, but I commanded them to silence, and they stopped.

Carlo turned to me, put his arm on my shoulder, and said, "Go, now, Mark. Go to Stefania and Max, get something to eat (how did he know?) and come back here with both of them in exactly four hours. A vet will be needed. Four hours. Got it?"

I got it. I began to leave. I stopped, kissed Carlo on the cheek, which made him laugh, and walked. I walked towards my Jeep, towards the road, and hopefully towards the end of this madness.

Carlo opened his cell phone again, and made a call.

***

41 – There's a Sandwich For You, Remember?

I drove back to my house in stunned but comfortable silence. My head was still wrapping itself around all of it, but I felt so happy to be alive I almost forgot that the most important thing had yet to be resolved. I breathed out forcibly, made myself relax, and drove.

When I reached my house, Stefania and Max were standing in the driveway. I drove up, got out, and wrapped myself around Stefania. I began to cry. To her credit, she said nothing, and hugged me back fiercely. I was not the only one who had deepened in scope in the past few days.

Stefania led me inside, and I followed with no fuss. In the kitchen, at our center of operations - the center island   -   she sat across from me and waited.

I spilled. I spilled, and spilled, and spilled. Her mouth formed an 'O' after the first minute or so, and she said nothing until I had completed my diatribe. For a long minute after, she remained silent. Then, the real Stefania came back.

"That mother-fucking…ooooo…oooo. I want to kill him myself! Oooo!" she sat down heavily again (she had risen to pace while muttering the ooooos) and looked at me. "You did good, Mark." She said to me. I did not agree at the moment.

I then explained that Carlo wanted us back at the mill four hours from when I left, which was about three hours from now, and she nodded. I told Maxie too, since he was to come along.

As we sat there, I should have remembered the sandwich Stefania had made for me. I did not, and I forgot about my hunger for the time being. There was nothing left to do but head back to the mill when Carlo had indicated. We waited.

I rose, and went upstairs. I looked for the engagement ring, but could not find it. Then I remembered I had hidden it in my office.

I quickly went down the stairs, and met Max in the hallway.

"Come on Maxie, help me look for something." Max's tail began to wag, and he followed me into my smelly, but slowly drying, office.

It was still there. I almost laughed aloud with relief when I saw it. Craig, in his damaging of my office, had not found this box. I looked up, closed my eyes, and squeezed the box.

I went back to the kitchen, and I suppose I should have thought this out before, but I did not. It was very funny looking back at it later.

Without a word, I handed Stefania the box and said, "Open it. I'm tired of the nonsense. It's about time, don't you think?"

She did, and her jaw dropped. She looked at me, and said, "Mark, I…"

I laughed aloud. "No, you idiot, it's not for you – it's the ring I bought for Sarah!"

She laughed with a combination of embarrassment and relief, and finally said, "It's awesome. She's going to love it." She started to cry softly. I hugged her, kissed the top of her head, and asked the powers above to find someone on this vast planet of ours who would love Stefania as much and in the way I loved Sarah.

Comfort. Comfort and peace. Those were the feelings in my kitchen on Florida Lane as the three of us passed the time. No one spoke. No one moved. This was nice. This was good. This was how it was supposed to be. This is what friends are for. I had teased myself at the mill that I was becoming more patient. Partly, it was no joke. I felt calmer, and if you can understand my usage of the word – older. I did not feel tired, I was not drained. I was simply more veteran at this thing called life. It felt good.

At the appointed time, Stefania, Max and I climbed into my Jeep and headed out. There had been no word from Sarah, or Sophie, or anyone for that matter. I still had not eaten, either.

I saw the lights from quite a distance. As we approached the Horton Mill, we saw law enforcement vehicles of every shape and size, lights blaring in the early morning lightening sky, reflecting from every tree in the area.

We parked as closely as we could, and exited the Jeep. I grabbed my medical kit from the back, grabbed Stefania's hand

and Max's leash, and made our way to the mill.

Stefania took everything in as we walked, understanding all of it more as we approached. Max simply walked. He was as cool as his owner was. Terrible term, owner, let me try that again. He was as cool as his best friend, Carlo. Better.

We waited at the open east door of the mill, where a uniformed officer greeted us. "Help you folks?" he asked.

Carlo appeared along with two other gentlemen in suits, and said, "Ah, yes, he is the veterinarian I asked for, officer; please let him and his entourage through." Carlo shot a purposeful look at Max, who, incredibly, understood it to mean "do not greet me in an outward fashion my friend." Max stayed by my side.

Carlo briefed me as we walked, as if I had never been there before. The gentlemen with him, active detectives from somewhere or another I assumed, let him take the lead.

"Dr. Canis – we have quite a situation here. Apparently, there was a puppy mill operating here, and there are quite a few dogs here that could use ministration. Is that possible?"

I thought about what to say for a moment, and replied, "Sir, the numbers here seem to be quite large, I would recommend a call, if possible, to your colleagues in Suffolk County (which was east of here) who have a very well stocked mobile animal facility that I'm sure could be here in rapid order. That would be my recommendation."

Carlo smiled at me. He knew I was going to say that. Wow.

"A superb suggestion sir, thank you, I had forgotten about that." One of the suit guys nodded to the other, and left to make the call.

Stefania and I, hand in hand, walked through the facility with Max in tow. I was sickened still by what I saw, but now had a renewed sense of hope. These dogs would be seen to, and I hoped, adopted. Their nightmare would soon be over.

Carlo returned to us, and said, "Well done, Mark. Perfect." He looked at Stefania. "The gentleman known as Craig has been charged with more than one hundred counts of animal cruelty, trespassing, breaking and entering, and a whole other gamut of charges that will ensure he is away for a long time." He stopped, and looked back at me. "One thing I would like you to see, Mark, then you can take the lovely Stefania back to your place, or hers if she prefers. Keep Max with you until tomorrow."

"Tomorrow?" I asked.

"Yes, tomorrow. Tomorrow evening at six o'clock, come to my house to return Max. I am going to need some serious sleep. But before you go…" his voice trailed off, and he pointed to a cage in the corner, and walked away.

Again, we often take for granted the watershed moments. It is not because we do not care about them or give them their fair due. It is because they are sometimes so sudden and precipitated without warning we have no idea we are swimming in them until we almost drown.

I looked at the cage Carlo had indicated, but saw no movement. I moved closer, and noticed a large female dog lying motionless on her side. She appeared to be dead. I opened the cage, intending to feel for a pulse. I did not need to, the body was already cold. Something moved. I saw the movement in the corner of the cage, and reached in.

"Here, little one, come here, that's it, it's okay."

A trembling, tiny, frightened, and now motherless creature was huddling in the corner, emitting what could only be described as terror. I tried to sooth it, but he or she did not respond. I reached in, slowly, and grabbed the infantile puppy by the scruff of the neck and raised him or her out of the cage.

I looked her over (it was a she) and then froze for a second. Stefania, who had tears in her eyes, said, "What? What is it, Mark?" I do not know if she meant "What is it" to me, or "what is it" meaning the type of dog. She would not recognize the breed, but I did.

I turned; my eyes filled with tears, and carried out my new best friend. I tried very hard not to crush the tiny thing in my emotion, and managed not to. I was now the proud owner of a tiny, newborn, female Norwegian Elkhound.

***

42 – I'm Still Hungry

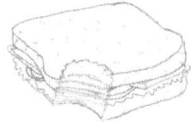

Once home, I immediately went into my office and looked over my new friend carefully. She appeared a bit malnourished, but otherwise fine. I had tears in my eyes the whole time, which made it difficult to focus, but I managed. She looked so much like my beloved Chelsea it was surreal and jarring. Same coloring. Same eyes. Same ears. I laughed as she daintily wagged a miniature version of the same tail.

I walked across my examination room, and thanked those up above again. A cabinet on my wall, in which I kept exactly what I needed at this moment, was apparently alcohol free.

I removed a small baby bottle, a can, and went back to the examination table.

Stefania and Max walked in, and they stood and watched me.

On the way home from the mill, Stefania clearly stated she was coming home with me, no question about it. Max, incredible soul and friend that he is, cleaned and washed the puppy the entire ride home. He covered her with his neck when he ran out of spit, and the little dog seemed at peace.

I picked up the little Elkhound, and cradled her in my arm. I brought the bottle to her tiny mouth, and she drank. She drank, and drank, and drank the milk that I had for her. She drank, and drank. I cried and cried.

Stefania came over to watch, and cooed, "Ooo, she's so cute. Ohhh."

As if she realized that as much as I loved this little female in my arms, she also realized there was still one more out there that I would hurt over forever. She hugged me.

After downing an entire can of puppy milk, my little friend promptly fell asleep in my arms. I walked her into my den, Stefania and Max in tow, and I asked Stefania to bring me a towel from the linen closet next to the bathroom.

I laid the tiny pup on the towel, on the floor, by my chair, and sat down heavily. Max dutifully laid down next to her, on guard duty apparently. I looked at Stefania, and said, "I'm starving."

She let out a quick laugh, and said, "Moron" as she headed off into the kitchen. She returned with the sandwich she had prepared for me earlier, and a box that I had forgotten I had in the closet. It was full of Mallomars.

In our den, there are two couches. As six o'clock was still hours away, Stefania took one, I took the other, and wordlessly the three of us joined our new little friend in the blessed land of slumber.

***

43 – Six O'Clock

When I awoke, Stefania, Max and the puppy were already awake. Stefania smiled at me, and said, "Come on, sleepy head, it's quarter to six." I jumped.

Stefania knew something. Her smile gave it away. "What?" I asked.

She said, "Oh yeah, right, Mr. I'm Not Telling You Nothing all of a sudden wants information. Yeah, right. Nothing, mister, just get up and let's get out of here. I'm just happy everything is working out."

I was immediately sad. The way Stefania had called me "mister" reminded me so vividly of Sarah. I missed Sarah.

Stefania offered to drive, but only if we could take the BMW. What the heck, you only live once, right? Besides, it probably needed gas by now. I did not remember the last time I had filled it up.

Stefania expertly maneuvered the car onto the parkway that led, at least for me, to only one place - Carlo's. I think I might hurt Stefania's feelings if I told her what I was thinking. My situation was almost perfect – the two dogs – one in the back seat and one in my lap - the convertible top down, but the wrong girl was in the driver's seat. Sorry, Stef.

We rode in silence, except for the occasional cooing I did to my new little friend, who as of yet, did not have a name. She stared at me the entire ride, and I sensed a tiny little hint of something from her, but could not tell what it was.

The drive was quick, the weather was perfect, and almost

everything was right in my world.

We arrived at Carlo's about ten minutes late, but I was not worried about Carlo being upset about that. I had so much to thank him for, so much to be grateful for, and so much I needed to say.

Max ran into the house as we pulled in, seeking out his best friend.

Stefania, carrying a baby Norwegian Elkhound (she insisted), and I made our way towards Carlo's house.

In that incredible way that he has, as we reached the threshold I heard Carlo call, "Out back! Come around the side!"

We stopped, and turned towards the back of the house.

I stopped, and all of the waves I had felt, all the fear I had felt, all the angst I had felt were nothing compared to what I felt now.

Sitting, not ten feet away from me, on Carlo's backyard patio, on a chair, looking like the angel she was, was Sarah.

I could tell she had been crying. I joined her in that. I could not move. I saw Stefania move towards her, hand the puppy to a surprised Carlo, and embrace Sarah. They were both crying now.

Stefania turned to me, wiping tears from her eyes. Sarah's wet eyes were fixed on me, and her crooked smile was only half formed on her face.

I moved slowly, purposefully, and silently. I crushed Sarah against my body so hard I heard the breath rush out of her. I did not care. Breathing is so overrated anyway.

After a long while, I pulled back and looked at my Sarah. MY Sarah. Her smile and eyes told me I was right. I was at a loss for words. I put my head on her shoulder and I wept. "I'm so sorry" was all I could manage. I could see Carlo now as my head was facing him. He was smiling, holding up my new little friend. I owed my world to this man. He nodded, as if he read my thoughts.

I kissed Sarah, hard, and it felt even better than that night at the dock. I was home.

Sarah looked at me, wiped her eyes, and said, "I love you, Mark."

I said, in broken voice, "I love you, Sarah. I always will."

After a time, Sarah looked at Carlo, and said, "Thank you." He simply nodded, still smiling.

Sarah noticed for the first time, the tiny baby that Carlo was holding. She crooned, "Oh my, oh my, who's this?"

I came up behind her, took the puppy gently from Carlo, turned to Sarah, and said, "Sarah, I would very much like you to meet Chelsea the Second."

***

David I Schoen

44 – My Meeting With My Editor/Agent/Critic

The barbecue at Carlo's was the most anticipated social event of the year. Okay, that may be overdoing it a bit, but you know what a sap I am by now.

Only a month or so had passed from my visit and near-death experience at the Horton Mill, which I will forever think of as *The Whining Mill*. I spent the next few weeks starting the process of making good on the vows I had made sitting behind the bush waiting to be discovered.

I gave Sarah the ring that very night we came home from returning Max to Carlo. She accepted it, and told me Crazy Glue would not be necessary, she would never take it off.

Stefania has become almost a daily part of our lives, and there is a new comfort level we enjoy that eclipses anything we experienced during our previous relationship, way back when. It is nice.

I was called in to consult on the disposition of the myriad dogs from the mill, which I am sure Carlo arranged, but I cannot prove it. One day, I received a call from the ASPCA asking me to come in to discuss the situation. They were so impressed with my actions they told me they were planning to hold a dinner in my honor next month. I asked them to change the theme of the dinner from a celebration of me to a fund-raiser for the other lost animal souls in our area. The lady from the ASPCA actually asked me if I were an angel sent from God. Talk about boosting one's ego. I would look good with a halo.

I found a way to get Emily and Stan back for the kitten incident – wait until you hear this stroke. I had made several visits to the large animal hospital where the animals from the mill had been taken during my consultations, and on one particular visit I asked for a list of the breeds that had been identified and catalogued. I saw immediately what I wanted. There was a single

Great Dane on the list, a survivor of the mill's horrendous conditions. She was female, which was perfect. I wanted some remembrance of Spirit and Cindy, who had moved away and left no contact information. The dog was given to me immediately after I filled out the adoption papers. Unannounced, I showed up at Emily and Stan's with their new best friend. Jordyn and Jacob instantly fell in love. There was nothing Emily or Stan could do about it. Hey, look at it this way – at least the vet bills will not bankrupt you, I know a guy. Now when we visit my sister and her husband, which is much more frequently, Chelsea the Second has a friend to play with at my sister's house. Moreover, I never stop smiling. Stan has stopped making me great drinks, though. Now I get only soda. A fair trade. At the rate the Dane is growing, (they named her Princess) I know what I am buying Jordyn for her birthday this year – a saddle.

Carlo is Carlo, and will always be Carlo. Friends like this are golden, rare, and to be treasured. We have a regular dinner weekly now, once at his place, once at ours. In fact, the barbecue today is part of that wonderful cycle we have established. Max and Chelsea the Second are inseparable.

Speaking of Chelsea the Second, maybe it is the breed, but I am constantly eerily reminded of the original Chelsea by this affectionate, intelligent, loving dog. She makes the same motions, runs around with the same graceful gait, and learns new things just as quickly as original Chelsea did. Sarah absolutely loves her, which is wonderful to observe.

I arranged with my parents for us all to go on a weeklong cruise in the coming fall. When my mother mentioned that there was a wedding to plan and many other things to do, I simply told her I did not care, and we should go anyway. That surprised her a bit, but we are all booked for the trip. Guess who is watching Chelsea the Second when we are away? Thanks again, Emily.

Stefania met a new guy who looks nothing like Craig (thank goodness,) likes the same sports teams I do, and I am starting to feel the planets are all where they belong. Stefania is also taking it much more slowly with this one, which is a good thing. Maybe I should tease him that I saw her naked not that long ago. Think so?

Sarah has adjusted well to her parents moving very far away, and she keeps in touch with her mother surreptitiously through that wonderful medium of text messaging, which you know by now I am a huge fan of. I plan to encourage Sarah to bring her mother out for our wedding, but Lou can stay home. Sorry, Lou. By the way, he never paid me anything as Carlo had instructed him to do, but I looked at that as added insurance he would never venture this way again.

As I sit here reflecting, enjoying, and taking the time we often forget to take, I revel in the fact that I am very lucky. I also remember another vow I made that fateful night, which was to never take a single day for granted. I know there are more things to come. More injured animals, more strange owners, and more excitement.

Max is now running into the house, trailed by Chelsea the Second, and is bringing me sheets of paper. I have no idea why he is doing this. After placing each sheet in front of me, he looks at me for a minute or so, then goes and gets another. Stefania's friend, his name is James, hands me a pen and jokes that the dog probably wants me to write down the story I have told and retold for the past month. I start to write, Max settles down, and you know the rest.

If you take nothing else from this memoir, take the lessons that I have learned. Life is precious. The people we love are precious. Do not waste a single moment with them. Do not ever take them, your life, your peace, or your happiness for granted. It can all be gone in an instant.

I do not know why we are on this planet, but I do know this – I have made others happy in my time here, and I found out what I get in return. I am happy too. What more can one ask for?

The next time you smell a freshly mown lawn, think of me. The next time you spot an eclipse of moths circling a light, think of my old buddy Oscar. When you pass a park with a metal merry-go-round, think of my old girl, Chelsea. I know she would be happy there is a new Chelsea in my life, and even happier to know there is a Sarah. I leave you with this sincere wish: I wish all of you, my dear friends who now know my story, a lifetime supply of your very own Sarahs, Carlos, Stefanias and Chelseas. Oh yeah, and an occasional Max too, just to keep things honest. *** * ***

ABOUT THE AUTHOR

The author teaches and tutors high school students for the SAT and ACT standardized tests. He is the author of seven books (so far) in that non-fiction genre.

The Whining Mill is his first foray into fiction, and whether you like the book or not, you can be sure the grammar is pretty good.

He lives, teaches, and writes in New York City.

You may write to the author at the following:

randomscholasticpress@gmail.com

Be sure to include the author's name in your email: David I Schoen

Look for The Meowing Mansion, another appointment with Mark Canis, coming in 2013.